the

TEMPORARY LIFE

Eric Wasserman

La Questa
PRESS

WOODSIDE, CALIFORNIA

ISBN 0-9644348-5-7

Library of Congress Control Number: 2004114097

The Temporary Life
Copyright © Eric Wasserman
All rights reserved

Cover and text design by Kajun Design
Front cover photograph by Thea Ledendecker
Author photo by Joel D. Wasserman

La Questa Press
211 La Questa Way
Woodside, CA 94062
www.laquestapress.com

Grateful acknowledgment is made to the following publications in which these stories, some in altered form, first appeared: *Allegheny Review*, for "The Temporary Life" (first published under the title "Who Said Anything About God?"); *Beacon Street Review*, for "Next Year In Kona"; *Monster Press*, for "Being Secular"; *Sparks*, for "Replacement"; *Writers Corner*, for "Nina the Useful." "He's No Sandy Koufax" was awarded First Prize in the Thirteenth Annual David Dornstein Memorial Creative Writing Contest, sponsored by the Coalition for the Advancement of Jewish Education (CAJE) and appeared in *Jewish Education News*. "Layla Tov" and "Reunion" appeared as part of the author's master's thesis for Emerson College, Boston, Massachusetts.

ACKNOWLEDGEMENTS

While writing this book I accumulated a lot of debts I can only repay with friendship and gratitude. Those who have assisted me along the way know who they are, and I offer each of them my appreciation, especially all of the wonderful people who have provided insights and advice regarding the various drafts these stories went through.

My heartfelt thanks go to Kate Abbe and La Questa Press. My sincerest appreciation to my agent Dan Green at Pom Inc. for his straight talk and expertise. Alex Tennent was always willing to give me a fresh perspective and, without fail, continually forced me to put myself on the line as a writer. The incredible Thea Ledendecker assisted me with capturing the Russian dialect for "Nina the Useful". Sarah Bunin Benor provided a superb understanding of Hebrew and Yiddish. Andrew "Doc" Mendenhall verified the medical details for "Reunion". My brother, Ryan Wasserman, helped me to work out the baseball facts for "He's No Sandy Koufax". My uncle, Michael E. Wasserman, provided the necessary legal terminology for "The Involved Congregant" and made both personal and professional moves possible. Matthew Negrin and Debby Wasserman took a close look at nonliterary items. John Zamparelli, Albert Neal, Michael Atwood, Mike Pettit, Nina Schneider, Yuliana Min Kim-Grant, August Adams, Trent Masiki, Aaron Reid, Carmen Corral-Reid, and 2716 3rd Street all provided feedback and support that I will never forget. All my thanks to Todd and Scott.

I would like to express my deepest gratitude to Frederick Reiken for his steadfast encouragement and for holding me to the highest standards, and to Anne Whitney Pierce for her critical eye and for giving me a woman's point of view. I am indebted to Joseph A. Soldati for his continued camaraderie, advice and editorial scrutiny. I would also like to thank Rick Hillis for being an early believer and somebody who pushed me to begin this project.

The June 12, 1999, issue of *Sports Illustrated* featured a piece by Tom Verducci titled "The Left Arm of God" which inspired one of the stories in this collection. I would like to acknowledge Mr. Verducci s influence.

I cannot thank my family enough, particularly my parents, for their unconditional love and support. And finally, everything spoken and unspoken to Thea, who arrived and guided me out of the shadows. I love you.

To my mother and father

And to Thea

CONTENTS

You have to laugh with us,
at us, and take us seriously
all at the same time
or you're going to miss the point.

—*Abbie Hoffman*

$\mathcal{N}$EXT YEAR IN KONA

$\mathcal{E}$VEN as the plane descended, Gabe Allen thought of how fond he had always been of his nephew. That was why he decided to fly to Los Angeles for the bar mitzvah. It surely had nothing to do with not seeing his family since his last visit. As far as he knew, nobody had died recently. And in the Allen family, only funerals required attendance.

Now almost forty, Gabe, a man with prominent hooded eyes who had only recently lost his boyish complexion, was constantly aware of his mortality. He demanded a seat in the emergency exit row of the airplane, and not for the comfort of his giraffe-like legs. He had even taken to reading the evacuation manual before takeoff, and gave undivided attention to stewardesses instructing passengers how to secure oxygen masks in the event of cabin pressure loss.

He had no wish to even see the family, except for his nephew, Jeremy. The calculated life of his older brother Mason, a psychiatrist, was unimaginable to Gabe: married at twenty-two, three children each separated precisely by two years, a spacious home in Brentwood, where Jeremy attended a private performing arts school. Gabe had fled Los Angeles after law school, determined never to succumb to domesticity. Unlike Mason's life, Gabe's was a series of airport terminals, courtrooms, and evenings of take-out meals in his condo, which was more of a second office than a home. His time was not his own, and he preferred it that way.

He rarely dated anymore. To Gabe, bars were like meat markets displaying various cuts of divorcees not looking for love, but rather somebody adequate to remedy loneliness. Only the week before he had gone out to dinner with a thirty-seven-year-old dermatologist. He still didn't know if he wanted to see her again. She was pretty. Not beautiful, but certainly a woman who took care of herself. He imagined she had a membership to a fitness club for women. But there was something about the way that she had written CALL ME! on the back of her business card—handing it to him after a chaste good night peck on the lips—that made him feel that he had just been on a job interview. She had talked about her younger sister's children all night. It turned him off. There was always something about women that seemed to turn him off.

As a child Gabe had enjoyed flying, exhilarated by being thousands of feet above the earth in the grip of sky alone. "This is as close to God as you will ever come," his atheist father had once said. Flying had been as thrilling as discovering a duplicate rookie in a pack of baseball cards. Now flying had become a necessary chore. Only three days earlier he had flown to Ann Arbor to take a deposition for a case he was certain to lose, knowing his client was blatantly guilty of bending the law, if not breaking it entirely. Then again, Gabe knew that it was his job to defend people from prosecution by those in his own profession.

He was tired, anxious about traveling to Los Angeles. His stomach coiled loosely, like worn bedsprings. "I'll order you a kosher meal for the flight," his travel agent had said. "They tend to be better." His digestive system was now paying the price. He was accustomed to brown, square pieces of meat that chewed like Styrofoam, accompanied by tiny bits of rubber-like rice. The kosher meal was worse. He had pushed the tray aside after a few bites and ordered a vodka tonic. But the damage was already done, and he spent the duration of the flight between his seat and the lavatory.

Just removing his seatbelt was unsettling. He had heard the stories: the tops of planes dislodging in midflight, stewardesses whisked away, plummeting to imminent death below, bodies never recovered. However, the trips to the lavatory were unbearably necessary.

He couldn't smoke on the flight either. Six hours of travel with only a forty-minute layover in Dallas allowing him to have three cigarettes was nerve-racking, more so than concealing his habit on that date with the dermatologist. That probably had more to do with his stomachache than the kosher meal he had nibbled. In Dallas he was forced to smoke in a room resembling a holding cell at the precinct station where he had once bailed a client out. At least the hotel room had been ready when he arrived.

From the lobby, the Beverly Hills Hilltop Hotel—recommended by Gabe's brother—was impressive: marble pillars, oak paneling, impeccably white carpets. No hint of the Formica countertops at the motels his firm reserved. Even the plants appeared to have been watered with routine care.

His younger sister, Ingrid, had insisted they share a room. "Bonding time, like when we were kids." But Gabe was not particularly accustomed to sharing space, especially with his twice-divorced, still childless sister.

Gabe and Ingrid talked on the phone once a month, whereas he and Mason obliged each other with calls only on holidays. Mason still lived in Los Angeles, Gabe had planted his new roots in Chicago years ago, and Ingrid followed each new boyfriend or husband around the country: Miami, Minneapolis, Phoenix, now Seattle.

"Mrs. Allen has already checked in, sir," the desk clerk informed Gabe, who was surprised that Ingrid had discarded her second husband's surname. Hearing his sister being referred to as Ingrid Allen, Gabe conjured images of a fifteen-year-old girl stuffing her bra with tissue paper.

Ingrid was not in the room when he entered, but he could hear her humming *Fiddler on the Roof*'s "Matchmaker" from behind the bathroom door. On one of the two double beds her charcoal suitcases—still displaying the monograms from her former life as Ingrid Esther Schulman—were open, exposing her wardrobe: black sweaters, black slips, black stockings, at least six pairs of black shoes for only three days in Los Angeles. "I'm here," Gabe shouted towards the bathroom.

"Great," Ingrid answered. "I'll be out of the tub soon."

The windows were open. He remembered that about Ingrid, her needing to sleep with circulating air, even in the winter. The memory almost brought with it the aroma of burning leaves. Of all his childhood recollections, those that included Ingrid were the most vivid, particularly that of waking early on fall mornings with their bedroom window open and the odor of burning leaves rising from their parents' yard.

He took the chair at the coffee table by the window, leaned back, and looked at the Los Angeles skyline, the sun setting over Pico Boulevard. The intoxicating hues of pollution glazed billboard advertisements for cellular phones and sport utility vehicles. He looked at the table and noticed a complimentary dish of mints, each sealed with the Beverly Hills Hilltop Hotel logo of a palm tree superimposed over an aqua-green shield. He was opening a new pack of cigarettes when he saw the card. *The Beverly Hills Hilltop Hotel thanks you for refraining from smoking.*

Gabe took the dish and dumped the mints, as if pollinating the surface of the table. He fitted a cigarette between his lips, lit up, and inhaled strongly. He exhaled, watched the smoke silhouette throughout the room from the fading sunlight; flicked ash into the candy dish. He then noticed a rubber band on the carpet, leaned down, and placed it in his pocket. Rubber bands caught his eye everywhere—on the street, in restaurants, airports.

His stomach coiled again, and he felt something creep downward into his lower abdomen. But the sky was gorgeous, nothing like the one he looked out upon from his office on the eighth floor of a Chicago high-rise.

Gabe took nervous drags from the cigarette, the tiny inhalations making him feel like a sputtering engine on its last cylinder. He felt his stomach drop again in rapid, loosening increments. That was it; another journey to the toilet, his sixth that day.

He smothered the cigarette into the dish and made a beeline for the bathroom.

Ingrid turned her naked body to her brother as the door opened. Soapy water spilled from the tub onto the linoleum, blanketing Gabe's wingtips.

"Gabe," she gasped, smiling.

He dropped his slacks and was already evacuating his bowels before his skin touched the toilet seat.

"Airplane food?" Ingrid asked, not looking at Gabe as he scrunched his eyes into crow's feet. "You should have ordered a kosher meal. They're always better." Gabe said nothing, just opened his eyes, looked at her, and sighed.

Ingrid now faced him from the tub, her tiny, pedicured toes protruding through the bubbles. Her breasts were exposed just as they had been in high school when she would bathe while practicing her clarinet. Neither she nor Gabe felt embarrassment. They had shared a bathroom in their childhood: brushed their teeth while the other showered, changed clothes in one another's presence. Ingrid and her girlfriends had even used Gabe to practice French kissing.

She set down a hardcover copy of English translations from the Hebrew Tanakh onto the shampoo rack. After her first divorce she had vigorously submerged herself in a kind of quasi-Judaism, mailing Gabe passages of scripture that he would feed into his recycling bin. But he always thanked her for thinking of his soul while he was occupied with the monetary salvation of his clients.

"Better?" she asked.

"I think so. Nice to see you."

"You, too," she said. "I like you without the beard, looks good. Oh, be careful, I think I saw a rat in the toilet. It might have been an acid flashback, but you never know. These older hotels look top-shelf, but the plumbing might have gone to shit. Oh, sorry, bad word choice." She laughed. "By the way, there are some joints in my purse, might help your stomach. I campaigned for medical marijuana use last year, remember?"

Gabe nodded. She hasn't changed, he thought. "Isn't there a dinner or something you should be at?"

"Me? We, Gabe." She stretched her arms over her head. Gabe watched the soap bubbles trickle from her wrists to her armpits, noticing that she was shaving them again. Her small breasts raised higher out of the water, settled again when she relaxed and ran her talon-like fingers through her damp black hair. "The whole family went to services. I can't stand Friday night services at Conservative temples; such a bore." They were all the same to Gabe. "Mason and Wendy had a fit about my refusing to go, even more so that you hadn't taken an earlier flight. Jeremy is just sitting on the bimah tonight, won't even participate in the service until tomorrow morning. I was just reading up on tomorrow's Torah portion. Wanna know what it's about?"

"Not really." Gabe was crinkling his eyes again. He could sense another approaching release, had come to recognize the warning signs. He turned away toward the sink, which was cluttered with Q-Tips, vitamin C tablets, skin moisturizers, and Ingrid's diaphragm. Sandalwood incense burned from a stick propped in a water glass.

"Not worth going to," Ingrid continued. "All of Mason and Wendy's ritzy friends will be there. They socialize with people who display bumper stickers that tell the whole fucking world that their children are honor roll students. It's all a big show."

"I thought they were Reform," Gabe said.

"What?" Ingrid asked as she began to finger through the book again.

"Reform. I thought Mason and Wendy belonged to a Reform shul. You said it was Conservative."

"Oh. I don't know, maybe they are Reform. Still, it's a bore. You at least go to temple on high holy days, don't you, Gabe?" No answer, he simply squinted his eyes in readiness for the assault of his bowels. "You're still Conservative, right?"

"No," he said to the violent splash of water. "I'm just a lawyer now," and flushed.

She bent her cheeks in disapproval. "But you still believe in God, right?"

"Yes, Ingrid," he sighed. "I still believe in God. We just don't talk that often anymore."

"Very funny," Ingrid said, closing the book. "I have this great idea," she continued. "Here it is. I see so much in common with Jews and American Indians."

"How so, besides genocide?"

"Genocide? I hadn't thought of that one. No, I was thinking how wonderful it would be to have a drumbeat during the Mourner's Kaddish at services."

Gabe looked at her, perplexed. Ingrid was always seeking to fulfill an inner life with something; attending Arizona retreats that taught the correlation between tarot cards and the Torah, campaigning to save obscure plant species. For a while she had reveled in garage sale hunting, thrilled by the potential treasure of other people's junk. After her last divorce she had taken up painting Jewish midrash with watercolors like some late seventies rabbinical dropout. "You're serious?"

"Absolutely!" she sang like a giddy schoolgirl. "I brought a small hand drum with me for Jeremy's bar mitzvah tomorrow. If it goes well, I'll introduce the idea to my own unaffiliated shul. What do you think?"

"Maybe you should just bring it up at your own temple before—ach!" Gabe felt an excruciating pain in his left buttock.

He leaped from the toilet. His feet tangled in the slacks at his ankles and he barreled over into the tub with Ingrid, his body smothering her tiny frame. He lifted his neck to breathe. She shook and wiggled to pull herself from the water, holding the book high.

"Oh, my God!" Ingrid gasped, and dropped the book into the tub. They watched as a pair of claws reached over the toilet seat, followed by the head of a large sewer rat. Ingrid screamed. The rodent answered with its own piercing voice and retreated into the toilet water. Gabe leaned out of the tub and slammed down the lid to the toilet seat.

"Find something heavy to put over it!" he shouted at Ingrid, the bath water now having drenched his entire body, his scratched buttock bleeding. But Ingrid was still screaming. She leaped from the tub and didn't stop to wrap herself in a towel as she bolted for the phone in the bedroom.

"Sir, we do not have rats at the Beverly Hills Hilltop Hotel," the manager told Gabe later that evening after calling a plumber. But the rodent had already escaped to the pipes. "This has never occurred before. I assure you that we will do everything possible to upgrade your accommodations and comfort." What Gabe had wanted was a new room, but the hotel was completely booked. Ingrid, more livid than she was after her pilgrimage to Roswell, New Mexico—convinced that the government was concealing UFO secrets—had demanded another hotel entirely, particularly after being mistaken for Gabe's wife. "Oh, your sister. I see," the manager had said. "We would appreciate you not mentioning this incident. The Beverly Hills Hilltop Hotel does not have rats, sir." Gabe settled on a forty percent discount and his inoculation shots at Cedars Sinai's ER paid for in full.

The doctor at the ER told Gabe that he shouldn't worry, that the inoculations, which were relatively painless compared to the rat scratches, should take care of any fears, including rabies. Gabe was told that he could see his own doctor in Chicago for a follow-up if he wished, but that it was not necessary since the rat had obviously not bitten him, only torn his skin with its claws. But for Gabe, just the idea that he could have been bitten by a rat brought about thoughts of imminent death. My God, he contemplated, I could die childless.

He couldn't wait until Monday; he wanted a second opinion immediately. And for some reason, the first doctor that came to mind was not his physician of the past four years, Dr. Charlesworth at Northwestern Medical, but that dermatologist he had gone on a date with the week before. He fished out her business card from his wallet, the one with CALL ME! written in her swirled penmanship on the back. Her name was Debbie. He remembered it being Denise, but he had to admit that Debbie sounded nicer, softer, sweet really. She answered on the third ring.

"Oh, Gabe," she said after he finally reminded her who he was. She then gave him a silent, heavy breath response after he described in great detail what had just happened to him. "It's really not my field," she said. "But yes, you should be fine if it was only a scratch and not a bite, just see your regular doctor when you get home." He thanked her and said that he would call her again when he returned to Chicago. She said, "Sure." Gabe liked her quiet tone. He decided that he was more attracted to her than he initially thought, and then proceeded to call Dr. Charlesworth's answering service to schedule an appointment for Monday.

Gabe and Ingrid stacked three phone books atop the toilet lid before leaving their hotel room for the bar mitzvah the next morning. He had not seen Jeremy in four years, but he was certain that the child would remember him. He called all of Mason's children on holidays. But Jeremy was his favorite. Had it been Kalia's or Daniel's special day, he might not have come to Los Angeles at all.

Gabe sat with Ingrid near the back of the synagogue's sanctuary, though they could see Mason and Wendy proudly situated on the bimah. The ceremony consisted of Jeremy falteringly reciting his hafto-rah and maftir portions in English, the rabbi, a plump woman wearing

Birkenstocks, openly correcting him a dozen times.

Ingrid removed the small drum from her purse during the Mourner's Kaddish and began to tap lightly. When bodies turned towards her, she steadily magnified the beat. Gabe could see Mason's face, mortified. He was amazed by how much Jeremy had grown. The thirteen-year-old was already at least five-foot-seven. Looking at Jeremy, Gabe wondered if the child had inherited his own rare height.

When the ceremony concluded, the guests bellowed, "Mazel tov," and stood up to leave. Jeremy was immediately congratulated, although he had probably spent more time on his waxed hair than on preparing for his participation in the service.

The number of guests was impressive, the children in attendance astounding. Perhaps every child from Jeremy's school was there. Gabe followed Ingrid, shaking hands with people he vaguely recognized. "Good to see you again, still in Chicago?" was repeated some fifteen times before he left the sanctuary. "How's the wind treating you?" Forced laughter. After five minutes of this polite, acceptable language of people so distantly removed by time, mind, and geography that they might as well have been dead, Gabe needed a cigarette.

Guests aggressively surrounded Mason and Wendy as if they were political candidates. Unlike Gabe and Mason's bar mitzvahs, the reception was not to be held in the basement of the temple, but at the banquet hall of the Beverly Hills Hilltop Hotel.

Gabe slipped on his sunglasses as he left the sanctuary for the arboretum lobby of the temple and followed the migration to the parking lot. He could see the children boarding a chartered Greyhound like ants in a colony, Jeremy standing like a celebrity among the prepubescent entourage. "My God," Gabe said, "Mason rented a bus for them to travel seven blocks?" He and Ingrid had walked that morning. His buttock was still sore from the scratches and inoculations, and the less he sat the better. For the first time in years he had slept on his stomach and not his back.

He turned to see Ingrid standing with her off-black dress and charcoal shawl fluttering in the light Los Angeles breeze, her horn-rimmed sunglasses slipping from the bridge of her sloped raven's beak nose as she pontificated to a stranger about the spiritual void her parents had created by not allowing her to have a bat mitzvah when she was a young girl. She was still stoned from the two joints she had smoked that morning. "I'm really experiencing a new channeling of my displaced aggression," she was telling an old man wearing a baby-blue polyester suit with brown suede Hush Puppies. Gabe shrugged and lit a cigarette.

Ingrid carried Jeremy's gift in one hand, her opposite arm looped through Gabe's elbow as they walked into the hotel. She was giving Jeremy *The History of Jewish Feminism*, a book Gabe was certain his nephew would write a gracious letter of appreciation for and never read. At least Ingrid had thoughtfulness going for her. If she didn't know what to give somebody, she purchased an item that conformed to her own interests. Gabe had simply written out a fifty-four dollar check, the Jewish equivalent of triple chai, and placed it into a money holder. He had wanted to buy Jeremy a chess set, maybe instructional videos on acting; he knew the boy was enthusiastic about dramatics. But the Ann Arbor deposition had kept him too busy.

"I don't know any of these people," Ingrid whispered as they followed the crowd towards the banquet hall.

"Me neither," Gabe said. "I need another cigarette."

"Just relax. You can't leave me here alone, I might have to explain to somebody why I don't have a husband anymore." Gabe was certain that that was exactly what she was hoping for.

The reception was not the balloons and streamers display Gabe had expected. On the far wall was a ten-foot cardboard replica of a projection camera spinning enormous Styrofoam film reels. To the left of the camera lens, *Happy Bar Mitzvah, Jeremy Allen!* was spelled out in blue and gold twinkling bulbs. Canister lights swiveled from the corners as if the reception were a movie premiere: "There's No Business Like Show Business" hummed from speakers while the hired band members arranged their instruments. A shadow of Hitchcock blanketed the dance floor. Even the caterers looked like movie stars. Placed on each table were plastic souvenir replicas of the small wooden tefillin boxes that Orthodox Jews prayed with each morning. The boxes themselves traditionally contained pieces of parchment with selections of scripture.

These spun open with potpourri inside. And suspended by cables from the ceiling was a miniature reproduction of *The Titanic* with an enormous black and white photo of Jeremy dressed in a tuxedo positioned at the ship's bow. Gabe thought that his nephew looked more like the main attraction at a gay nightclub than Leonardo DiCaprio.

"Sushi, sir?" Gabe turned to see a young girl dressed as Marilyn Monroe spreading her glossed lips at him.

"Excuse me?" Gabe managed to say.

"Sushi?" she repeated. "They're California rolls."

His bowels cringed. "No. No, thank you."

The girl smiled and moved on. A waiter dressed as James Dean passed her with glasses of champagne craned in his arm. Sushi was not what Gabe expected to be served at a bar mitzvah. He wouldn't have minded some champagne, though.

Ingrid tossed her present onto the gift table. Gabe refused to place a card with a fifty-four dollar check on a table. Besides, he wanted to congratulate his nephew personally. He knew there would be more time to speak with him at the private family brunch at Factor's Delicatessen the next day. Today was for Jeremy to be with his friends, to acknowledge congratulations. But Gabe still wanted to see the boy.

"There's Mason and Wendy," Ingrid said. Taking Gabe by the arm, she maneuvered her slender frame through the maze of cologne and perfume-scented bodies. Every other woman in the room seemed to be wearing a black velvet dress. Even the thirteen-year-old girls wore black velvet dresses worth a fortune that they would outgrow in less than a year.

"Wendy!" Ingrid said, swinging her slim arms around her sister-in-law, who was wearing a black sequined dress with a necklace of modest pearls around her ostrich-like neck. Mason's wife held herself like a window mannequin. She was a Lutheran convert to Judaism and had paid to have trees planted in Israel for every guest in attendance. Gabe had clipped the certificate he received from the Jewish National Fund to his refrigerator.

"Hi, Mason," Gabe said, extending his hand. ˙

"So," Mason said, "you made it."

"I told you I would," Gabe said, releasing Mason's hand.

The tense crinkle of Mason's brow was unmistakable as he looked up to his much taller younger brother.

"Hello, Wendy," Gabe said, and kissed her cheek.

"You decided to come?" Wendy said in the condescending tone typically reserved for seasoned schoolteachers. She was the sort of woman who confused her acquisition of wealth for having acquired intelligence. Then again, Gabe knew that rich people could afford to be stupid. He had had plenty of clients prove that to him over the years. Wendy took a glass of champagne from a waitress dressed as Audrey Hepburn.

"You think I would miss my own nephew's bar mitzvah?" Gabe said, as he too took a glass of champagne.

"Why not?" Wendy said. "You've missed every family event over the past four years. Excuse me, I need to make sure the cake has arrived." Gabe thought it was the perfect excuse for a woman who earned her family a needless second income coordinating events for a Santa Monica party planning company.

"Don't worry about her," Mason said, sipping his champagne as Wendy left. "It's good to see you again."

"You, too," Gabe said.

"Jeremy did well today, didn't he?" Mason said. It was more a rhetorical statement than a question.

Gabe appreciated it that his brother, unlike their own father, was proud of his children's accomplishments. He wondered if Debbie liked kids, assumed she wanted them.

"He was wonderful," Ingrid said.

Mason refrained from commenting on her drumming. "Oh, shit," he said. "It's Uncle Edward."

"He's still alive?" Gabe asked.

"Yeah, don't worry, you didn't miss his funeral, yet."

"There's my little Ingy Ingy. Give your Uncle Edward a kiss."

Ingrid didn't have the heart to request that her uncle not call her by her childhood nickname. To avoid kissing his Old Spice-soaked cheeks, she put her arms around him and squeezed. Their uncle was affectionate with women: kisses, hugs, pinches to the butt. Firm handshakes were sufficient for Gabe and Mason.

"The boy was good," Edward said.

"Thank you," Mason said.

"Your father should have lived to see today," Edward continued, pulling at his polyester slacks, which were elevated over his ankles by the assistance of safety pins. He was easily in his late eighties and had managed to retain more hair than Mason had at forty-five. "Have you been watching that new television show, *Get Rich Quick?*"

"Sure," Mason said. "Every Thursday night."

"Haven't seen it," Gabe said. He owned two televisions and was lucky if he caught the local news, occasionally a Cubs game. Gabe was well aware of Edward's fascination with game shows. The old man had once been a contestant on *The Price Is Right.*

"It used to be a good show," Edward said. "Smart questions, ordinary people. Now they have celebrities. Terrible, just terrible. This is a serious program giving the average Joe the chance to be a millionaire, and now they have celebrities. I never watched *Hollywood Squares* for that reason. Look what happened to *Wheel of Fortune*; low ratings and they bring on big stars. Now it's happening to *Get Rich Quick*. Serious questions, serious people, and they ruin it. Not for me. If it's not serious, I don't watch it. I'm sticking to *Jeopardy*. Your father would have done well on *Get Rich Quick*, though, would have known the final question last week. What was it? You know, that Russian proverb he used to say?"

"Oh," Ingrid said. "To not become a father is to never become a human being. Something like that." Gabe stared at her coldly.

"Yes, yes," Edward said. "That was the answer. If your father had been on the show he would have been a rich man, could have sold that lousy furniture store of his before it went under. See, serious questions." He turned to Gabe. "So, when are you getting married?"

Gabe glared at Ingrid again. "Oh, you know how it is, Uncle Edward."

"No, I don't," said Uncle Edward. "I may be old, but all men want a little pussy." Mason almost spit up his champagne through his nostrils. "You're not queer, are you?"

"No!" Gabe gasped. He was uncomfortable around older people, especially since he was gradually becoming one of them himself. He suddenly felt like one of those sets of matryoskas, Russian nesting dolls his mother had collected that Ingrid routinely broke as a child;

being opened one by one until his smallness was revealed.

"Well, think about getting started. Mason here was married almost ten years before Wendy had Jeremy. Find a nice girl and get it out of the way, Gabe. That's my advice. Sooner you begin, the sooner you can get rid of them, send them off to college and have your own life."

"Uch, my babies!" shouted Edward's wife, Edith, as she approached, a pear-shaped woman with thick ankles. "Ingy Ingy, give your Auntie Edith a hug." Edith's enormous bosom pressed a flap of gold sequins into Ingrid's face. Gabe and Mason both kissed the cosmetic foundation of their aunt's cheek. "This is such a classy reception, Mason. I remember our Philip's bar mitzvah. It wasn't fancy-shmancy like this. We only had a magician there to entertain the kids after the ceremony. Back then we didn't even know you had to have a theme."

"By the way," Gabe said facetiously, "I love the guys over there setting up instruments, the ones dressed like The Commodores."

"They are The Commodores," Mason announced.

"Wow." Ingrid had a dreamy look in her eye.

Mason shrugged. "Wendy plays bridge with their manager. They do a few weddings every year, usually ask for six thousand, but I got them for less. If they still had Lionel Richie, I'd pay at least five."

"Oh, here," Edith said, reaching into her purse. "Let me take a picture, the three of you are never together. Your mother would want me to if she was still alive." The three siblings squeezed each other close. "Okay," Edith said, lifting the lens of the instant Polaroid to her eye, her arthritic hands shaking. "Say, 'Mazel tov, Jeremy.'"

"Mazel tov, Jeremy," they said in unison, as the flash made a miniature explosion and the film cartridge dispensed the slowly developing white sheet.

Edith handed the picture to Gabe. "You keep that."

"Thanks," Gabe said, placing it into the liner pocket of his suit jacket with his cigarettes.

"May you all have much mazel in your lives," Edith said, affectionately.

"I need to check on things," Mason said. "It was good seeing you." Gabe was certain they would not see him again until the family brunch at Factor's Delicatessen the next day.

"You coming to Seth's bar mitzvah next year?" asked Edith as Mason disappeared into the sea of black dresses and three-button suits.

"Who?" Gabe asked.

"Seth," Ingrid turned to Gabe. "Seth, our cousin Philip's son, Edward and Edith's grandson in Hawaii."

Gabe instantly conjured images of a reception with hula dancers wearing grass skirts and coconut halves for brassieres, maybe lox and bagels arranged on surfboards.

"You should come," Edward added. "Philip got that big coffee company management job on the big island's Kona Coast. Philip killed a big fish. What was it called?"

"A marlin," Edith interrupted. "So big it was. We eat fish every time we visit." She turned to Ingrid. "You'll love Kona, dear. Beautiful, warm. Remember to bring a hat; you shouldn't get too much sun." She nodded her head with authority. "Oh, you would have loved my friend Ruth's grandson's wedding, absolutely exquisite."

"Feh!" Edward grunted. "It was like being trapped in an episode of *Dynasty*."

"Oh, hush you!" Edith snapped.

"Well," Edward sighed. "It's time for my pills."

"His blood pressure," Edith informed Gabe and Ingrid. "It's good the two of you don't smoke. You kids are so much smarter than we were."

Edward kissed Ingrid on her lips, then pinched her butt. He extended his hand for Gabe. "Well, I guess until Seth's bar mitzvah. Next year in Kona, huh?" he laughed.

"What?" Gabe said.

"Next year in Kona. You know? Like saying 'Next year in Jerusalem' at the end of a Passover seder."

"Oh, right," Gabe said. "See you there."

"Why did you say that?" Ingrid asked as Edith and Edward walked away.

"Say what?"

"That you'll be there. You aren't going to Hawaii. You haven't seen Philip in fifteen years; you don't know his kids. I'd be surprised if you're even invited."

"Oh please, they'll forget what I said in five minutes. Besides, since when does anyone need an invitation to a family event?" Gabe's buttock was hurting, the three aspirin he took earlier having worn off. "You wanna get a drink?"

"Sure."

They made their way across the room, noticing replica Oscar statues on each table. Gabe really wanted a cigarette.

"I'll have a White Russian," Ingrid said.

"You got it, kid," the bartender said in a perfected Humphrey Bogart tone. "What about you, pal?"

"Vodka tonic," Gabe answered, still looking about the room in amazement.

Ingrid's eyes ballooned, scoping the banquet hall for potential single men.

"Hey, Cary Grant," Gabe said.

"Bogey, pal," the bartender corrected.

"Whatever. Can I smoke in here?"

"Sorry, pal," the bartender kept up the act. "This is California, no smoking anywhere, especially in the Beverly Hills Hilltop Hotel." He handed the vodka tonic to Gabe. "There you go, kid," he said to Ingrid, sliding the White Russian to her. He winked and excused himself to dispense ginger ales to several thirteen-year-old girls with identical sitcom hairdos and tiny French manicured fingernails, a kind of children's chorus, Gabe thought, to this tacky event.

"I wonder if Jeremy will buy a car with the money he gets," one of the girls said as she handed her Chap Stick to a friend. From the size of her chest, Gabe concluded that she hadn't even begun puberty.

"I'm saving my money," another girl responded. "My mother won't let me get a nose job until I'm eighteen. Have you seen Jenny Silver's nose? Not the best. I wonder who her surgeon is. Jenny: deviated septum? I think not."

Near the girls, guests were lined up where a man was processing written messages into a fax machine to be sent to an office in Jerusalem, where they would be received, then inserted into the cracks of the Wailing Wall. Gabe sipped his drink, his mind wandering.

Mason was not the observant type. He was a man who wrote

out checks and asked his wife few questions, no longer the boy who thumbed through *National Geographic* to see the bare breasts of Third World women. He paid membership dues to a synagogue simply for professional prospects; in Mason's estimation, the Jews of Los Angeles were in severe need of psychiatric assistance and were willing to pay well for the service. Wendy was a different creature, a convert whose kitchen contained more sets of dishes for kosher meals than she would ever use, although she ate treif outside the home. Even their cat had separate meat and dairy plates. Wendy had the taste of whatever catalogues deemed stylish. Gabe wondered what Debbie's kitchen was like. She had dressed modestly on their dinner date, seemed to be sensible about food, had ordered a boneless chicken breast instead of a salad, which was not what he had expected. He wondered what her family was like, couldn't remember if she had mentioned any of them besides her younger sister's children. He looked at Ingrid.

His sister always had something to submerge herself in. Her last business venture was an attempt to remedy the cultural propaganda of the female body for Jewish American girls. She had designed a toy series called The Earth Woman, a plastic doll with a small bosom and wide hips, dressed in a tie-dyed gown and hemp sandals, her coiled black hair falling to her enormous butt. "The more accurate depiction of a woman for little girls to admire." Ingrid paid to have prototypes constructed and used Mason's daughter, Kalia, for a trial session, and was heartbroken when the child discarded Earth Woman after ten minutes for her Barbie dolls.

Although Ingrid had never ceased her quest for a third husband, she desired a child now more than a spouse. Thinking of his sister, Gabe wondered if there was any lot of people in America—on the planet— that were more lonely, bitter, and desperate than the legions of childless single women in their late thirties. He had certainly dated enough of them. Is Debbie one of those women? he wondered. After Ingrid's last divorce, after discovering her second husband's mistress's love letters by reconstructing debris from his office shredder with Scotch tape like some basket maker from the Old Country, she was set on becoming a mother. At first she placed classified ads. "SJF seeks SJM who enjoys karaoke and Gertrude Stein. Must want children immediately." Not one response came. Ingrid's yearning for affection and companionship, her longing for someone to love unconditionally, emanated from her like skunk scent. If she didn't find a husband candidate soon, she had decided to adopt an orphan from Korea. Gabe suggested that she take in a cat from the Humane Society instead. It was worse than her sporadic vegetarian diets, wielding control over her life with the simple choice of what she ate. She had forgotten where their parents came from, was now blessed with the privilege of never knowing what it's like to be hungry.

Mason was less complex, a shrink who believed in rationalizing with children and discussing feelings. Unlike their father, Mason saw barbarianism in the timeless philosophy that the only way to discipline was to drop the child's pants and deliver a spanking. Instead, Mason adhered to calculated psychobabble. "I'm not angry with you, I'm angry at what you did," he would say to his children.

And Gabe had long observed both of them, everything from Ingrid stuffing her nose with cocaine before her nursing school graduation to Mason's constant pretentiousness. Yet Gabe, too, was consumed by emptiness. The last time he was in Los Angeles he had astonished the family with a bearded face. "What's this shmatte?" Ingrid had teased. Gabe said he had grown it because a stress rash from a big case had made shaving excruciating. The truth was too confusing even for himself. Gabe's work had somehow become all he knew; it was his entire life, without intrusion. The beard had been his new anchor, an identity beyond the law. Even his given name, Gabriel, was bewildering. Why had his parents named him after a Christian archangel? He had grown the beard out of a dubious attachment to ethnicity, as if he might be able to embody the wisdom he saw in those sepia-toned family portraits from Russia, men he was certain held a simpler, more absolute vision of the world. He had tried keeping kosher for a week, thought of joining a Jewish singles group, but continued to prefer spending what little free time he had watching Cubs games on the tube. Then a disgruntled employee walked into the office of a dot-com company on the thirty-ninth floor of Gabe's building and fired a twenty-two-caliber bullet into the CEO's forehead. It convinced Gabe that not even those old men had the answers. Nobody did. They had been as messed up as everyone else he had ever known. Gabe's world was devoid of reverence. His Judaism consisted of teacups from Odessa, coffee table books on Israel, watching Charlton Heston portray Moses in *The Ten Commandments* on television once every year. His Jewish identity in America was nothing more than knowing he didn't celebrate Christmas and Easter. His Judaism was the beard. It came right off, and he returned to worshipping Michael Jordan and Sammy Sosa. That's when he started dating again, no longer caring what a girl's religious background was.

There was a time in law school when Gabe thought he might settle down and raise a family. Had Gabe been born a woman, he would have wanted to be born as Kathy Morgan. She had been his female counterpart; a dedicated law student, more interested in old Billy Wilder films than television, politically progressive, raised in Los Angeles but determined to forge a new life elsewhere. They even smoked the same cigarettes. While other women in their law class took fashion direction from *Cosmopolitan*, Kathy was as naturally beautiful and graceful as a swan dropping to a lake.

And he broke her heart, all because she confessed that she could not convert to Judaism as Wendy had for Mason, that she could not pretend she was something she was not, that even to do so symbolically was to deny her true self. "You've always said that Judaism is concerned with the law, Gabe. How can I be expected to be an advocate of the legal profession and lie to myself about who I really am?" Kathy had said in her idealistic young voice. After almost fifteen years of being a lawyer, Gabe now found her argument painfully humorous. But the twenty-five-year-old Gabriel Allen had not.

The past few years now seemed like a four-act play Gabe was certain he had enjoyed but could not possibly recall the plot of. The stock market had treated him well; he owned a BMW, a spacious condo, wore a Rolex. For God's sake, he often thought, unlike my friends with kids I can afford to spend seven hundred dollars a month for a parking space in downtown Chicago. And still the world was far from being his oyster; it felt more like a damp cardboard box.

He watched his nephew pose for photos in front of a five-foot-high plaster replication of Mann's Chinese Theater; a neon HOLLYWOOD sign propped against plastic Walk-of-Fame gold stars that served as the backdrop. A few years ago Jeremy had been interested in learning to play chess. Yet Gabe's last visit to Los Angeles had been less than thrilling, watching the Academy Awards with Mason, Wendy, and the kids, amazed at how the family applauded from their couches and recliners for nominees and recipients as Hollywood congratulated itself. Now Gabe wondered if he were not related to these people, would he even want to know them? He certainly didn't want Debbie to know them. There was no reason for her to. As Gabe's father always told him, the Ten Commandments can be condensed down to one: stay out of other people's meshugas, you've got your own nonsense to worry about. His father always thought Gabe was breaking that rule by becoming a lawyer.

He sipped the last of his drink.

"Want another, pal?" the bartender asked.

"No, thanks," Gabe said. He turned to Ingrid. "I'll be back in a minute." He slipped slowly off the barstool, his butt still sore from the rat scratches and the shots, and began making his way towards the reconstruction of the Hollywood Hills where Jeremy now stood.

Throughout the banquet hall were people Gabe was certain he should know, faces long forgotten or transformed by life, the way Mason's face seemed to have aged a decade in the year following their father's death.

"Gabe Allen!"

He looked down. At work Gabe enjoyed his height, the physical authority he carried into courtrooms. But he had forgotten the abnormality it brought when around his family.

"Aunt Alice," he said, thankful he could quickly place a name to the face, contorting his body to hug the woman, who wrapped one arm around his waist and leaned the remainder of her weight on a leopard-spotted cane. She had small features that let one know she had not always suffered from obesity.

"I hear you're going to be coming to Seth's bar mitzvah next year. Have you been to Hawaii before?"

"No, I haven't."

"Will you be bringing somebody?"

Gabe paused. "Probably not," he answered politely, then thought of Debbie again.

"Still a bachelor? Wonderful. I have the perfect girl for you. She's lovely. Her first marriage didn't work out." Alice lowered her voice. "Embezzlement. Her ex is doing twenty years in San Quentin. You'll love her. Her therapist says she's ready to date again."

"Great," Gabe said, wishing to God he might come down with some assaulting ailment instead of simply the discomfort of the rat scratches to his buttock.

"Look," she said, holding out her palm. "I found another paper clip."

Finally, he thought, a relative with simple sincerity. He smiled, reached into his pocket to amuse her. "Wow, Aunt Alice. I guess we have something in common. I found this rubber band this morning and one last night."

"Really? I find paper clips everywhere."

"Same with rubber bands for me."

"That's wonderful, Gabe. We really do have something in common. Tell me," she whispered. "Do you hear the voice, too?"

"Excuse me?"

"The voice. I think the voice has something to do with me finding these paper clips. That's why I keep them. I think she's going to tell me to do something with them. Mason recommended a psychiatrist I see each week, Dr. Miller, a very nice man. He says there's no connection, but I know otherwise. You must hear the voice, too."

Aunt Alice had always been a sweet woman, if not a little peculiar. But in all honesty, Gabe realized that he hadn't seen her in over a decade. "Well, I'm going to say hello to my nephew."

"Okay. It's nice to see you again." She lowered her voice to a hush. "Do you smoke, Gabe? I could really use a cigarette." So could he.

Gabe smiled, reached into his pocket, and gave her one.

"Thanks, Gabe. We should talk some more. You might be the only one who understands. See you next year in Kona."

Jeremy was now standing with his sister, Kalia, a small child with black pigtails who wore a back brace for scoliosis. Gabe wondered if she still hoarded food under her bed, Wendy having placed her on a diet since age seven to become sitcom-thin. Kalia frightened him. Most children did. Jeremy was the only child he had ever enjoyed spending time with. He wondered if that would change if he and Debbie worked out.

"Congratulations, Jeremy," Gabe said.

"Thank you," Jeremy said in rehearsed fashion, staring absently.

"Don't you remember me?" Gabe asked, somewhat hurt that he was not immediately recognized. He thought that he would enjoy the children being older now, that he would not have to speak to them in the tone people typically reserve for their pets.

"Uncle Gabe!" Kalia shouted. "You shaved your beard." The little girl lunged at her uncle.

"Whoa there," Gabe said, lifting Kalia by her armpits above his head. "How's my girl?"

"I lost another tooth," she exclaimed.

"Let me see." She spread her plump lips, exposing a tiny gap, which she promptly squeezed her tongue against. "Guess you'll be getting a visit from the Tooth Fairy."

Kalia's face froze. "Uncle Gabe, there is no Tooth Fairy."

He set her down. "Well," he said to Jeremy. "Do you have a hug for your Uncle Gabe, who came all the way from Chicago?"

Jeremy moved reluctantly into Gabe's body. Gabe held the boy tightly, pleased to see him so big. Releasing Jeremy, he avoided the temptation to affectionately kiss his cheek, or worse, finger his rock-like hair.

"So, how's the acting coming along?"

"Okay," Jeremy said, smoothing down his double-breasted suit with his soft hands. Gabe could not help noticing how nicely trimmed his nephew's fingernails were.

"Do you like your performing arts school?"

"It's all right," said Jeremy, indifferently, perhaps not knowing that his father paid more than most people's entire income for him to attend. "They're making me act, but I'm really a director. I'm beyond acting now."

"Is that so?" Gabe said, trying not to laugh.

"Yes. Film's my medium. I'm very influenced by Andrei Tarkovsky and John Cassavetes. My parents found me an agent and want me to audition for commercials, but I think it's beneath what I'm worth. Acting's out."

"I liked Billy Wilder films when I was your age," Gabe said. "Have you seen *Some Like It Hot?* It's my favorite."

"That's such fluff," a prepubescent voice piped up from behind Gabe. He turned to see a boy not yet five feet tall sipping a soda through a straw. His fragile frame was consumed by a shimmering blue suit with enormous shoulder pads that practically eclipsed the peach of his face.

"Excuse me?" Gabe said.

"*Some Like It Hot*, all of Billy Wilder's films."

"You've seen them all?" Gabe pressed, wanting to tear the studded earring from the kid's left lobe.

The child leaned out his left foot like an amateur ballerina. "No, but I'm sure they're all the same. Fluff director." He sipped his soda.

"You go to school with Jeremy?"

"Uh huh."

"Michael is giving a speech later," Jeremy said.

"Really?" Gabe said, turning back to Michael, staring down ominously.

"Yes," said Michael. "Jeremy and I have been through so much together. I only hope I don't become too emotional."

Gabe wondered what they had possibly been through at thirteen. "You act with Jeremy at your school?"

"Yes, but I'm really a screenwriter. My brother is Richard Rose."

"Who's that?" Gabe asked.

Jeremy gasped melodramatically. "Richard Rose, Uncle Gabe? He plays the younger brother on the new FOX show, *What a Life We Have.* Irene Reynolds stars as the single mother, you know?"

The name of the actress sounded vaguely familiar. "I guess I don't watch enough television. I work."

"It's a good show," Michael continued, "except for the writing. I could do better."

"Your brother must be pretty talented if he's on television."

"He does what he can with the lousy scripts," Michael said. "It wasn't that hard for him to get the part." Both he and Jeremy erupted into laughter.

"What do you mean?" Gabe asked.

"He's talking about the competition," Jeremy said. "Every fall L.A. is flooded with wannabe child actors who know nothing about the industry. They come out here with their stage-moms from all over the county, even some from Canada, of all places." More laughter. "They stay at motels and audition for pilots."

Gabe wouldn't have minded a room at one of those motels right now.

"It's really funny to see," Michael added. "Those kids will be lucky if they get work as extras. They have no connections. What can you expect?" He shrugged. "My father's a producer at FOX-TV."

Gabe could not help feeling that had these children attended public school with him in his own youth, they would have had to enroll at private academies just to insure their physical safety. At thirteen, Gabe's sole interest had been collecting baseball cards.

"Are you coming to Factor's tomorrow, Uncle Gabe?" Kalia asked.

"You bet." He looked to Jeremy, whose eyes were focusing on the thirteen-year-old girls lined at the bar. Gabe understood. He would have a better chance to spend time with his nephew eating deli the next day. "Well," he said, producing the envelope. "Happy bar mitzvah. You earned it with all that hard work. You were great today."

"Thanks," Jeremy said more cheerfully.

Jeremy impatiently pulled the money holder card from the envelope, not bothering to read the eloquent letter of fondness that Gabe had written, simply opened to where the check was placed, and clutched it.

"Get yourself something you want," Gabe said. "Really, you earned it."

Jeremy paused for a moment. "Fifty-four dollars," he finally said. But it was not the excited tone of disbelief Gabe had anticipated. The boy stared blankly at the check. "What can anyone get for fifty-four dollars?" He looked up to his uncle.

Gabe's face became numb. He no longer heard the clamor of voices or the clanking of dishes; he no longer smelled the odor of perfume and cosmetics. He had the inclination to crack the brat across the nose. But he managed to relax his tense lips and retain a smile. He reached out his large hand and plucked the check from Jeremy's fingers. The boy's eyes bubbled, startled. Gabe ripped the check into two pieces and placed them in the liner pocket of his suit jacket. He took Jeremy's face forcefully with both hands and kissed the boy's cheek. "Happy bar mitzvah," he said and turned back towards the lobby. The Commodores broke into a funky rendition of "Hava Nagila" as he left the banquet hall. He lit a cigarette as he reached the elevator, his bowels beginning to simmer again.

Room service had remade the beds and replenished the dish on the coffee table with a supply of mints. Gabe peeked into the bathroom and saw that the lid to the toilet seat was down, but the maids had removed the phone books. His buttock was still aching. He knew he could sue the hotel if he had the energy, but he didn't. In truth, he didn't have the desire to make another journey back to Los Angeles. Gabe was tired, more so than he could recall for some time. Here he was, after a four-year absence from his family, and all he really wanted was to be left alone. Kona was now a jettisoned thought: what was one more disappointment?

Ingrid had left her vibrator on the bathroom counter atop the water-damaged copy of the Tanakh. Gabe laughed and popped one of her antacid tablets for his stomach, swallowed three more aspirin for his buttock. For all he knew, he could be dying right now of some sewer rat-transmitted disease and would be forever childless, having never become a human being. He returned to the bedroom.

"What can anyone get for fifty-four dollars?" he grumbled to himself as he lifted the three phone books under the nightstand and went back to the bathroom to place them on the toilet lid. "I should have bought the little shit a chess set. No, I shouldn't have even come." He needed another cigarette. At least he knew tobacco. There was a truth smoking brought, a dependency more based on not facing himself, rather than just an addiction. Gabe was now aware of what he had been denying for some time: he really didn't know his own family any longer and maybe he didn't want to. They simply spoke a language he had lost fluency in. He was comfortable in the sensible logic of the law, of a world governed by established rules and balance. This crap is Jeremy's right of passage into the tribe? he wondered.

He thought of Kathy Morgan, whose heart he had broken out of an instilled obligation to raise Jewish children. He thought of Kathy occasionally, but at that moment, although he had lost touch with her, he wanted to dial a phone number, write a letter, somehow apologize for once believing her love was less important than a religion he didn't even practice. If this was Judaism, he surely wanted nothing to do with it.

He lowered himself into the chair at the coffee table; the windows overlooking Pico Boulevard were closed. Thinking of Ingrid, he propped them open again. He took the candy dish and spilled the mints over the table, then fished through his jacket pocket, locating his cigarettes, along with the ripped check and the Polaroid. He fit a butt between his lips, lit up.

Gabe stared at the Polaroid, pleased that Edith's shaky hands had not cut their heads from the picture. Ingrid had cocked her body to the side, as though she was still a teenager showing off a new dress. And for all of Mason's shallow affluence and petty demeanor, he appeared content, as if he possessed everything he had always wanted. Gabe wondered if they had noticed that he had aged, that youth and possibility had somehow slipped from him like a forgotten promise.

He then noticed a handwritten card on the table; it reminded him of the note Kathy left the morning of her departure from his life, after he terminated their engagement. He took another drag and picked it up, flicked ash into the dish. *Dear Mr. and Mrs. Allen.* Gabe laughed and thought of his sister downstairs on her third husband hunt. *Please accept our complimentary breakfast buffet, courtesy of the Beverly Hills Hilltop Hotel. We apologize for your inconvenience.* He tossed the card into the wastebasket.

What would have been justice? Had Mason been like their father, Gabe could imagine suitable discipline. At his tenth birthday party, Gabe had been spanked by his own father in the presence of eight grade school classmates, all for a crime he no longer recalled the details of committing. Perhaps it was that type of humiliation Jeremy needed. Would that be fitting, to have Mason erupt like a water heater and yank Jeremy's pants right to the dance floor and spank the thirteen-year-old at his own bar mitzvah reception? A sardonic smile spread across Gabe's face just thinking about it, imagining his show-off brother blowing his precious, dignified facade. But the boy? Gabe thought, does Jeremy deserve that? What had happened to the nine-year-old learning to play chess who once won Gabe's heart by asking why the knight couldn't be called a horse?

A thought came to him and within two cigarette drags, he was dialing Debbie's number. Once again, she answered on the third ring.

"It's really not my field," she said coldly after Gabe told her that he was still in pain, still worried. He had expected her to tell him not to worry, that things would be okay, that he would heal.

He quickly changed the subject, mentioned that he was flying home to Chicago and suggested that they have dinner again, maybe catch a movie.

"Listen, Gabe. You're a nice enough guy, but I'm not used to men calling me twice from Los Angeles after only one date. I don't think I'm what you're looking for. Take care and try to quit smoking; it's one of the leading causes of cancer. Please don't call me again."

He shut his eyes and sighed after hanging up the phone, not even caring that she had figured out that he smoked, perhaps by his sporadic drags through the receiver.

Eating brunch alone tomorrow might be more pleasant than dining with the family at Factor's Delicatessen. He smothered the butt into the candy dish and lit another cigarette, stood, and went to the bathroom. He lifted the three phone books, hesitated, and peered at the rim of the toilet where the rat's claws had been the night before. Maybe Mason would like to hear about how the hotel he had suggested had treated his younger brother with a sewer rat that had the lungs of an Olympic swimmer, Gabe thought. Mason, big brother, I'm not angry with you, I'm angry at what you recommended. He set the books back down for safety and went to the phone in the bedroom, taking nervous drags from his cigarette. What Gabe needed was a real vacation, a new life. He dialed Information.

He waited patiently, dragged the cigarette to the filter. "Pilgrim Airlines, please. Yes, reservations." He set the phone down, rushed to the candy dish, dropped the butt, and lit his last cigarette. He skipped back to the phone, cradled it in the nook of his shoulder, and for a moment he could faintly smell the aroma of burning leaves from the yard below the childhood bedroom he had shared with Ingrid. "Yes, I have a reservation for Monday morning to Chicago's O'Hare from LAX. I would like to change my meal from kosher to the regular selection. No, I ordered a kosher meal, but now I want the regular meal. Yes, I'm sure." He took a long drag. "Yes, I'm positive." Pause. "Oh, could you tell me what the price of an economy ticket to Hawaii from Chicago runs, say, for this time next year? No, make that first class. Which island? I don't know. Any except the one Kona is on."

REUNION

"I CAN'T BELIEVE Noodles is gone," Mia said, setting down the listings for bed and breakfast spots on the Oregon coast as she clicked on the Volvo's radio. She had brought a few cassettes with her from Portland, but Howard's car didn't have a tape deck. "She was probably dead before you stepped into the garage," she continued, turning the channel knob for a clearer frequency as snowflakes descended against the windshield.

"I still feel terrible," Howard said.

"The cat was twenty years old. Her time had come."

"Noodles was twenty-two."

"Really?" Mia said. "Has it been that long?"

Howard shrugged. "Twenty-two. We got her the first year we were married and Ben was born three years later, remember?"

"I guess you're right. Think, twenty-two years old. Cats just aren't supposed to live that long. I think you were the only one Noodles ever liked: you always did spoil her." Mia found a station playing Cyndi Lauper and returned to the bed and breakfast listings. Howard had suggested they rent a motel room, but Mia wouldn't hear of it.

Noodles was a scrawny, malnourished tabby kitten with a crooked tail Mia had brought home after picking flowers outside the commune shortly after their wedding. Neither of them could have predicted that the cat would grow to the size of a healthy possum or that she would favor Howard over Mia, following at his heels more like a dog. Howard had recently run over Noodles with his Volvo while pulling out of his garage. He didn't go to work that day, simply called his son, Ben, in Alaska and wept shamelessly.

Mia was humming along with the radio. Howard was not. After

their marriage ended Mia had begun listening to contemporary music: Huey Lewis and the News, Duran Duran, Wham, Hall and Oates. At least she still likes the Beatles, Howard thought. For him, it never got better than the music of his youth: Bob Dylan, the Grateful Dead, Creedence Clearwater Revival. He couldn't even appreciate the new synthesizer-induced Springsteen; it just wasn't the same. Mia had recently suggested that he try listening to Journey because the group's guitarist once played with Carlos Santana, but Howard didn't take to it. He'd rather keep listening to "Oye Como Va" on his scratchy vinyl copy of *Abraxas* than try something new. With utter contempt, he had sold all of his Buffalo Springfield records at a garage sale after Neil Young praised Ronald Reagan in 1980. The Cyndi Lauper song was driving him nuts. He rolled down his window a smidgen to dilute the reception with the chop of wind.

Mia was the kind of woman who kept love letters, categorized shoe boxes with Valentine's and Mother's Day cards their son had given her over the years. She still wore her straight black hair to her shoulders, unlike most of the women her age who had succumbed to manageable perms. She enjoyed long walks, maintained a strict vegetarian diet, religiously checked her horoscope in the *Oregonian* every morning. But she now carried herself without so much nervous energy.

The years had not been as kind to Howard. He was the type of man who stood in line at the post office every April fifteenth to insure that his taxes were mailed on time. He still ate three eggs every morning and preferred his steaks cooked blood-rare; sprinkled salt over almost anything he placed into his mouth. By noon, without three cups of coffee and a sizeable coating of nicotine to his lungs, he couldn't even function. He breathed heavily, but this seemed normal to Mia. Howard had always slept as if hibernating for his next life. She wondered if he would keep her awake. It had never been a problem when they were married, but they hadn't slept in the same bed for almost a decade.

Although he had recently gained almost forty pounds, Mia still thought Howard was attractive. He had retained a full head of hair and the gray patches around his ears seemed distinguished. But his cheeks appeared to be one tuck of flesh folded over the other, slightly hidden by his thin beard, which had grayed around his lips where red bristles once sprouted. Mia liked the beard; she had not seen Howard with one since Ben was a toddler. Nevertheless, she knew Howard had let himself go. He was now prone to lying about his house in old jogging suits every weekend, rotating cable channels from the couch. It disturbed her, knowing that this man she had once been married to didn't care about himself any longer.

o   o   o

The two had met twenty-three years before in Eugene. Howard was back from Vietnam, cooking at a pizza parlor near the University of Oregon campus. Mia needed something to fall out of the sky, something tangible to focus upon. She took one look at Howard and told herself: That's what I want. That is what will make me happy. With his shaggy curls, dense beard, and silver-rimmed glasses, she never guessed he had been stationed as a company clerk in a war she was protesting weekly outside the university's administration building. But there he was, tall and muscular, a man who hummed along with the radio as she did, especially to Beatles tunes. She declined his first invitation to go for a ride on his Norton motorcycle because his name sounded too much like Herbert, her father's name. But the second time he asked she couldn't resist. He was just too polite to turn down again.

Howard won her over with little effort. He opened doors for her, had the habit of saying "please" and "thank you," spread a gentle smile. Her friends thought these traits were old-fashioned, but not Mia. She even grew to disregard his stint in the Army when she learned that he had not held a rifle since learning to fire one at basic training. And although it was certainly not a prerequisite for him to date her, she liked that he was also Jewish, that he didn't mind attending Shabbos dinner with the rabbi from whom she had been seeking spiritual direction.

Rabbi Reznik was raised in the chicken ranching community of Jewish communist immigrants in Petaluma, California: "The Egg Basket of the World." When he told Mia and Howard his plan to start a commune in eastern Oregon, they didn't need persuasion. Mia dropped out of college at the end of her freshman year, Howard quit his job, and by late summer they were married at the commune known as Shalom

Hadash, New Peace. With the birth of their son, Ben, three years later, Mia began to slowly reconstruct a relationship with her father.

Following the bankruptcy of the commune, Mia and Howard settled in Portland. Most of the commune members fell from their lives like discarded clothing, and the ones they did keep in touch with managed to disappoint them. Rabbi Reznik abandoned his rabbinical life and moved to New York, where he invested so wisely in the stock market that he now drove a Cadillac and owned a spacious home on Long Island. The last they heard, Reznik was working on whittling down his golf handicap. Many of their friends simply returned to college. Mia enrolled at the Northwest School of Massage Therapy, again disappointing her father. "It pays well," she told him, "and God knows we need the money."

Mia thought Howard, who had always loved to cook, should have opened his own restaurant. Instead, her husband opted for a job with Portland Social Services, training disabled adults, helping to mainstream them into the workplace. Howard was determined to retain his ideology, even as Mia pleaded that he should pursue a vocation more financially rewarding for the family.

The divorce, when it came shortly after Ben's tenth birthday, was amicable. They only saw each other inserting bread into the toaster each morning, or in front of the bathroom mirror handing over toothpaste. Being good parents for Ben seemed to be the only subject they had any mutual interest in. The happy first years of their marriage on the commune now seemed like the memory of an adolescent summer camp romance of holding hands and kissing after singing songs around campfires.

One day Mia came home from the grocery store, saw Howard with the cat on his lap, surfing channels by remote from the La-Z-Boy, and accepted that she was living with a complete stranger. Since leaving the commune she had slowly watched the man she fell in love with fade away, dissolving into something unrecognizable. Howard was like a double exposure: He was with her and somewhere else at the same time, and that other place had already pulled him away from the person he had once been, the person she thought she would be eternally connected to. Mia felt closer to the checkout girl she saw each Thursday at the market. Howard had become a silent being she only shared a dwelling with, a creature who filled ashtrays with cigarette butts while watching ball games. She had heard his same stories for over a decade, the same jokes she had once laughed at hysterically. They didn't even eat dinner together any longer, just nibbled silently on stale popcorn while cheering for Ben from sports bleachers. Howard's own father had never gone to any of his son's high school wrestling meets, but Howard never missed one of Ben's baseball games.

Howard wasn't surprised when Mia began sleeping on the sofa in the living room. When Ben began to inquire, Mia could only say, "I had trouble sleeping; your father snores very loud." For Mia, Howard was no longer approachable; he was almost as socially challenged as the disabled adults he trained. He had slowly denied her access to his life. When she sat down on the edge of their bed that morning, she was overcome with a sense of failure, knowing neither of them had attempted reconstruction. There had been no major fights, no discussions over the necessity to compromise. Unlike other couples they knew, they had never taken a save-the-marriage vacation to someplace warm when things got rough, hoping that their problems would just wash away with a tropical tide. That unconditional love, that belief that Howard was the person she was meant to spend the rest of her life with because she could not imagine anyone loving her more than he did, simply didn't exist any longer.

"Morning," she said, knowing Howard was already awake. She placed her bird-like hands on his large knuckles. "What do you think about getting a divorce?"

Howard was silent for a moment, then looked at her. Mia was still beautiful, even with her tired expression. "Okay," he said, and that was it.

It was a marriage that died with a whimper rather than a bang. Howard kept Noodles and Ben lived with Mia.

Howard came to enjoy solitude, could no longer fathom why he had once chosen to live communally. Sometimes he wondered if his marriage would have lasted had they made aliyah to Israel, to live a socialist life on a kibbutz; one of many unrealized dreams. He often wondered what kind of life his ex-wife was leading until the day John Lennon was killed and Mia called him to talk about something other than Ben for the first time since the divorce. "My God, did you hear?" she asked when Howard answered the phone, and the two slowly started to become friends again.

The two began to see one another sporadically, though Howard was constant in helping Mia care for her father in his final, painful months, suffering from liver cancer. When Ben was in high school, they occasionally went to the movies together, after sitting together at his baseball games. People seemed to come and go with differing intensity in Howard's life, but Mia remained a stable constant. He couldn't get rid of her, and he didn't want to, ever. Since their son's high school graduation though, the two had not spent much time together. Then Ben came home from Alaska, where he had chosen to live rather than go to college.

It began with a phone call. Ben had not felt well for several months. Mia told him to see a doctor in Fairbanks; Howard mailed a check to pay for the examination. Their son had been born with weak lungs, but that wasn't the problem. The symptoms were not specific; further analysis was suggested. Howard and Mia bought Ben a plane ticket and took him to a specialist in Portland, then to another in Seattle. One diagnosis after another led to the same conclusion. Their son's stem cells, which are produced inside the larger bones, were slowly being depleted. Ben was in serious need of a bone marrow transplant. He would die in three years, perhaps less, if he did not receive one.

It was a simple procedure. Once a candidate was successfully screened, liquid marrow would be removed from the pelvic bone and transferred to Ben, whose body would hopefully accept the substitute. But a compatible donor could not be located for Ben's rare marrow type.

Howard and Mia felt as if the earth had suddenly ceased to rotate. Time no longer proceeded in its dictated arrangement; a week became more like a day, hours moved like minutes. Ben had no health insurance. The diagnosis alone cost a fortune. Both Mia and Howard tapped their retirement funds. Howard even took out a second mortgage on his house. Ben eventually went back to Alaska to be with his girlfriend, Kelly, for the short time he had left. He didn't cry, although his mother did.

"Seventy percent of those needing a marrow transplant must find a donor outside the family," the doctor told Mia and Howard. "It would be more optimistic if you had had another child." But they had never thought of having more children. In her socially conscious youth, Mia was convinced that the world would crumble from overpopulation, even when Rabbi Reznik urged her to help the Jewish people replenish their numbers from the Holocaust. She resented the doctor's comment, feeling that he was blaming her for their limited options.

"I know you are divorced," one doctor had suggested, "but if you are not uncomfortable with the idea, you might consider in vitro insemination. Genetic counseling has recently become more successful. I can recommend several specialists. The technology is getting better. We are hoping to have new fertility drugs by 1990." Ben didn't have that much time. "There is a chance, twenty-five percent to be exact, that another child's marrow from your gene pool will match your son's."

Mia and Howard sat together over bran muffins and burnt coffee in the hospital cafeteria. In vitro would bankrupt them. Howard held Mia's hand as he thought of his son, how Ben was so much like they had been. Every two weeks he would call Ben in Fairbanks and listen to the details of the life his son was building, the girl he was seeing.

"Well, son," Howard had asked shortly before the shattering news came. "Is it love? Is Kelly the one?"

"I don't know, Dad. I guess we'll see," Ben answered. And when Howard heard this, he was shocked to hear the voice of his own distant, once youthful, ambivalent self coming from his son.

"If only we had the money," Mia said. "I'm only forty-one, you know. I'm still young enough to have another baby. It's possible."

Howard couldn't help thinking that he was going to turn forty-four the next month. "It's too bad we aren't still married," he had said, attempting to make her smile, trying anything to relieve her pain for a moment. "Then we could just do it the old-fashioned way." He forced a nervous laugh.

But Mia hadn't laughed. She released her ex-husband's hand and looked at him with new optimism. "I don't have a problem with that," she said.

There was no certainty that a new baby's bone marrow would match Ben's, but Mia and Howard were desperate. They had not had sex in almost ten years. Their only touching had been Howard's gentle kiss to her cheek when he brought Ben back to her house after weekend visits; that, and the recent support of hand-holding.

Unlike Howard, who had always handled tragedy with contemplation, Mia was her typical impulsive self. Some people broke down under pressure. She switched into overdrive; became emotionless, logical, coldly focused. She immediately made plans for the two of them to go to the coast together at the end of the month, when she knew she would be ovulating.

∘   ∘   ∘

"What do you think of Kelly?" Mia asked.

Howard took the opportunity to turn down the radio. "I don't know, I haven't met her."

"I think she's lovely," Mia said. "I spoke to her on the phone for the first time last night. She's a vegetarian, too. Do you think Ben will marry her after the transplant?"

"Ben's a little young, don't you think?"

"We married young."

"Maybe too young," Howard said.

"Yes, we should have waited longer."

"We could drive up to Fairbanks and meet her," Howard encouraged Mia, playfully.

"Great idea. They would love for us to see where they live; young people are like that. It took having Ben to get my father to see where we moved to. Will this car make it there?"

"Probably. Volvos are good cars."

"Mine would die, it can't even make it up Burnside to get out of Portland to the suburbs. When we go to Alaska, remind me to bring a portable tape deck."

He glanced over to Mia.

"You really can't stand this music, can you?" she asked as a Culture Club tune began.

He grinned.

"You're such a doll, Howard. You always were. I can't believe you put up with me as long as you did." She clicked off the radio and returned to the bed and breakfast listings. "All of these places are so expensive." They could have attempted to conceive at one of their houses, but the idea of a trip put them both more at ease.

"We can still stay at a cheap motel."

"No. Motel rooms are so smoky. Bed and breakfasts are quaint. I like that." Howard refrained from saying that he could do without doily decor.

"I can't believe how different it is out here," Howard said, snowflakes melting on the windshield. "Remember when we were in college, this whole drive was lined with trees."

"I know," Mia said, looking out at the wasteland of deforestation, snow blanketing enormous stumps that once supported thousand-year-old Douglas firs. "Remember when they first started clear-cutting this area? Ben came running home with a permission slip to volunteer with his Boy Scout troop to replant. You hated the Boy Scouts, but you went along with all those Nixon-loving dads. You were so pissed off when none of them believed you went to Vietnam."

"They didn't, they thought I was some hippie."

"Oh, you were, dear," Mia said and laughed.

"Those other dads were so macho. You should have seen it." She had heard him tell the story countless times. But she let Howard tell it again. "I got up there and they were making fun of me. But within fifteen minutes I'm the one instructing the kids how to plant the baby trees. All those fathers were just there to help the kids earn a merit badge. Ben must have replanted ten times as many trees as the other kids. The whole troop nicknamed me Fungus. I was Fungus and Ben was Little Fungus." He turned to Mia. "Hey, we did okay, didn't we? Raising Ben, I mean."

She smiled. "Yeah, we did."

The snow fell less, transforming into a modulation of ice and rain that collected into slush cones amongst the exhaust-tinged embankment as they exited the Sunset Highway.

"There should be an inexpensive bed and breakfast on Seashore Drive," Mia said.

Neither of them had been to the coast in years, not since taking Ben to spend time with Mia's father when he was young. That was years before the liver cancer, before Herbert Segal's home overlooking the Pacific Ocean was sold to help pay for his experimental surgery.

"Damn," Howard said, steering onto Seashore Drive, "they've really built up this area."

"I know. When I was a kid there was practically nothing but fields and homes. There must be fifty antique shops now."

"Not to mention the hotels."

Mia said nothing. The motels and bed and breakfasts had begun sprouting up like weeds by the time she left for college. The big hotels came later, the fortress-like Sand Dune Hotel's parking lot obliterating her father's beachfront property.

"There it is," Mia said.

Howard steered the Volvo into the parking lot, the car's exhaust pipe scraping over the sidewalk like fingernails running down a chalkboard. He cut the engine. "Well," he said after a short pause. "We're here."

"Yup," Mia said, staring at the windshield, watching the slush collect now that the wipers had ceased to flap. Howard reached into the back seat for his wool coat and Mia's rain slicker.

"This gonna be warm enough for you?" he asked.

"Oh yeah," she said. "I've got this turtleneck on and my mittens with me. I'll be fine."

"Ready?"

"Yup," she said, having not removed her seat belt yet. Howard stepped out into the coastal breeze, snow meshing with his beard. He opened the trunk and unloaded his duffel bag, took both Mia's suitcase and cosmetic case in one hand. Mia didn't wear makeup, never had. But the cosmetic case had been her mother's. Mia never really knew her mother; had only vague recollections of a kind woman who always smelled of applesauce. But Mia liked to take the case on trips. She always thought if she had a granddaughter that she would give her the case.

Howard opened Mia's door. She still hadn't removed her seat belt, had taken out the listings again. Her head snapped when she heard the door open. She looked at Howard. He still had manners, still opened doors for her. "There's supposed to be a good fish house a few blocks away. They'll have clam chowder. You like clam chowder."

"I'd like to shower first," Howard said.

"Okay," Mia said, and unfastened her seatbelt.

Mia stretched out across the bed of the pastel-decorated room, her shoes on the carpet beside the television. She breathed slowly and went about her short yoga routine.

Howard undressed in the bathroom. Carefully setting his glasses on the counter, he removed his sweater and looked into the mirror; placed his hands on the carpet-like patch of hair insulating his stomach, which appeared to be harboring a small watermelon. Mia was still slim, sexy with that black hair he had once enjoyed combing his fingers through. But thinking of his ex-wife in the next room, Howard wondered if he could actually go through with this. He thought of Mia simply going about the motions, tolerating his now enormous stomach pressed against her small ribs. He turned on the shower.

The water was comforting, tiny streams flowing between the bristles of his beard. There was a time on the commune when Mia would hear the shower and quietly creep into the bathroom, undress, and surprise Howard. But he didn't anticipate such romance now.

The water was dense. It reminded him of the hospital water he had bathed Mia's father in. Sponge and soap in hand, Howard had washed his former father-in-law's failing body.

∘ ∘ ∘

"Not so rough," Herbert Segal had said as Howard ran the sponge over the man's skin, folds and creases draping his backside and shoulders like a suit of flesh. Herbert had been a domineering presence in Mia's life. She calculated everything against what her father's reaction might be. Howard had always known this, even before meeting the man three years after he married Mia.

Mia's father was as different from Howard as one could imagine. Howard was drawn to wearing loose fabrics, solid colors that he could match without the effort of coordination. He hadn't been much different on the commune when they were married. While Mia and the other members paraded about barefoot in denim shirts with embroidered flowers, Howard's long brown curls, pulled back into a ponytail, had been his only sign of social rebellion. To Herbert Segal, Howard was simply sloppy, which translated into irresponsible. Howard's military service was among the few qualities Herbert ever found redeeming in the man Mia had chosen.

It took a great toll on Herbert's pride to allow the former son-in-law he never cared for to bathe him. Herbert liked to drink his coffee black, preferred a money clip to a wallet, never went more than two weeks without a trim at the local barbershop. He shaved meticulously and distrusted men with facial hair. His neck was never without the aroma of Sea Breeze.

"Too rough, too hard," the old man complained with each swipe of the sponge.

"Sorry, Herb," Howard had said. He had never referred to the man as Dad. Even when they were in-laws, he knew he was not welcome to.

Herbert Segal was a righteous man, the founder of the first Reform synagogue on the Oregon coast. For him, there was a certain way things were done: a right way or not at all. A daughter simply did not see her father without clothes on. After Herbert insulted a black orderly, Howard volunteered to bathe the old man.

"Fine," Herbert said reluctantly. "I won't stand on ceremony. Everyone leave the room and let me get this over with."

The two talked little during the sponge bath, but they had never spoken beyond cordial small talk in the past, usually sticking to safe subjects such as sports and automotive maintenance. Politics was off-limits.

Herbert saw Howard as the catalyst for Mia's disappointing him. He always hoped Mia would find a boy who might take over the liquor store he ran. The store had been one of Herbert's small successes. He had a reputation with the police for not selling to minors, for running an honest establishment. Herbert thought of himself as a responsible citizen. He even made donations to the local fire department. At the age of fifty, he decided he wanted a college education. Two years later he had an associate's degree from the local community college framed on his living room wall beside little plaques of service to B'Nai B'rith and financial contributions to the Anti-Defamation League.

Howard had been more annoyed than angered by his father-in-law. The man's overly cautious driving, spotless dishes, his habit of correcting everything Mia did from the way she toasted bread to her indifference to Ben wearing an earring. "My grandson looks like a queer. What's next, is he gonna date a colored girl? Feh! The boy's got too much of Howard in him. Mia, you never should have married that bum." It was naturally Howard's fault that Ben was never bar mitzvahed. In truth, both Howard's and Mia's spiritual motivation had gone bankrupt with the commune. Neither of them even thought about religion any longer.

The commune was something akin to blasphemy for Herbert. "This isn't Judaism," he said every time he visited after Ben was born. "You call this being closer to God, living in poverty? You think being poor is fun? We spent thousands of years pulling ourselves out of the shtetls and ghettos and now you want to put us right back there. My parents brought me to this country with nothing. Nothing! Now I've got my own business. That's work, not sitting around and smoking dope out here in the middle of nowhere."

Herbert Segal couldn't stand idleness, and the commune exemplified that to him, right down to the shit-covered floors of the dilapidated chicken houses. Herbert actually knew Rabbi Reznik, which increased his hatred for the commune. His visits reminded him of his repulsion for the Petaluma community he and Reznik were raised in, where their parents referred to each other as "chaverim." He thought that the commune members might as well address one another directly as "comrades" and have a hammer and sickle flag suspended from the hayloft. Sitting around the table in the barn, Herbert would ridicule the jam jar being used as a kiddush glass.

But Mia's father could be tender. Before each Sabbath dinner began he would stand behind Ben and place his hands upon his grandson's head. "May you be like Abraham and Isaac and Jacob and Moses and all of the great men that have come before you," he would say, then lean down and whisper into the child's ear, "and may you hit a home run your next time at bat." Then a kiss to the cheek. He would bless each child at the table; children dressed in what Herbert referred to as "rags."

The commune parents watched as their kids were spoken to, wondering why Howard and Herbert were not close since Mia's father seemed to be so gentle in these moments. Herbert would always end by standing behind Mia, placing his hands upon her head. "May you be like Sarah and Rachel and Rebecca and Miriam and all of the great mothers that have come before you." Then, leaning close to his daughter's ear, he would force himself to say what he did not honestly believe. "Your mother would be very proud of you, we both still love you very much." But he never stepped behind Howard.

Herbert believed that the divorce was Howard's doing, convinced there was another woman. He had little belief in the loyalty of the men of Howard's generation. "Selfish bastards," he would mutter, "wiping the flag with their asses." He considered Ben running off to Alaska instead of attending college to be a result of Howard's fatherhood. "Benjamin could have been a somebody. It's a shame, a real shame."

"How's that?" Howard asked, moving down to Herbert's lower back, rotating the sponge in tiny circles.

"Good, that feels good," Herbert said.

"They're having Hanukkah in the hospital tonight," Howard said. "The doctor says you're well enough to go to the children's ward. You like kids, it might cheer you up."

"Hanukkah in the hospital? What kind of hullabaloo is that? Let me tell you something: Hanukkah in the hospital? Why not Passover in the hospital? Huh? Why not Sukkot in the hospital? I'll tell you why, because Christmas is so close to Hanukkah and this place doesn't want to piss off an old guy like me who might call the ADL. See that nail on the wall above the sink; used to have a cross hanging there. They removed it because I checked the box on my background form that lets them know I'm not a Jesus freak when I die here."

"So, will you go to the children's ward? Lean forward so I can wash your neck." Herbert did so. "You could tell them the story of the Maccabees and the miracle of light, the way you told it to Ben when he was young. Remember?"

"Yeah, yeah, I remember. Sure, I'll go."

"Good," Howard said, taking the hand-held faucet and rinsing Herbert.

"Hey," Herbert said. "Thanks for doing this."

"Don't mention it," Howard said.

"Yeah, well, I just did. Thank you."

Thirty-eight years of selling liquor and Herbert had never taken a drink, but the doctors opened him up and assumed he was a closet alcoholic. The surgery was experimental, risky. The doctors planned to freeze the cancer and remove it from his liver like crystallized ice cream from the top of a bin. But they cut Herbert open and saw that they could easily remove half his liver and not help. A week later he fell into a coma.

Howard remembered that his former father-in-law had always had a passion for Irish music. He stopped by a record store on one of his nightly drives to the hospital and purchased everything Irish he could find—Celtic, Gaelic, folk. He even bought a Van Morrison album. Ben played each tape on the cassette machine that he brought from home to the Intensive Care Ward, including a U2 album after strong protest by Mia. Herbert Segal died to a Chieftains tune. The official cause of death: internal bleeding. But Howard knew it was more than that. And Mia, whose father and son had been her only family left, held tight to Howard's arm at the funeral, as if they had never been apart, as if only he could understand.

∘　∘　∘

Howard cut the shower, stepped out, and looked at his damp, middle-aged body in the mirror. A horrifying thought emerged: the possibility of playing Van Halen and Rush albums for his dying son in the hospital. He liked to think that he would cry if Mia did not get pregnant and Ben died. Chances were that at her age she wouldn't conceive, and that scared him—the chances. He had cried when Noodles died, but he knew he wouldn't for Ben. And that shamed him. How long would it take? he wondered, knowing that it had taken him five years to cry over his own mother's death. If Ben dies, he wondered, who will take care of me when my time comes? And he could only think of Mia. What if she doesn't get pregnant? he kept thinking. She's already in her forties, it just won't happen. Some girls in their late twenties have to keep trying for six months. He couldn't imagine Mia being willing to sustain a sexual relationship with him beyond this weekend. He certainly knew he couldn't do that. He combed his hair back, ran his fingers down his beard, and wrapped a towel around his waist.

"Better?" Mia asked, sitting at the foot of the bed atop the quilt comforter as Howard emerged from the bathroom. He nodded. "You look nice," she said.

"Thanks," he said, staring more at the bed than her, conscious of the towel and his damp body. He turned his back to her and went to his duffel bag.

He took out his clothes, placed them on the dresser. As he reached for clean socks, he felt the touch of Mia's dry hands on his shoulders. He froze as her palms ran down his back to his waist. Her breath fell against his skin. She took the tuck of the towel and released it to the floor. Pulling at Howard's arm, she turned his naked body around to face her.

Her turtleneck was tight. She had a slight tummy that he had not noticed before, but nothing like his own Buddha-like bulge. She gazed up at him, her small brown eyes wide. She leaned inward, tipped upward on her toes, and pressed her lips to his. Howard watched as her eyes closed, unable to do the same. She released and placed her cheek to his wet chest. He lowered his face to her scalp, inhaled. He knew what was at stake. This wasn't like when they were first married and had yet to discover what desperation was. This was about their son's life. With this, there was only one option left. He closed his eyes, untucked the back of her turtleneck, and ran his fingers over the small of her back. He hesitated, then raised the turtleneck. Mia's arms lifted and he pulled it from her. She smiled as he fiddled like a schoolboy with her bra. She stepped back and removed it herself, exposing her breasts, which she quickly pressed against his torso. They kissed again, clumsily. She took his hands in hers and stepped backwards toward the bed, her movements choppy until Howard gained the confidence to take her in his arms. His feet tangled at his ankles and his body barreled over hers onto the bed.

"Sorry," he said, his voice rushed.

Mia laughed. "That's okay." She kissed his forehead. "Give me a second."

He watched as she removed her socks, unfastened her belt, and hastily slipped off her jeans. She pulled at the sheets and slid beneath them. Her hidden body wiggled until one of her arms protruded and she dropped her panties to the floor. She had never concealed herself to him when they were married.

"Okay," she said. Howard didn't move. "Oh," she giggled, "don't tell me this is your first time. What was your name again?" Howard grinned. "Come on," she said. "I won't bite." She paused. "That is, unless you want me to."

Howard erupted into nervous laughter. She allowed him to move on top of her. Her body was warm against his. They kissed again. She liked the way he pulled at her earlobes with his lips just as he had when they were married. They continued to kiss, her fingers combing through his beard until, slowly, he entered her.

Howard paused, unsure, then pressed harder. Mia let out a pained groan. "I'm sorry," Howard said.

"Stop apologizing, silly." She laughed. "Hold on, this isn't working." She pushed his body to the side, tossed off the sheets, and went to her cosmetic case. Howard could now see her shadowed, naked body in full, watched as she removed a half-empty tube of vaginal lubricant from the cosmetic case, and came back to the bed. He felt that she could not possibly be enjoying herself. They never needed assistance when they were married. He wondered if the foreplay they had enjoyed during married life was still appropriate. More so, he wondered if lubricant would decrease their chances of conceiving.

Under the covers, he heard Mia squirt a glob of lubricant to her fingers before shuffling about. Then, with another glob, she leaned over and cupped Howard's penis with her hands, smiling. Howard was startled, wondered when she had begun using this, what lovers she had had or might possibly still have. Was there somebody she was not telling him about? If so, how would she explain this weekend to him, how would that person feel about this if they were lucky enough to conceive? Howard was uneasy with the thought that he had somehow intruded on a possible life that Mia kept from him. Had she assumed this weekend would be passionless? He simply did not know, and that frightened him: the thought that he no longer knew her. On the commune they had openly had extramarital affairs, but placed one another over all others. They had not agreed to be monogamous until Howard insisted on it after the commune went bankrupt and they moved to Portland.

"All right," she said, teasingly. She lay down again and pulled him back on top of her. He became excited as Mia began to move her hips. But having not been with a woman in almost three years, he climaxed quickly, with little more than a slight convulsion of his body, silent.

Mia was still; her palms held against his shoulder blades as he slowly shrank inside of her. Howard's being quick would have been forgivable when they were first married, even flattering. But there was too much to risk now. She patted her palms against his back as if burping a baby and he removed himself to stretch out beside her. She was no longer concerned with the sheets. Unlike when they were married, she did not immediately get up to pee, but instead brought her knees to her chest and held them there, leaning back, lying on her shoulders. Howard couldn't look at her. Strangely, he was thinking of Rabbi Reznik eighteen years ago, lecturing on the rabbinical teaching for a husband to satisfy his wife before himself.

"I'm sure it will last longer tonight," Mia finally said, still tucking her knees tight to her chest.

Howard was surprised. In truth, he had assumed they would only do it once.

"Are you hungry?" she asked after a long silence.

"Sure, I can eat," he said.

"Good," she said, then kissed his cheek before sliding from the bed to dress.

It had stopped snowing as they walked down Seashore Drive back toward the bed and breakfast. The ashen clouds were still heavy, as if holding something back. Howard was satisfied from his clam chowder, Mia from her lentils and rice. They passed numerous antique shops, Mia peering through windows at items she could never have.

"So," she said, "what should we name him?"

"The new baby?"

Mia laughed. "Don't tell me you're still nervous. What do you think about a name, old man?"

"Well, old lady," he said, "I thought Herbert would be nice, after your father."

Mia continued walking. "Oh, that's so sweet of you, Howard. You always were thoughtful. But isn't that a little old-fashioned? Herbert Goodkin isn't exactly with the times."

"How about Herbert as a middle name?"

"And what about a first name," she continued, pressing him.

"I don't know," Howard said. "How about Noodles?"

"Noodles Herbert Goodkin? Very nice." She removed one of her mittens and held Howard's hand as they continued to walk. "Let's think on that one."

"I don't know," Howard said. "I like the sound of it."

"It could be a girl," Mia added, thinking how nice it would be to leave her mother's cosmetic case to a daughter.

"Could be."

The wind was gusting, intoxicating them with the odor of salt, the air crisp, tingling as they collided with it.

"Candy?" Mia gasped like a giddy child seeking permission. They had stopped in front of a sweet shop. "We have to go in."

Mia's sugar tooth had annoyed Howard in the latter years of their marriage, but he found it amusing now, recalled how she complemented even a breakfast of jam and toast with a handful of chocolate chips. He fished out his cigarettes; he hadn't smoked since picking Mia up that afternoon.

Howard's eyes squinted, his lips spread into a smirk. "You go ahead," he said.

"Listen," Mia snapped in the manner she might have scolded Ben as a child, her hands firm on her hips. "Let's get something straight. I don't comment on that disgusting habit of yours and you leave my own weakness alone."

He slipped a butt between his lips. "Whatever you say, darling," he mumbled, and she disappeared into the shop.

Howard looked to the reflection of the window and, for a moment, saw the way he had once posed with his Norton motorcycle outside a pizza parlor twenty-two years ago; waiting until the new weekend hostess, a girl named Mia Segal, got off her Saturday evening shift. He remembered what a confident young man he had been when he had asked her if she wanted to go for a ride even though she had turned him down the night before. Mia was more drawn to guys with Volkswagens, but Howard's smile had been irresistible.

Howard lit another cigarette, ran his hands together against the chill. He thought of ways he might improve his performance later that night, tried to recall what had pleased Mia when they had been married. Still, he could not stop thinking of Ben. Is what we're doing right? he kept wondering. They hadn't told Ben yet, wanted to wait until Mia was sure they had conceived. They had no idea how to explain it to him. That was almost as frightening as knowing how slim Mia's chances were of getting pregnant in one weekend. They just couldn't bring themselves to discuss it. They couldn't even talk about where the baby would live if it entered their lives. Howard simply assumed it would be with Mia.

He watched the wind pick up speed, the trees swaying, snowflakes catching air like dust particles. The sky was darkening into charcoal; he could hear the tide creeping over the Pacific's shore. He thought of Ben with his short spiky hair in Alaska: his horn-rimmed glasses, spectacles that were stylish in Howard's own youth and now the definition of anti-style for Ben. He thought of Ben's choice to keep a kosher diet, wondered where that came from, surely not from him or Mia.

The early years of Ben's life were the most vivid. Howard cherished the memories—how he and Mia would sleep on the hay-covered ground beside Ben's cedar-wood crib in the barn of the commune. Howard rose every two hours to listen to his son's struggled breathing, adjusting the humidifier Herbert had bought when he learned his grandson suffered from weak lungs. Howard recalled how easily he would wake with the slightest change in Ben's breathing, launching himself to the crib to see if he needed the oxygen tank they had invested in. Nothing but Ben could wake Howard. He had spent hours teaching himself how to secure the mask around his son's tiny face, knowing just how much oxygen to gauge. That time seemed almost dreamlike now; the long hikes

Howard would take Ben on, the annual outings to the Oregon Country Fair and to Portland for the Rose Festival Parade with Ben high on his shoulders, his son's curiosity for everything from sand castles to the geological formation of Crater Lake.

Howard always thought Ben would become something more than Mia and he had been. In high school Ben had talked about becoming a dentist: traveling to Israel and volunteering to examine Russian immigrants. "I wouldn't do it for the money," he told his father. "I want to help people." He was disappointed when Ben said he was no longer interested in dentistry or Israel. "It was just a phase," he had told his father. "I can't see myself looking into other people's mouths all day."

"Well, then," Howard had said, "how about gynecology, you could look into something else." And when Ben scolded his father for such a chauvinistic comment, leaving the house with a door slam, Howard felt that he had somehow betrayed Mia and everything he had once believed in, that he had grown into somebody he no longer recognized.

Howard's life had not been relegated to an hourglass at nineteen, but his son's had. At Ben's age he was filing casualty forms in a Saigon office while other boys his age were fighting the war in the paddies and jungles of Vietnam. What about my son? Howard thought, can't God give a few of my years to Ben, even one extra year? I've lived enough. Then, he thought again, what if Mia doesn't get pregnant? She probably won't. Will we keep trying? If she doesn't get pregnant, then what does this weekend mean?

Mia opened the door to the candy store, came out holding a bag of chocolate-covered pistachios. Howard stamped out his cigarette under his shoe.

"I have an idea," Mia said. "We should celebrate, shouldn't we?"

"Absolutely. What did you have in mind?"

"Well, remember when I found out I was pregnant with Ben? I woke up the morning after we...you know." She smiled. He nodded. "I just knew I was pregnant, remember? And from that moment on, I didn't smoke grass for the next nine months. What do you think about sharing my second pregnancy with me?"

Howard swallowed hard, his Adam's apple lifting and bobbing like a metronome. He hesitated, then reached into his pocket and reluctantly relinquished the cigarettes with a sigh. "Done," he said, handing Mia the pack. He then checked his other pocket to make sure the fresh pack he had bought that morning was still there. But as he stared at Mia, he realized that in all the years of knowing her, he had never lied to this woman. He reached back into his pocket and handed over the unopened pack, to Mia's surprise. She smiled and dropped both packs into her purse.

Howard stared at this woman to whom he had been married and had once thought he would grow old with, a woman he had retained in his life as a constant while his youthful idealism had been compromised by practicality. Seeing Mia now, he felt unhelmed, spun to the ground like a fallen leaf. What if? he thought. What if we could fall in love again? And the thought fluttered away just as so many had before.

Mia edged against his warm torso, shielding herself from the cold. He placed his arms around her, squeezed. He kissed her forehead, his whiskers tickling her.

She giggled and looked up. "My God," she said. "An eyelash." She tweezed the eyelash resting on the bridge of Howard's nose between her fingers. "Make a wish for me to have a baby, a little girl, with a matching bone marrow for Ben." She paused. "Are those too many wishes?"

"Let's make it twins," Howard said, "double our luck."

"Okay," she said, shivering. And Howard gently blew the eyelash into the coastal breeze, not looking to see which way it went.

"Can you feel it yet?" he asked. "Do you think we're pregnant?"

Mia looked down at the damp sidewalk, not wanting Howard to see her eyes, not wanting him to see what she was painfully aware of, what she assumed he was not accepting.

"I guess we'll know tomorrow morning if I feel it or not," she said. And she looked up at her ex-husband.

"But what if you don't feel it? What if we don't...?" and he stopped.

She tried to smile, but couldn't; instead took one of Howard's large hands with both of hers. She said nothing more and slowly led him back to the bed and breakfast, knowing that she would still need the lubricant, knowing that after that night they would never be with each other in this way again.

$\mathcal{N}$INA THE USEFUL

$\mathcal{N}$INA WAS NOT accustomed to such hot weather, although her pride would never allow her to admit it. Since it was going to be one hundred and five degrees that day, Nina's daughter Ida had her husband Alex drive into the city to bring Nina back to the comfort of their air-conditioned, West Hills home in the San Fernando Valley. Nina had always thought air conditioning was strange. However, it was not as strange to her as living in Los Angeles had been the past year. After her father Abe died, Ida brought Nina down to Los Angeles and moved her into a modest city apartment that Alex leased a few blocks off Pico Boulevard. Nina had expected to be moved into the guest bedroom of her daughter's spacious suburban home, but Ida would rather have left her mother in an assisted living community back in Saskatchewan than endure such a situation. Nina was touched by the apartment proposal, believing her daughter was being considerate of "an older lady's need for privacy."

"Is not necessary to haff own place," Nina had said.

Ida panicked and quickly concocted a story that Alex was planning to use the apartment as a tax write-off and that it was necessary for Nina to live there for the time being. Nina still did not understand. She wanted to live with her daughter's family as her own mother had lived with her in old age. It was the expected tradition.

Nina, now in her early eighties, lived within five minutes walking distance of a supermarket and bus stop. The supermarket was an odd concept for her to grasp, having a baker, butcher and grocer all in one place. But Nina had grown to appreciate Los Angeles buses since Ida now refused to allow her behind the wheel of a car, having forced her to sell Abe's Buick before leaving for California. There had been no buses in Russia when Nina was a young woman, not even in Odessa before she and Abe had been able to leave. The only bus she had ever known until then was the Greyhound that occasionally passed through the small town of two hundred in Saskatchewan where Ida had been raised.

Thees place I liff now vill do, yes not bad, Nina often thought to herself. It only bothered her that she could not take the bus into the Valley to see her daughter's family. She prayed for the day when Ida would ask her to come live with them.

"Alex is coming to get you, Mom," Ida had said over the phone that morning.

"Vy Alex should come to get me?" Nina said, "I am fine."

"Mom, it's supposed to reach a hundred and five degrees today and you don't have air conditioning. You're coming out here to stay at the house."

"Everyone tell me vat to do. Vy you do thees?"

"I'm not arguing with you, Mom. Alex will be there in an hour, so be ready to go." Ida hung up the phone.

Nina could not understand what the fuss was about. She had survived the winters of both Russia and Canada. *How different heat in Los Angeles?* she thought. *Von extreme no different from next.* She knew extremes quite well. But she also knew that Ida, who never minced words, was serious when she said Alex would arrive in an hour. She began straightening things around the tiny apartment in preparation of leaving for the day.

She liked Alex. "Such a nice man," she often told the checkout clerks at the supermarket. Every time, without fail, while her purchase was being bagged, she told the clerks how Abe had owned a small grocery store of his own for twenty-two years in Saskatchewan. She talked about Abe, Ida, and her son-in-law constantly. But what she loved most was removing photographs from her purse and talking about her grand-daughter, Rachel.

Nina had had a brother, Alexei, who had not survived the pogrom that came through Odessa shortly after she and Abe had left. Alex always seemed to remind her of Alexei, whom she still affectionately referred to as her Sasha. That was why she had coaxed Abe into attending the wedding in Los Angeles when Ida announced that she intended to marry Alex less than a year after her divorce from Rachel's father. Nina could accept that Alex was not Jewish. What mattered to her was that he presented himself as a responsible father figure for her granddaughter.

Sweat was condensing over every inch of her skin, but Nina would not let it bother her. She had refused to allow Alex to install an air conditioner in the apartment. Staying in the Valley for only the day, she packed light, only a handbag and her favorite purple sweater. She was sure it would get chilly that evening. *Such hot temperature vill not last long,* she thought. Before leaving the apartment to wait outside by the curb she looked at the picture of Abe that hung above the table in her boxy kitchen, right next to the creased photograph of her two sons, the older brothers Ida had never known, from a life in Russia she had never been able to escape hearing about. "Look to vere I go, Abe. You have such nice daughter, alvays tink of me from time you gone. I come back later."

From the fridge, she took two dollar-sized pancakes she had saved from Denny's the night before, still wrapped in the syrup-soaked napkin. She stuffed them into her bag, then locked the apartment.

Nina smiled and waved as Alex approached the curb. She despised his German-made car, but was always silent about such things, never wanting to make a fuss. She was a petite woman, not even five feet tall. Alex routinely asked her how such a tiny lady was strong enough to give birth to three children. It was flattering to her when he said such things, but she could not help thinking of Ida's twin brothers who had not survived their childhood in Odessa, could not help wondering if she would have been living with one of their families now that Abe was gone. She had always been convinced that they would have been educated men; not merchants as Abe and her own father had been. She had been successful for quite some time in not dwelling on her two abortions before she left Russia. Ida did not even know about them. That was easy, those children she never knew. But not the twins she had borne and breast-fed. She could never forget her own babies being skewered on bayonets and danced around the street by the same soldiers who had dowsed her own brother with gasoline to be burned alive before her eyes, only to have his throat slit when the flames failed to end his life.

She was thankful that Ida had gone to college, believing a woman needed an education in the modern age. Every time she saw Rachel's good marks on school reports, Nina was certain that her granddaughter would become the first woman president of the United States.

Alex parked and immediately rushed around the curb to assist Nina into the Mercedes. She liked it when Alex took the time to do this; it was not as much of a tormenting experience as when Ida helped her. *Vat a gentleman, such a mensch*, she thought.

The drive into the Valley was bright. Alex helped Nina turn down the visor on the passenger's side to shade the sun, even though she was so short that it did not help much. Noticing that Alex was wearing sunglasses, she reached into her purse and removed a pair that were ridiculously too large for her own face; thick black plastic shades with purple rims. She put them on and Alex laughed. *How strange Alex ees sometimes*, she thought. She had bought them while spending an afternoon with Rachel at the mall.

"You look cool, Nanna," Rachel had said. That was all the incentive Nina needed to purchase the glasses and a matching pair for her granddaughter.

·Nina enjoyed the words her granddaughter taught her: cool, awesome, etc. She occasionally attempted to teach Rachel a few Yiddish phrases, but never when Ida was present. "Don't teach her that crap," Ida would say. "My daughter is not a greenhorn."

As Alex drove down the freeway into the valley he turned the radio dial from one news channel to the next in search of political talk shows. Alex loved politics. Nina often giggled at the way he salivated over poll results. He definitely reminded her of her brother, Alexei, her only Sasha.

The air conditioning blew furiously. Nina discreetly slipped on her purple sweater. Finally, she rolled down her window. Alex left the air conditioning on and smiled politely. Nina could not understand his obsession with controlling the environment, particularly in automobiles. She liked breathing free air, watching the sequoias pass by as the car descended into the Los Angeles suburbs. Never as a young woman in

Odessa would she have thought that such trees existed.

It was almost eight o'clock when they reached the West Hills home. Alex helped Nina out of the car, opened the front door of the house, and gave her a kiss on the cheek before leaving. He pocketed the five dollars she had left by the gearshift that she hoped he would use to buy some breakfast before work.

Ida was bustling about when Nina walked in.

"Hi, Mom," Ida said, running into the living room and then returning to the kitchen with a thick manila folder. The toaster popped as she shoved the folder into a glossy black briefcase. She took the bottom half of the bagel and swiped a quick lump of nonfat cream cheese over the top, then sandwiched it with the other half. "I gotta get going, Mom. I'm late for work. There's a whole pile of mending I put on the couch in the living room for you." Ida, in anticipation of leaving her mother alone in her home for the day, went through old clothes and made as many discreet rips and tears as possible. She even pulled a few buttons off some of Alex's flannels, hoping the mending would keep Nina occupied until the evening. She knew that her mother would meddle into something or another if not left a project for her to feel useful.

"Ida, now you go vork and only eat bagel? Sit, I make breakfast." Nina was convinced Ida was anorexic, shocked at how the designer suits she wore to the office hung loosely from her jazzersized body as if on a coat hanger. She doubted that her daughter's thighs, hidden under those dark stockings and short skirt, even touched each other. Nina imagined two skeletal bones chopping air like the Ethiopian children on television that she donated money to every month. Even when pregnant with Rachel, Ida had never appeared healthy to her mother.

"Mom, I gotta go."

"No, you sit. I make eggs and pancakes, vay you like ven you leetle girl."

Ida rolled her eyes, tossed her thick, ironed-straight, black hair out of her face and kept lifting the scattered pages of the morning *Times* in search of her keys. Nina noticed that her daughter had failed to flatten several of her natural curls that morning.

"I should be home around six, Mom."

"Vat about Rachel and Alex?"

"Alex is flying to San Francisco. He'll be there for the next two days."

"Rachel?"

"She'll be home after school, then she has softball practice." Ida tossed the newspaper to the floor. "Where are my goddamn keys?" She slipped off her heels and ran into the living room again.

"Ees very late for such leetle girl to be out," said Nina as she began putting away the cream cheese and wiping the counter. "Ees not healthy for leetle girl outside after dark."

"Okay," said Ida, rushing into the kitchen with her keys in hand and slipping her heels back on. "I'm leaving."

"I make dinner for ven you home," said Nina, closing the fridge. "I make roast, vay your brothers like ven they leetle boys."

Ida stopped and looked right at her mother. She hated hearing about the two brothers she had never known beyond the pictures Nina kept. "No, Mom. Don't touch anything. Just do the mending I put out for you."

"Vat, I should not eat in such a cold house? Vy you need thees air condition?"

Ida quickly slipped on her two hundred dollar sunglasses. "Make a sandwich if you're hungry, Mom, but absolutely no cooking. Understand?" She turned her back and headed for the front door. "I'll see you around six. We'll go out for Chinese or something. The number for my office is on the fridge if you need it. And don't go anywhere. Stay in the house." Door slam.

Nina soon heard the sound of Ida's car pulling out of the driveway. Alone. She hadn't even had a chance to offer her purple sweater to Ida to cover those thin shoulders and arms from the potential cold if she removed the jacket of her designer suit.

She went to the living room and saw the pile of mending Ida had left on the couch, knowing full well the reason for it being there. *Such dear daughter*, she thought, *worry I be bored in house all day.* She scooped up the pile of clothes into her arms and went to the laundry room to place it in a basket.

Nina slid the door open and quickly found the light switch. She could not believe the condition the room was in. *Poor Ida*, Nina thought, *she vork so hard, haff no time to keep laundry room nice.*

She spent the next hour emptying every item from the laundry room, then rearranging and reorganizing until it was properly ready to be used in an efficient manner. After starting a load of whites, she opened the linen closet and spent another hour refolding every towel, sheet, drape, and washcloth the proper way. *Poor Ida,* Nina thought again, *she never fold towel right vay I teach her as leetle girl. Alvays her own vay, not dz right vay.*

After preparing herself a scrambled egg Nina relaxed, reading an article from the *Time Magazine* she had found while searching through drawers in the room Ida and Alex had converted into a study. After devouring every word of gossip on Britain's royal family, she was horrified by an article describing in detail the rituals of a particular University of Arizona's fraternity's hazing, where pledges had been forced to drink mass amounts of water until they could drink no more. The article focused on the result of this popular entrance requirement; the death of a seventeen-year-old freshman. *Die from drinking votter?* Nina thought, *I never knew.*

She finished the egg and went to the front room to sit and write out a list of things that needed to be done to the house. Passover was approaching in less than a week. *Poor Ida,* Nina thought, *she so busy she have no time to start cleaning for first night seder.* After rummaging through Alex's record collection, she put on Carly Simon's *No Secrets* album. Two Neil Diamond records were left out for later. Nina liked feeling as though she was still knowledgeable about modern music. She knew she might find an even more modern selection in Rachel's bedroom, but would never consider going in there. *Leetle girls need privacy,* she thought. Besides, her granddaughter had only recently forgiven her for sewing dark denim patches over the strategically ripped knees of her favorite stonewashed jeans a few months before.

Nina sat on the recliner and began writing out the list of things Ida needed done for the preparation of Passover, tried to ignore the slight pain in her arthritis-stricken hands. She would accomplish as much as possible that day, then come back and finish over the next week, certain that this would compel Ida to consider having her move into the guest bedroom. She didn't even need to look over the house, the list of the obvious tasks simply came to her as she hummed along to Carly Simon singing "The Right Thing to Do." The list was extensive, everything from washing the kitchen floor to clearing the entire house of all grain products.

Several hours later Nina knew there was much more to accomplish, but she also wanted to begin preparing dinner for when Ida came home. *Such considerate daughter,* she thought, *tries to make easy for me dzat I not cook. Ida need good dinner ven Alex and Rachel ees not home.*

It was then that Nina heard the front door slam. She glanced down to the silver watch she wore on a chain around her neck, then looked sharply at her granddaughter. It was only noon.

"Rachel, vat are you home so early? Vy you not in school? You sick?"

Rachel tossed her backpack to the floor and skipped over to throw her arms around Nina, squeezing tight.

"Hi, Nanna. We had a half-day of school." She let go and skipped to the kitchen. "I gotta run. I've got softball practice in an hour."

She followed Rachel into the kitchen and pulled her by the arm away from the refrigerator.

"Vat you doing?"

"I'm gonna make a sandwich."

"Sit, I make you kasha."

"No, please don't make me kasha. I'll throw it up."

"Fine, I make sandwich."

"But I was going to make myself a sandwich."

"No, you sit, I make sandwich."

"But Nanna—"

"I say sit. Such beautiful face, but too thin, just like your mother."

Rachel giggled, remembering her mother's instructions to occasionally humor her grandmother. She kissed Nina on the cheek. "Okay," she said.

"There," said Nina, "sit at table." *Such a happy child,* she thought, *Ida do vell raising her.*

Still giggling, Rachel went to the kitchen table and pulled a chair out.

"No no no!" Nina said, racing to her granddaughter.

"What?" said Rachel. "What is it?"

"No sit on corner of table, bad luck."

"What?" Rachel giggled.

Nina pushed the chair away from the corner to the middle of the table, clutching Rachel by the arm. "No sit on corner, you not get married for seven years if you sit on corner."

Rachel erupted into laughter.

"Vat? Vat ees funny?"

"I'm only twelve, Nanna, I'm not getting married any time soon."

"Yes, but in seven years you be nineteen, and then be different."

Rachel did not say another word about the matter. She sat and thumbed through an issue of *Seventeen* until Nina brought two grilled cheese sandwiches to the table.

"Vat you read?"

"Oh, nothing. Just stuff about boys."

"Vat about boys?'

"Just stupid stuff, like being honest about your feelings with them. Dumb things."

"You shoult alvays be honest." She slapped the table with her palm. "Eat, I get you milk."

Rachel smiled and bit into the sandwich, the cheese oozing out the sides from the bread and sticking to her lips.

After Rachel was finished and obediently followed her grandmother's demand to drink two big glasses of two percent milk, she went to her bedroom, changed into her softball uniform and tried to fill a large thermos with water from the kitchen sink's filtering tap.

"Vat you do?" asked Nina, finishing her own sandwich.

"It's hot out. I'm gonna take some water with me to practice."

"No no no!" hollered Nina, swiping the thermos from Rachel's hands. "No drink votter. Boy die in Arizona last veek drinking votter."

"But—"

"No, no drink votter. You promise your Nanna, you not drink any votter." She grabbed Rachel by the shoulders, looking up into her enormous brown eyes, arms almost trembling. "Now, you promise. No drink any votter. Say so to me."

Rachel was perplexed, but her mother had always instructed her both to humor her grandmother and to respect her.

"Okay," said Rachel.

"No, promise again."

"I promise." She gave her grandmother a long hug.

Nina finally pulled back and took Rachel's face by one hand. "Good girl."

After Rachel left for softball practice, Nina discovered two frozen chicken breasts in the freezer. She preheated the oven to defrost them, then opened a drawer in search of a dusting rag. It quickly occurred to her how disorganized Ida's kitchen was. She could notice nothing in the proper or practical place. *No sense to have kitchen with things in crazy places*, she thought. Painstakingly, she began unshelving each item from every cupboard and drawer, then categorized everything on the kitchen table and surrounding floor. She went to the garage and retrieved a stepladder to reach the pots and pans, which were in an inconvenient place beside the Jell-O molds. While putting away the molds in their new home, she decided to make a Jell-O dish for Rachel. There was not enough time for her to completely defrost and excavate the freezer.

It was almost four o'clock when Nina completed straightening and reorganizing Ida's kitchen, having also scrubbed the kitchen floor twice on her hands and knees in addition to perfectly preparing dinner. She concluded the project by accumulating all the grain-products she had discovered and dumping them in the trash outside, with the exception of a challah and bag of bagels she had found which she immediately placed in the foot-cabinet where Ida had previously kept plates and bowls. She secured the two-hinged doorknobs to the cabinet with an elastic band to symbolize that it contained bread and should not be opened until after the Passover holiday was over. She then looked over the kitchen with pride, imagining that after seeing what a wonderful job she had done, Ida would instantly ask her to move into the guest bedroom.

Nina then took a short break to eat the dollar-sized pancakes she had saved from Denny's. Exhausted, she went to the living room and put on one of the Neil Diamond records she had taken out earlier. She lowered her hearing aid and turned up the volume to the amplifier as high as possible before lying on the couch to take a short nap. She loved the company of singing as she fell asleep. It reminded her of when Abe had occasionally sung to her before bed. Lying down on the sofa, she made a mental note to begin reorganizing the pantry after she awoke.

Ida arrived home at five o'clock. She knew Nina preferred to eat by sunset but would wait, even if starving. Therefore, she had arranged to leave the office early. The piercing static of Neil Diamond's voice could be heard from the driveway. She opened the front door and found her mother asleep on the couch.

Nina awoke as the needle was removed from the turntable and looked down at the silver watch she wore. She turned up her hearing aid. "Oh, vy you home early, dear?"

"How was your day, Mom?" Ida was irritated by the records being out, but felt secure that her mother was only sleeping. She could already smell the chicken, mapping a trail to the kitchen.

"Oh, it vas good."

"Did you keep yourself busy?" Ida asked, walking towards the kitchen. She wanted nothing more than to sit down with a glass of wine and relax. She had promised herself on the way home that she and Nina would not quarrel that evening. She tossed her briefcase to the floor by the kitchen table, noticing it was already set for three, then kicked off her heels.

"Oh yes," said Nina, following Ida into the kitchen, "I vas fine, no problems."

"Good," Ida said. She walked towards the cupboards above the coffee maker and felt the dampness of the recently washed floor seeping through her nylons. The chicken and Jell-O dishes on the counter were impossible to miss. She felt an intense tightening begin to form in her throat but stayed calm. *Fine*, she thought, *we'll just eat here. Besides, the kitchen actually looks clean for once. Why fight?* Since marrying Alex, Ida had come to refer to cooking as reservations. A home-cooked meal was actually a pleasant thought.

"Mom," said Ida, "why don't you put the chicken on the table for us? I just want to get a drink. Then we'll eat."

Nina dashed across the slippery floor to retrieve the two dishes, ecstatic at being able to feed her daughter. *She look so thin in dzat crazy suit-dress she vear to vork*, she thought. *She vants to look like a man? Shoult have given her Abe's suits.* They had actually been donated to a homeless shelter.

"Vee shoult vait for Rachel to be home. You like vay I make thees chicken, Ida. It same vay your two brothers like before you vere born."

Ida closed her eyes. Tonight she did not want to hear about the brothers she had never known. She only knew that it would please her mother if she ate the chicken.

Opening the cupboard and expecting to find wineglasses, she instead discovered her cooking spices, lined alphabetically next to the sugar bowl and flour container. She slammed the cupboard and turned around to open the drawer she kept the corkscrew in, finding only her dishtowels. Looking down, she noticed the elastic band holding together the cabinet doors where plates and bowls had always been kept, finally realizing exactly what had happened.

She marched to the kitchen table. Nina was already sitting with a napkin over her lap and a proud smile. Ida slammed a fist onto the table, jolting the chicken dish to the edge.

"How could you?" Ida cried. "How could you?"

"How could I vat?" said Nina.

Ida let out a shriek and hit the table again, with both fists this time. The chicken dish jolted once more and tipped over, turning upside-down with the sauce spilling all over Ida's custom-tailored skirt before it hit the floor.

"Ugh," Ida grunted, then picked up the Jell-O dish and lifted it to her chest.

"No," said Nina, "I make for Rachel."

Ida slammed the Jell-O dish back on the table, stood, staring over Nina. "You know, Mom, sometimes I wish you'd just disappear. Can't you ever do that, can't you ever just disappear?"

"You not vish such ting," said Nina.

"No, Mom, I wish you'd really disappear."

"And vat if someday such ting happen to me like happen your brothers and father, then vat you tink?"

Ida closed her eyes, clenched her fists, and breathed slowly through her nostrils, just as her analyst had instructed her to do when she was stressed. The heat outside was no longer unbearable. She was ready to take her mother back to the apartment in the city.

The phone rang.

Pausing to force a calm tone to her voice, Ida answered the third ring. It was Rachel's softball coach, asking Ida to come for her daughter who had fainted from dehydration.

Early the next morning, Nina's phone rang. It was Ida.

"Hi, Mom, it's me. Listen, the reports say it might be even hotter today than yesterday. It's supposed to be the worst heat wave to hit L.A. in ages. I'm gonna come get you and bring you back to the house."

"I vill not go to house," said Nina.

"Mom, come on. I'm sorry about last night. I overreacted, okay?"

"I have ting to do, I am good here."

"Mom, you don't have any air conditioning. Listen, let's just forget about last night. I know you meant well. You can make dinner tonight. Rachel will be home. It'll be just the three of us, come on."

"No, Ida, I have much I do. You not vorry, I not mad, but I stay here."

There was a long pause. Ida thought of how much time she would save by not having to drive into the city to pick up her mother, come back to the Valley, and then leave for the office.

"Okay, Mom," said Ida, "but I'm gonna come by your place on my lunch break to check up on you, all right?"

"Dzat ees good," said Nina, "I promise I vill have ice tea ven you come, vay you like ven leetle girl."

"You have a fan, right?"

"Yes, I have fan."

"All right, Mom, that sounds good. I'll see you at one o'clock. And we'll still have dinner together, the three of us, okay?"

"Fine," said Nina, "have good day making money."

It was almost nine o'clock. Nina went to the window sill of her tiny kitchen and glanced at the plastic temperature gauge that hung by the branch of a geranium. Eighty-four degrees.

Dzat not hot, Nina thought, *more hot yesterday, never trust vetterman report.*

She slipped on her favorite purple apron and went to the bag of groceries she had purchased only a half-hour earlier at the supermarket. There was a roast, three grapefruits, a bunch of onions, garlic, a bottle of concord-grape Manischewitz, and then the item that truly brought her joy. Nina had used Quickie-Tight Plastic Food-Wrap for years and now it was available in a light shade of purple. *Ah, thees Los Angeles place finally have pretty ting dzat ees useful,* she thought.

She set the wrap on the counter, having already preheated the oven to three hundred and fifty degrees. It was important to begin preparing the food for Ida's Passover seder. She had decided that morning that she would cook everything in her own apartment so that there would no longer be a reason for them to argue. *Maybe I make good food for Ida's seder, then she ask me to live in guest room,* she thought.

After preparing the roast, then letting it marinate, she set the dish in the oven. The heat knob was turned up five more degrees for cooking.

Nina soon felt sweat trickle down her thin black eyelashes. She wiped her brow with a washcloth then felt a scratchiness forming in her throat. It would have felt refreshing to open the kitchen window for air, but she considered it as much bad luck to have a window open while cooking a roast as it was to not bring salt and bread into a new home. She would open the window once the roast was finished cooking, none of that air conditioning nonsense for her.

As for her throat, Nina thought she might be getting a cold. She took all three grapefruits from the counter and chopped them into thin, almost transparent slices, then ran a pot of water from the stove. Turning the burner to high, she dropped the slices into the pot. She had learned the remedy from her own mother as a child in Odessa. She never understood why Ida adamantly refused to use it for Rachel when she had contracted strep throat the previous winter. When the water finally evaporated in an hour there would be a residue of pure quinine at the bottom of the pot: perfect treatment for any ailment. *Doctor not needed for simple throat ache, Rachel vould been better next day.*

Nina then recalled her promise to have iced tea for Ida at one o'clock. She took a teakettle and ran faucet-water into it, then turned on the second burner. The tea would be iced once the bags had soaked into the boiling water. *Good vife know best vay ees first soak tea in hot votter dzen put in ice, not taste right if boil votter first, it lose flavor.* She looked at Abe's picture above the kitchen table. "Look, I make tea for Ida, Abe. Vay she like as leetle girl, like you alvays like, too. It vill be done in leetle time. Maybe today she ask me to live in guest room." She took a dust rag and wiped Abe's picture frame, then the frame containing the creased photograph of her sons.

She stared at their round faces then turned back to Abe's portrait. She smiled at him, her top lip almost curled enough to reveal the jiggled, loose fit of her dentures, the same way she always did when he had charmed himself into her good graces.

"Remember dee gift you give me on our vedding day, Abe?" she said aloud. "A big frying pan. Remember vat I say? Vy you give me such big frying pan? Ees only two of us. And vat you say? Soon ve'll need big frying pan." She gave a girlish giggle, wiping the top of the frame again for assurance, then looked to Ida's infant photo to the left of his, then back to the twins. "And you vere right, I did need big frying pan." She lightly rubbed the frame of Ida's picture, then refolded the rag and returned it to its proper place in the drawer with her party napkins.

Feeling mildly lightheaded, Nina sat at the small kitchen table and looked through the morning's *Times*. She read through the complete obituary section twice for possible familiar names, then took a few glances at the front page: mostly political headlines and statistics on the polls concerning the upcoming race for mayor. She smiled, thought of her Sasha, and then of Alex. She wondered if Alex was enjoying his business trip to San Francisco, was concerned to know if he was eating enough, if they fed him well at his hotel.

The kettle whistled. Nina carefully poured the boiling water into a large thermos and dropped in several tea bags, closing the lid as tight as her arthritic hands would allow. She made a mental note to ice the tea before Ida arrived, then went to peek into the pot of boiling grapefruit. *Still long vay to go,* she thought, then turned up the heat knob on the stove. "Grapefruit not best kind, Abe," she said, looking at his picture again, "not fresh like you alvays had in your store. Thees supermarket ting not so super."

Nina suddenly felt a sharp pain in her chest. She almost fell to the floor, but she caught herself on the counter. She then brought a palm to her chest and felt the sweat soak into her now-drenched purple apron, right through from her lavender dress. The thought of calling Ida at work came to mind. The number was posted in large, permanent marker on her fridge. *No, I call ven I take roast out, if pain still make problem.* Carefully she went to the chair.

After reading the complete morning's *Times*, Nina rose from the chair just as the timer for the roast went off. The pain came back, striking sharper than before. She brought one hand to balance herself on the counter and the other to her chest. The bun of hair at the back of her head felt tight. Released, her hair fell long like damp straw, gray strands sticking to the perspiration of her cheeks.

Composing herself, she opened the oven and felt the heat assault her frail body. She took her two favorite purple oven-mitts and removed the roast after basting it. The pain struck again and she dropped the pan onto the counter. The arthritis in her hands was almost as unbearable as the chest pain itself.

She bit her tongue. *Maybe ice tea help*, she thought, and unscrewed the thermos top, then poured the steaming liquid into a large, ceramic serving-gourd. She opened her icebox, enjoyed the cold wave of moisture colliding with her creased skin, then removed both ice trays. She struggled several times to break the ice from the plastic, then dropped the cubes into the gourd. *Maybe I open vindow*, she thought.

Nina went to the counter to get her newly purchased purple plastic food-wrap. The pain struck again, more intense than before. She grabbed her chest with both hands and smelled the sweat tainting the conditioner in her hair. Carefully, she stretched the wrap over the roasting pan. The pain struck once more, this time bringing her to her knees. She wanted to scream but found that she couldn't. She looked up, and saw that she had forgotten to close the door to the oven. With all her strength she brought one arm up and closed it. She could not reach to turn off the oven heat knob, or the burner for the pot of boiling grapefruit. The pain struck one more time and Nina dropped to the hot, rubbery, linoleum.

When Ida found Nina at one o'clock, the pot of grapefruit was still boiling on the stove with quinine-residue collecting at the bottom. The roast on the counter was covered in purple plastic food-wrap. A gourd of iced tea was waiting for Ida, just as Nina had promised, the way she had liked it as a little girl.

*L*AYLA TOV

"*W*HEN did she start crying?" Nathan asked.

"Well, there were a few times after we left Patrick. But she's cried every night since I put the dog to sleep." Carol checked her reflection in the microwave, squeezed her glossed lips together.

"So, is it because of Patrick or the dog?"

"Probably the dog. José always slept on Katie's bedroom floor. Seven years is a long time. She'll probably wake up crying sometime after you put her to bed. I'm not trying to freak you out, but you should know." She pulled a casserole dish from the fridge. "Okay," she said, "just re-heat for ten minutes and you should be fine."

Sliding over the hardwood floor of the hallway in her pantyhose, Carol went to Katie's bedroom to say she was leaving. Nathan downed the rest of his beer, tossed the bottle into the trash under the sink, and opened the fridge for another.

"All right," Carol said, returning to the living room. She slipped into her heels, turned her back to Nathan, and dropped something concealed in her palm into her purse. She snapped it shut and spun around. "How do I look?"

"Beautiful," he said. And she was beautiful, more so than when they had dated almost a decade before.

"Do you really mean that?"

"Yes, you look absolutely gorgeous."

"But will he think I'm pretty? Be honest, Nate."

Does she even need to ask? he thought. "Carol, he'll be drooling over you."

She smiled. "Thanks again for watching her. Really, you're the best for doing this." She looked up at him, her soft cheeks rising, then reached out and squeezed his forearm. "See you around midnight, and don't let her watch TV."

◦　◦　◦

Carol and Nathan had dated for two years in college, living together in a one-bedroom Berkeley apartment their senior year. One semester before graduating, Nathan realized he did not want to marry this woman he had jokingly referred to as a "half-breed" since meeting her at a Grateful Dead concert at the Greek Theater. Carol was not the woman he wanted to be the mother of his children.

Nathan simply wasn't the egalitarian Carol believed him to be. He had only volunteered to work on All-Campus Women's Liberation Day to score points with her when she was still guarding her virginity. At first she was a science project of sorts. He even wore a button that said "Proud To Be a Male Feminist" until she relented and slept with him after three months of coaxing. Two years later he overheard Carol tell a friend she would never change her last name if she ever got married, and Nathan was finally turned off. But he was smart enough, so he thought, to not break things off because she was a feminist. She said she wanted to follow him into the Peace Corps, but Nathan also couldn't tell her that he was looking forward to sleeping with other volunteers. He knew he didn't love Carol, even though he often told her he did. He thought he might eventually be able to love her, but that didn't mean he wanted to swear off other women. Nathan needed a convincing lie, something he felt she would agree was not reconcilable.

As they lay in bed together after quick morning sex before Carol's Renaissance Art class their senior year, Nathan told her that he would not marry a woman who had a Jewish father and a gentile mother. He said that while he was not religious, his Judaism meant too much to his identity to be compromised by her own interfaith background. He even went so far as to say that since Carol's father was Jewish and her mother wasn't, she really wasn't Jewish at all, because the legitimacy of the faith was passed through the mother's bloodline. He expected her to cry. She gave him a black eye instead. His performance had been more convincing than he had anticipated.

"But I'm half-Jewish," she screamed. "This is the twentieth century and we're a fucking melting pot, you idiot!" Nathan didn't respond. The black eye was a shock. Until then Nathan had never heard Carol's voice raised except in giddy excitement when she was stoned. She had always proclaimed herself independent of men. He assumed she didn't want to marry anyone. He thought he was being easy on her. "You don't even believe in God," she continued as she hastily dressed herself from the laundry basket. That was true. Nathan had always been more inclined on Friday nights to light his bong than Shabbat candles.

In June, Nathan left for the Peace Corps on a two-year assignment to a remote village in The Gambia. He wrote Carol several letters during his first months there, but stopped when it became apparent that she would not respond. Shortly before his assignment was completed, he received a letter from her with a Boston return address. It was a lengthy letter, her spidery handwriting covering the front and back of each page. She went into great detail about the course of her life since their separation, repeatedly asking Nathan to forgive her for how she had treated him. Nathan paused during these sections, believing it was he who needed forgiving.

Carol had fallen in love, or so she said, with a man more than thirty years her senior: a wealthy contractor named Patrick, who conducted business in several Middle East countries. She moved to Boston to be with him and he had, as she put it, left her pregnant, alone, and penniless. She now had a job lined up but was broke, and the security deposit for the studio apartment she had just leased was due. Carol's parents disapproved of the older man and had cut her off even before she became pregnant. Around the sixteenth page of the letter Nathan came to the point he had already guessed. Carol needed money, and she needed it fast. He read this with satisfaction. She needs me, he thought.

Nathan had been given monthly living-expense funds from the Peace Corps, but since he was stationed in a rural village, he spent little. He also had a substantial readjustment check coming to him in three months when he returned to the States. The next day he walked thirteen miles to the nearest town and wired Carol one thousand dollars. All this time he was thinking that she was pregnant with another man's child, while after two years in the Peace Corps the only woman he had slept with was a forty-one-year-old divorcee volunteer, and that was only because he was drunk. A week before he was to return to the States, Nathan received another letter from Carol explaining that Patrick had returned to her. She was living with him in a Boston suburb and included a phone number.

When Nathan booked his flight home shortly after receiving Carol's first letter, he planned an extended layover in Boston. When he arrived at Logan International, he considered calling her but instead rebooked his flight to San Francisco for that afternoon. He never asked her to reimburse the money.

∘ ∘ ∘

"You're not hungry?" Nathan asked Katie as he removed the cap from his third beer. He was sitting next to her at the small card table that functioned for both meals and where Carol figured her clients' taxes at night.

Katie was small, practically a miniature version of her mother except for her green eyes. "She got those from her father," Carol had told Nathan, indifferently.

"It's cold," Katie said, spreading her food to the edges of her plate.

Nathan was still letting his own helping cool, having microwaved the dish too long. I'm not her father, he thought. The last thing he wanted was an argument with a seven-year-old who was lying to him. "How about ice cream instead?"

"Really?" Katie asked.

"Sure," he said, rising and walking to the tiny kitchen. "Just don't tell your mother."

"I won't," Katie said, "I promise."

Nathan scooped a bowl of chocolate ice cream then thought, What the hell. He opened the fridge and found the chocolate syrup before placing the bowl in front of Katie. "Our secret," he said, as she devoured her new dinner. Nathan took her plate and his beer to the kitchen and scraped the uneaten helping into the garbage disposal.

"Thanks, Uncle Nate," Katie said.

Nathan paused, then turned around. "What?"

"Thanks, Uncle Nate."

He barely knew this girl, hardly knew her mother any longer. Was that how Carol had referred to him around Katie? He took another swig of beer.

◦ ◦ ◦

Nathan hadn't seen Carol in nine years. In that time he had earned his master's degree in education from San Francisco State. He had expected the Peace Corps to change him in some way, but he didn't think it had. For one year he taught at a private Jewish academy where his older brother was the principal and his six nephews were students. Boredom compelled him to resign and teach high school biology and chemistry for the Oakland Unified School District. Three months ago, he was at a Berkeley supermarket, heard his name called out, turned and saw Carol standing with a seven-year-old replica of herself, right down to the sandy blonde hair cut at the shoulders. The first thing Nathan thought was, This woman owes me money.

Carol had never married Patrick. The man had never asked. Nathan might not have wanted to marry Carol, but had she gotten pregnant when they were together he would have believed it to be the right thing to do. For seven years Carol and Katie lived with Patrick in his spacious home outside Boston. "We were more like guests than a family," she said over breakfast one Sunday while Katie was at the Unitarian Church with Carol's parents in Mill Valley. Patrick had routinely left them in Boston when he traveled on business. Carol was almost factual describing the man's numerous children with other women he was also not married to.

All of this was strange to Nathan. In college he had known Carol as a self-proclaimed feminist. She had given Katie Patrick's surname, a bewildering act for somebody who once told Nathan that just being a woman was to be oppressed.

Carol forged a plan once she decided she'd had enough. The moment she became a certified public accountant, she demanded both a lump sum of money from Patrick and his signature giving her full legal custody of Katie. Then she moved back to Berkeley. "My lawyer said I could have taken him for a lot more," Carol said, "but I just wanted the bastard out of our lives. That's when Katie's nightmares began. Then José was hit by the car and they became more frequent. I guess I could have saved the dog, but the surgery would have cost me a fortune. Six grand? No way. Katie's still a wreck about it. My father insisted I take her to this child psychologist he knows. What a joke, total waste of money. The goddamn witch doctor made her dreams worse."

Carol and Nathan began having breakfast on Sundays when Katie was at the Unitarian Church with her Jewish grandfather and gentile grandmother. Nathan only reminded himself he was a Jew every Rosh Hashanah and Yom Kippur by taking off work to play golf. Carol didn't talk much about her parents, but Nathan guessed that their taking Katie to church was part of a reconciliation agreement, as was moving back to the Bay Area. Nathan had enjoyed attending college at Berkeley and now living there again as a bachelor. But he couldn't imagine why Carol was raising a child in a place where heroin deals were as frequent as morning fog. Just as Nathan had begun to wonder if he should rekindle a romance with Carol, she told him that a client was interested in dating her, only she didn't have a babysitter.

"Wow, Nate, I can't believe you're single," Carol said, sipping her decaf latté in a café near Telegraph Avenue one Sunday morning. The café had been a jazz club when they were in college. Now neo-hippie wannabes with perfectly styled dreadlocks and hemp necklaces worked behind the counters instead of passing out political flyers on the sidewalk. "I always thought you'd be settled down with some nice Jewish girl by now, raising half-a-dozen kids or something. I saw a few other guys without Patrick knowing over the years, but nothing serious. He was away so much that I didn't even have to sneak around. But I just don't feel comfortable having this Derek guy coming to the apartment with Katie there, especially on a first date. I don't want to start bringing men home and having her think of them as potential fathers, you know? I'd rather just meet Derek at his place. So, I was thinking, if you're not busy next Saturday, maybe you could watch her."

Where else was Nathan going to be? Maybe grading multiple-choice tests at home and drinking beer alone. He didn't have to coach his YMCA basketball team on Saturdays. He was free. "I'd be happy to," he said. At first he was a little jealous of Derek, but brushed it off, thinking, Why on earth do I need to be in a relationship with a thirty-one-year-old ex-girlfriend who has a seven-year-old daughter?

∘ ∘ ∘

"Time for bed," Nathan said, sipping his fifth beer.

"Not yet," Katie begged, "please?"

They had played some twenty hands of *Go Fish*, and he had read her a picture book about dolphins. Katie was certainly more pleasant than his nephews, or the high school kids he taught during the week. But Nathan wanted a break. Baby-sitting was far more tiring than teaching.

"Well, why don't you get your pajamas on and brush your teeth. Then we'll see."

He turned on the television, watched the sports news to catch up on the Forty-Niners, and within five minutes Katie was sitting cross-legged on the floor. He took note of her sleeping attire: one of Carol's T-shirts with a faded Earth Day logo. He handed Katie the remote. "Watch whatever you like," he said and went to the kitchen to remove the last four beer bottles from the trash and place them in Carol's recycling bin. He returned to the recliner and found Katie mesmerized by a nature special.

"How long do I get to stay up?" Katie asked.

"Until I finish my beer, all right?"

"Okay," she said.

Nathan watched a special on the bears of Yellowstone National Park, occasionally examining Katie. He couldn't get over how similar she was to Carol, right down to the cowlick in the back of her head. Aside from the green eyes, he wondered what else the girl had inherited from Patrick.

"Is that true?" Katie asked after hearing that bears were the most instinctively protective mothers of all mammals.

Nathan wished his students had this much interest in his classes. "Yes," he said.

"That's neat," Katie said. "Have you been to Yellowstone?"

"Yes, I have," Nathan said, having taken a group of high school juniors there for a field study three summers ago.

"I bet it was fun. We never go anywhere." She turned back to the television.

Nathan liked to imagine Carol as a mama-bear, protective of her daughter. He had expected her to call by now to check on Katie, but the phone hadn't rung once. Nathan looked at his watch. It was twenty minutes past Katie's bedtime. He decided to hold off on the beer until the special concluded. What harm is another ten minutes? he thought.

The front room looked like the display floor at Goodwill, only with scattered plants. The couch along the wall was practically a replica of one Nathan had made out on during high school in his parents' basement while listening to the Eagles. Unlike Nathan's condo, Carol's apartment complex looked like a technical building that hadn't been renovated since its construction in the mid-sixties. Nathan wanted Carol to have nice things, but she didn't, and that bothered him. At least she has cable, he thought.

At nine-thirty the nature special ended and Nathan swallowed the last of his beer. "Well," he said, standing. "Time for bed."

"No," Katie said, still sitting.

He took the remote control and turned off the television. Katie had been relatively agreeable all evening, unlike Nathan's six nephews, who were like a little pack of wolves. No child could be this perfect, he confessed, and prepared for the struggle of getting her to bed.

"Come on," he said. "Didn't I let you stay up late and watch TV? What about all that ice cream? Why not go to bed?"

"I'll have bad dreams," she said.

Nathan had no idea what to say. He believed that a father would know how to handle the situation; that it was an ingrained parental skill he lacked. He didn't particularly get along with his brother, but he wanted to call him at that moment and ask what he should do.

"How about if I sit with you?" he said. "You don't have to sleep, just lie in bed." He figured she would fall asleep anyway.

Katie contorted her face into a frown. She stood, folded her arms over her chest, and stomped to her bedroom. It was easier than Nathan had expected. He took his empty beer bottle to the recycling bin, then went to Katie's room. She was crouched at the foot of her bed.

"Are you going to say my prayers with me, Uncle Nate?"

Nathan couldn't help thinking that this was the influence of Carol's parents. "Please God, let me get my period," was the only thing close to a prayer he could recall having ever heard from Carol during a scare their junior year at Berkeley. She couldn't even sit still long enough to attempt yoga in college. Nathan reluctantly bent down to the floor and mimicked the child's palm-to-palm position.

"Lord," Katie began. "Please look after José and give him bones to chew on in heaven. José was a good dog and a good friend. Please make sure José has space to run around and play since he didn't have a backyard when we moved here. I hope José has friends. And I'd like another dog, one just like José. Amen."

He glanced at the girl, waiting for her to say something about her mother, but she didn't. She just crawled into bed. As Nathan rose, he realized that every light in the room was turned on, including a bedside lamp in the shape of a clown's face that looked more sinister than comforting. On Katie's nightstand was a framed photo of her with a Labrador he assumed was José. Picture books were scattered everywhere: *The Story of Jesus, Celebrating Kwanzaa, My Best Friend the Buddhist, Lucy and Her Two Mommies, What Is Hanukkah?* It was obvious to Nathan that Carol hadn't completely grown out of her naive, utopian mentality. How egalitarian, he thought, now she's imposing that politically correct crap on this innocent child. He was thankful that Katie preferred the book on dolphins. He pulled the small chair from her desk and removed the crayons and coloring books.

Nathan sat silently until he could see Katie straining to keep her eyes open. "Well," he finally said, "layla tov."

The child gave him a quizzical stare and he remembered that she was not Jewish. Although Nathan was not a religious man, he liked the way his sister-in-law said, "Good night" in Hebrew to her children. He would say it as well when he was occasionally at their house and took part in tucking his nephews into bed.

"What does that mean?" Katie asked.

He brought the comforter to Katie's neck. "It means you won't have bad dreams."

"Really?" she asked, suspicious.

Teaching high school, Nathan was accustomed to getting away with being condescending. This situation seemed to require a bit more sincerity. "Yes," he said. "When you say 'layla tov' before bed you don't have bad dreams."

"Lya toov," Katie said.

"Layla tov," Nathan corrected her, and smiled.

Unexpectedly, Katie wrapped the tiny fingers of her left hand around one of Nathan's thumbs. "Layla tov," she repeated correctly, not letting him leave.

Nathan sat with her until her eyelids closed. He couldn't tell if she was asleep. He stared at the child, thinking of his lie, knowing that Katie had one grandparent who was Jewish. Had he been her father she would have had three. The math boggled him, as if he were one of his students who couldn't comprehend why a grease fire reacts aggressively to water. "Half," that's what Carol had called herself when Nathan had lied to her nine years before. Had Katie been his daughter, what would that make her: three-fourths? If Katie were his daughter, he wondered if she would be such a replica of her mother. He doubted that she would have that sandy-blonde hair. More likely she would have his brown curls. He was certain that she would still be a small child, more certain of that than what Carol's reaction would be if he confessed that he once lied to her about something that still didn't matter to him.

By the tiny bounce in Katie's breathing, Nathan could tell she was asleep. He carefully slid away his thumb, and that's when he noticed the half moons near the cuticles of her fingers. They were genetic; he and Carol both lacked them. That was what Katie had received from Patrick: half-moons under her fingernails, a supposedly half-Jewish mother Nathan had possibly loved and lied to who had a daughter with half moons. He turned out the lights and shut the door.

Nathan went to the fridge and opened that last beer, then walked to Carol's bedroom, which was directly across the hallway from Katie's. He opened the door, turned on the light, and stepped in.

The room was smaller than Katie's. Aside from the bed there was a dresser and a nightstand with a framed portrait of Carol meeting Paul McCartney backstage at a Wings concert when she was in high school. On the wall above the bed there were other pictures: Katie as a newborn, Carol's parents, José at Christmas surrounded by torn wrapping paper. No Patrick.

Nathan opened the top drawer of the nightstand: hand lotion, reading glasses, a dog-eared paperback romance. He closed the drawer and opened the one below: stationary, stamps, a necklace of rainbow-painted uncooked macaroni strung on yarn that Katie might have made at a summer camp. He closed the drawer and sat on the floor. He felt a little drunk. Leaning against the nightstand, he looked under the bed, then pulled out a photo album labeled: "Baby's Book."

The first page contained a series of dated pictures of Carol at different stages of her pregnancy. At the nine-month mark she looked like one of those malnourished Third World children harboring a medicine ball that Nathan had tried to find compassion for in the Peace Corps but never had. He had forgotten how petite Carol once was. She was still small, but her pregnancy had left her with a grown woman's figure; hips that now shaped skirts, breasts that filled in stylish blouses.

He turned a page and saw newborn pictures of Katie, indistinguishable from all newborns. Nathan's nephews had looked the same. He wondered if one had to be a parent to recognize any distinction. He turned another page and that's when he saw the picture labeled: "Patrick 58, Katie 2 Weeks."

Patrick was not large. Nathan had imagined him as one of those older men who dressed in expensive suits and still wore a class ring. Patrick was the balding type. He wore khakis and a V-neck sweater and could easily have been dropped into a faculty meeting at Nathan's high school and not look at all out of place. He appeared to be the kind of man Nathan would ask to play a round of golf. But what he had expected, a large man who still had charming good looks, was absent. Patrick just didn't seem like he could woo a woman in the prime of her youth. Nathan wondered what Carol had been so attracted to, what led her to resign her youth to memory. But he finally saw what Katie had received most from her father. It was that indifferent stare—not mean, simply emotionless. The child carried a certain acceptance for what her seven-year-old life was.

Nathan returned the photo book to its place under the bed and took his beer to Katie's room. He opened the door cautiously. She was asleep, her body curled to the side, closed eyes facing him. A clump of her hair was in her mouth. He began to shut the door, then stopped. Quietly, he went to Katie's bedside and removed the hair from her mouth, tucking it behind her ear before returning to the living room.

He was rotating cable channels from the recliner when he heard the rattle of Carol's key unlocking the front door. He was already standing, smiling as she entered, hands stuffed into the pockets of his corduroys as if ready to speak with a favorite student.

"Hi," Carol almost sang as she entered the apartment.

Nathan noticed that she had the air of a woman who had just gotten laid after a long dry spell. He could tell, the same way he noticed the altered, confident stride of a student on a Monday morning who'd obviously had sex for the first time that weekend. His smile subsided.

"How was the date?" he asked.

"Great," Carol said, a lightness in her steps as she went to the kitchen and poured herself a glass of water from the faucet. "You should see his house, the view of the bay is incredible."

He was waiting for her to mention where Derek took her to dinner, what they talked about. But she said nothing. Nathan noticed that she was no longer wearing her pantyhose. This led him to believe that they had remained at Derek's home in Marin County all evening, fucking like bunnies. He thought of telling her that she still owed him money.

"I'm starving," Carol said, and opened the fridge. She pulled out the casserole and scooped a helping onto one of the plates Nathan had cleaned and placed on the drying rack. "How was she?" she asked, and set the dish into the microwave.

"An angel," Nathan said, joining her in the kitchen.

"Sorry I'm late," she said, touching Nathan's arm the way a grandmother might. "Things were just going so well, you know?" The microwave pinged. She removed the dish and began to eat, leaning against the kitchen counter. "How many times has she woken up?"

"Not once," Nathan said.

"Come on, Nate. You don't have to say that just to make my evening perfect. Really, was she difficult?"

"No, she's been sleeping since nine."

"Are you serious?"

"Yeah."

"My God, you're a pro." She took another bite of the casserole. "I guess it makes sense. No offense, but if you had told me in college that you were going to be a teacher I would have laughed. With all that acid you dropped back then I'd have pegged you for a pharmacist." She smiled playfully at him as she chewed.

"I should go," Nathan said.

"You sure?" she said in a tone he had heard from many women before: letting him know that she really didn't want him to stay.

"Yeah, I'm beat."

"Me, too," she said, and placed the dish into the sink. "Are we still on for breakfast tomorrow?"

Nathan thought about how he wanted to answer that.

The next morning at breakfast Carol walked into the restaurant and asked Nathan, "What's this 'layla tov' thing?"

"Huh?"

"Last night was the first time in months Katie didn't have a nightmare. I woke up at seven and she was still sleeping. I never have to wake her up for my parents to take her to church. She was just beaming this morning, kept saying 'layla tov' over and over again. Whatever it is, it worked—no nightmares. God, too bad you're not her father." She released a nervous laugh. "Katie said you taught it to her."

"Well, I didn't exactly teach her anything."

"But what does it mean?"

Nathan sipped his coffee, pushed his dish of eggs toward the center of the table. "It means whatever you want it to."

"Very cute, Nate," she teased. "Is it ghetto-jive or something? I know you teach in Oakland."

"What do you mean?"

"You know, Oakland. Come on, you know why the Bay Bridge is the longest bridge in the world, right?" She paused for effect. "Because it goes straight from Africa to Fairyland." She laughed. He didn't, although he liked her untypical, insensitive comment. He took it as a sign that she was maturing.

Carol shifted in her chair, cleared her throat, uneasy perhaps with what she had just said and Nathan's lack of anticipated reaction. "So, what does 'layla tov' mean?"

"It's Hebrew," he said, and she quieted, as if he had reminded her why Katie was not his daughter.

"Oh," she finally said, and took her coffee. They ate the rest of their breakfast in silence.

They no longer had Sunday morning breakfast together. But Carol's dates became more frequent and Nathan kept accepting invitations to watch Katie, even on weeknights, so that Carol could have an after-work drink with Derek. This meant that the child had to occasionally accompany Nathan to the YMCA while he coached fifth-grade basketball.

Nathan knew he wasn't ready to be a father, but he felt that coaching small children was more practical preparation for parenthood than teaching high school. He would never tell anyone, but he had yearned to be a father since his last nephew was born and he held the baby in his arms, making eye contact like a bird to its chick.

He coached practices every Monday, Wednesday, and Friday, and one game per week. After two consecutive years of being given kids who wouldn't listen to anything he told them, he volunteered to take on the "challenged" team nobody wanted to coach. It seemed rather cruel to Nathan, lumping the worst players into one team; but he had had enough of parents demanding that ten-year-olds play to win and their spoiled kids thinking they could take shots from the field whenever they pleased. He didn't care if the kids won; he simply wanted to give each child equal playing time.

The "challenged" kids, who called their team the Leprechauns, hadn't won a single game all season and only had three remaining to play. But for Nathan, it was more fun to coach the kids who couldn't remember any of the plays and ran aimlessly about the court, tossing up a ball that occasionally found its way into the basket. He was good with kids, always had been. If only I was as good with women, he often thought.

Katie sat in the stands of the gymnasium with her coloring books and crayons. That night's game was typical. Tony, the only boy who wore glasses, was so afraid of the ball that he stepped out of the way whenever it came near him. Malcolm, once again, pissed his pants when becoming nervous while playing defense. Peter, whom Nathan referred to as "snow-cone" because the child had a different color afro every week, stopped right at the top of the key to tie his shoe while the opposing team was on a fast break. And without fail, Ryan, who hadn't scored one basket all season, cried and had to be subbed out when he missed his only attempted shot. The Leprechauns lost fifty-five to eight. But Nathan gave a pep talk on how they had almost reached their goal of scoring ten points in one game as a team. Had Nathan wanted to, he could win every game by letting Brian, a Jewish kid who could actually dribble but was not allowed to attend Friday night practices because of the Sabbath, take every shot. Nathan actually wished Brian was on the regular team since his father was on par with the win-obsessed parents from his previous two years of coaching. Brian's mother was even worse, demanding that her son start every game even though he missed Friday night practices. "You of all people should understand," the woman had said, as if she and Nathan had a special bond he was betraying by making Brian sit out the first quarter of each game and letting the kids who attended every practice start.

Katie already had her crayons and coloring books collected into her backpack when Nathan was finished high-fiving his players. As he walked with Katie down the hallway of the YMCA she looked up at him and said, "Uncle Nate, are they retarded?"

He stopped and looked down at the child. She was serious. The players were simply terrible athletes. But he cherished how she had not said, "challenged," in that politically correct, understanding voice her mother preferred. Katie had used the term Nathan had been wanting to all season. However, he thought of Carol and how she would want him to act toward the girl. Reluctantly, he said, "They just need some extra help."

When they left the building and began walking across the parking lot, Nathan was startled by how Katie reached up and took hold of his thumb. They continued to walk, and Nathan finally took her entire hand and held it safely in his own until they reached the car.

Carol didn't call Nathan for some time. She had found a babysitter for Katie by placing a flyer in the youth lounge of her parents' Unitarian Church. After two weeks of not seeing Carol and three cancelled golf games, Nathan was lonely. All of his friends had children who seemed to occupy their lives in a way that he longed for. He was more bored than he'd been with his last girlfriend, a not-so-nice Jewish girl who forced him to light candles every Friday night before he left to coach.

Like an answered prayer, Nathan's phone rang that Sunday.

"Hi, it's me." Carol's voice was strained.

"What's wrong? Is it Katie?"

"Yes," Carol said. "I mean, no. Katie's fine, but I need to ask you a big favor."

"Anything," Nathan said.

"My babysitter got mono. Can you watch Katie tonight? I won't be out late, only a few hours."

"Sure, she can come watch me coach again; tonight's the last game of the season," he said, and heard a sigh of relief through the receiver.

"God, thanks, Nate. You're the best, don't know what I'd do without you."

Carol said little when Nathan arrived to gather Katie for the game and was out the door within minutes. In the car on the way to the YMCA Katie made another comment that Nathan's team really wasn't that good. Nathan explained to her that winning was not what was important. She shrugged.

Peter didn't stop to tie his shoe this time, but he did trip over his laces in the third quarter and had to have his mother come onto the court to look at his scratches. Ryan scored his first and only basket of the season, but still cried as if he had missed and had to be subbed out. Tony continued to dodge the ball every time it came near him, but for once Malcolm didn't piss his pants. With three minutes left in the game, Nathan resigned his belief in each player getting equal opportunity with the ball and simply told Brian to take every shot.

Katie asked to sit on the bench next to Nathan. When Brian scored a basket that gave the team nine points only fifty seconds before the end of another losing game, she stood on her seat and cheered, "Go Leprechauns!" Heck, Nathan thought, all the luck the better, let her scream if she likes. She then shouted, "Defense," her small hands cupped to her mouth, amplifying her voice, mimicking Nathan.

After the game, Katie unsuccessfully attempted to toss balls into the baskets while Nathan collected her backpack and the Leprechauns sulked about having not reached their goal for the season.

"She's absolutely adorable," Tony's mother startled Nathan, "such the little adult. She looks just like you, too."

"Thank you," Nathan said.

"She's your daughter, right?"

Without even thinking about it, Nathan said, "Yes, she is." As he said it, a tiny hand reached up and surprised him by taking his thumb. Katie smiled at him, cradling one of the junior-size basketballs in her free arm.

That evening Nathan bought Katie an ice cream cone even though the Leprechauns never scored ten points. He also invited her to the team's end of the season pizza party the following week. When they got back to the apartment, he bought thirty dollars worth of Girl Scout cookies after telling her she could keep one of the basketballs and he would teach her how to play. He scrambled her some eggs for dinner, which she requested, and let her watch whatever she liked on television. At nine o'clock Carol still hadn't come home. Katie willingly brushed her teeth and changed for bed.

Unlike the first time he watched her, only the lamp shaped like a clown was on when he tucked her into bed after her prayers for José's well being in heaven. As he brought the comforter to her chin, those tiny arms reached out from under the covers and gripped his neck. Nathan hugged her and when he released she kissed his cheek.

"I haven't had one bad dream since you told me to say 'layla tov,'" she said.

"That's great," Nathan said. He was prepared to sit with her, but thought he would take the chance that she was brave enough to fall asleep on her own.

"Are you my new daddy, Uncle Nate?" she asked as he was about to see if she could manage having the lamp turned off. He had wondered if she heard him speaking with Tony's mother. Why had he told her that Katie was his daughter? Driving to Carol's apartment that night he had thought of becoming her new father: trips to the beach, the zoo, Katie high on his shoulders as if she were indeed his own. He imagined taking her to the Humane Society to adopt a Labrador like José. He would even tolerate sending her to the Unitarian Church, if he had to. He imagined sleeping with Carol for the first time in nine years and giving Katie a baby brother or sister.

"Layla tov," he said.

"Layla tov, layla tov, layla tov," she repeated.

When she quieted, he turned off the lamp and returned to the kitchen. There was no beer in the fridge. He sighed, then went to Carol's bedroom. Bending to the floor, he looked under the bed again. He pulled out a blanket, a shoebox filled with costume jewelry, a sewing box. Then he gripped three photo albums he had missed before and sat with them on the floor. The first one had pictures of Katie growing up, the second pictures of Carol before Nathan had even met her. He opened the third.

The first page had a picture of Nathan with his arm around Carol. His hair was bushy, he had a mustache, was wearing brown jeans and a denim shirt. They were sitting on the grass of the Berkeley campus. Carol had her hair in two dangling braids, a T-shirt snug around her torso with "Peace" printed in English, Hebrew, and Arabic. Nathan looked at what Carol had written in the album under the picture. "Nate-Boy and me! All-Campus Celebration, March 26, 1979. Israel and

Egypt Make Peace." Nathan looked at the picture but simply could not remember being there. He certainly hadn't been a member of the Jewish Student Union; even the Campus Catholic Club scored better weed. But Carol looked beautiful. He had never considered her a knockout when they dated, not the looker she had become. But she was pretty. She really did love me, he thought, and maybe I really loved her, too.

Something had been missing from the women he had dated since Carol. Some of them were nice girls, really nice girls. But in truth, he had always wanted a prettier version of Carol without the feminism. He didn't recall that celebration for the Camp David Accords, but he did remember a night walking home across the campus, Carol smoking a joint with a girlfriend a few yards ahead of him, saying, "Nate's the best boyfriend in the whole world. I'll never find another like him."

Now Nathan truly wished he was Katie's father. He was convinced that he could love Carol. He thought, Now that she seems to be over that women's lib stuff, she's ready to be with me. He was prepared to tell her the truth, wanted to confess his lie. He thought about how he would go about it.

He crept into Katie's room and turned on the lamp. The child stirred slightly but did not wake. Nathan opened the book on dolphins and carefully lay down on the bed with the sleeping child. He imagined Carol coming into the room as he pretended to have fallen asleep while reading to Katie. Carol would see him and think about how sweet Nathan looked, asleep on the bed with the dolphin book and Katie, as if he was meant to be her father. A single mom will eat this shit up, he thought. But no pretending was necessary; Nathan really did fall asleep.

He woke to the gentle squeeze of Carol's slim fingers against his forearm.

"Hey, wake up," she whispered, slightly pulling at his arm, her face close to his, expressionless. She then left the room.

Nathan felt Katie turn over beside him, her breathing heavy, still asleep. He looked at his watch. It was almost midnight and his back was aching from lying on the tiny bed. He kicked a few stuffed animals off the end of the bed in frustration, turned off the lamp, and went to the living room.

"Sorry I'm later than I told you I'd be," Carol said, coldly, dropping her keys and purse on the card table.

"No sweat," Nathan said, surprised that he was already awake and alert without needing a late evening coffee as he typically did when grading pop quizzes.

The skin around Carol's eyes was red from crying. A fresh drag of lipstick had been hastily applied, maybe just before she walked through the door. Her hair was up in a bun, exposing her long neck. She went to the kitchen and filled a glass of water from the faucet.

Nathan munched down a Girl Scout cookie and walked to the kitchen, noticing with satisfaction that Carol was still wearing her pantyhose.

"You know, Nate, I'm really jealous of you," she said, her back to him.

"What do you mean?"

She turned around and stared at him. "My life is shit. You don't know how lucky you are. Look what you've done. You went into the Peace Corps, you got to live in Africa, you have a real career!"

"You're a CPA. You have a career, you—"

"No! I make sure rich assholes in Marin don't pay more taxes than they absolutely have to. You make a difference. I just have another fucking job. I don't even like math. In college I planned to teach art history to underprivileged kids someday, remember? I can't raise a daughter on that kind of money. I'm wasting my life and nothing will ever change. I pissed away my twenties on a man who never even took me to all those countries he goes to, and every other man turns out to be a creep."

He hadn't expected this. "Come on, there's still time to make things work out," he said, wanting to discuss what he thought could begin that. He imagined helping her pursue that career she wanted, his salary being plenty with what she would make, surely enough to raise Katie, even another child of their own. He had connections in the Oakland Unified School District, could make some calls after she got her teaching credential. He wanted to show Carol that not all men were creeps. "You're still young, babe."

She stared at him. Nathan had not called her "babe" in nine years, not since that morning he lied to her.

Carol turned her back and went to the sink again.

This was the moment Nathan had been thinking about. She saw me asleep with Katie, he thought, it'll work. As Carol refilled her water glass, he walked up behind her and placed one of his hands on her right shoulder. Carol reached back her free hand and gently squeezed his, as if to say, "Thank you for being here for me." Nathan then bent down and pressed his lips to the back of her neck.

Carol froze. She dropped the water glass; Nathan heard it clank in the sink then roll, the water rushing down the drain.

"Nate," she said quietly, "I think..."

He kissed her neck again, this time placing both hands on her small shoulders.

"Nate, stop," she said in that same controlled, quiet voice.

He kissed her neck once more, tasting her perfume this time.

"I said stop," Carol repeated, her words rushed, her voice rising slightly.

Nathan released his hands from her shoulders and stepped back.

"Please leave," Carol said, surprisingly calm, her back still turned to him.

"Carol, I...I'm sorry. I need to tell you something. I—"

"Nate. Please." He placed his hands on her shoulders again. She shrugged them off. "Please," she repeated.

"I'll call you tomorrow," he said. She remained silent with her back to him. He sighed.

That's when Katie's tiny voice called out from the hallway. "Daddy."

Carol and Nathan both turned to see the child, still half-asleep and facing Nathan, her eyes absent and unfocused.

"Daddy," she repeated, "can I have a drink of water?"

Carol looked to Katie, then to Nathan, then back to her daughter. She stood still for a moment then turned sharply back to the sink, her hands jittery as she took the glass she had dropped and quickly filled it with faucet water. "Okay, sweetie," she said, shutting off the faucet and taking the glass as she brushed past Nathan. She took one of Katie's hands in hers and walked the child back down the hallway.

From the living room Nathan could see the lamp flicker on from Katie's bedroom and feather out over the hallway carpet. He stood for a moment, sighed, and walked to the bedroom. Through the doorway he could see Carol sitting with her daughter, holding the glass to Katie's mouth.

"There you go," Carol said as Katie finished sipping and wiped her small lips with the sleeve of the T-shirt she wore as a nightgown.

"You thirsty? Is that it, sweetheart?" Nathan asked.

Carol and Katie looked up at him. Nathan was disappointed to see that Katie stared at him absently, unable to even register what he had said. It was as if she didn't even know who he was, as if he was no longer there with her.

She's still half-asleep, Nathan thought, the poor girl won't even remember drinking that water tomorrow morning. At least it wasn't a nightmare.

Carol kissed Katie's cheek and gently placed the empty glass on the nightstand. She stood and nudged Nathan's body out of the doorway back into the hallway. She leaned in close to his face, looked up into his eyes. Nathan was ready to kiss her, this time on those lips that his own had not touched in nine years.

"You always were obtuse," Carol said, coldly. "I needed a friend tonight." Then she whispered, her voice shaky. "A friend. Now get the fuck out of my apartment." She turned her back to him and disappeared into Katie's bedroom. Nathan heard her say, "Okay, sweetie, back to bed."

Nathan wanted to go into Katie's bedroom again but didn't. He walked to the living room and gathered his boxes of Girl Scout cookies. As he slipped into his sports jacket he glanced down the hallway.

I can just do it quickly, he thought, just take a peek to make sure Katie's okay. He began to take a step toward the child's room but stopped, and instead went to the front door. Just as he was ready to take the doorknob he turned around again, saw Carol standing motionless beside the television, staring emptily at him.

"Carol?" he said. She didn't respond, just kept staring at him. Nathan looked down to the carpet. "Good night," he said, opened the door, and stepped outside, leaving the basketball for Katie.

$\mathcal{H}$E'S NO SANDY KOUFAX

"$\mathcal{Y}$OU SHOULD wear the tie with the blue and yellow stripes," Leah suggests while applying lipstick, her plump face reflected in the mirror of her compact.

"Why would I wear the blue and yellow one?" Sid asks, his chin lifted as he loops the final tuck of a Windsor knot.

"Because that one has a mustard stain."

Sid looks down. "Damn it!" He tugs the tie over his head and tosses it on the dresser.

"You wore that tie to the Ziedman boy's bar mitzvah, remember?"

Sid doesn't respond; he's excavating the closet for the striped tie, the skin between his eyes crinkling. His wife being always right has tested his patience for almost forty years. Leah remembers everything; the dates of anniversaries, deaths, family medical history. She recalls it all, even the exact minutes separating the births of their twin sons, Robert and Harry. She rattles these facts off as if they are answers to the crossword puzzles she completes each morning.

Robert's and Harry's birthday is the only date Sid never forgets. He loves his sons more than anything, lives for their Sunday phone calls from Los Angeles when they lift his grandchildren to the receiver to gurgle and burp.

Sid pushes aside the twelve pairs of loafers he has retired to the closet over the years. He refuses to part with them, has no idea why his sons prefer to wear sneakers, even to the office. Sneakers are for going to the gymnasium, not to make a living in, he thinks. "I should have taken that tie to the cleaners."

"I told you to when we got home from the bar mitzvah. Don't you remember? Ask Eileen, she'll tell you."

Sid finally locates the blue and yellow tie. He swings it around his collar, folding the Windsor knot naturally. Sid once owned an impressive collection of ties, that was, until the late seventies, when he allowed Robert's high school sweetheart to sew a patch-dress out of them. "Sure, take as many as you like, dear," he had said, assuming the girl would one day become his daughter-in-law. In Sid's youth, a boy didn't date someone for two years with no intention of getting married; you didn't waste a girl's time.

Leah pops two of her diet pills. She swallows, then sees her husband. "You look quite nice," she says.

"Remind me to take the red tie to the cleaners, will you?"

"Sure," Leah says. She doesn't have the heart to tell him that the tie is as good as a dusting rag. She knows a few decent dry cleaners though, will see what can be done.

Leah never thought of her husband as particularly attractive, even when she married him. She had gone on their first date simply because Sid was the only boy she knew who drove his own car, not because he was the star varsity baseball player at their high school. Sid's looks only added to the disapproval of Leah's parents who, while Jewish, were more concerned with their daughter marrying well than for love. They would have been more pleased if she had been courted by a wealthy gentile than the son of an immigrant storeowner.

Leah knows that her husband has become quite attractive in his older years. She sees how the women her age look at him when they go to the grocery store. Sid still has most of his hair, which has receded into a widow's peak. Leah was the catch when they met. But she doesn't mind that her beauty has vanished, is happy to let her Sidney now be the pretty one. She snaps her compact and gently kisses her husband, leaving a thick map of her lips on his cheek.

"Oh, I'm sorry, dear. You just look so handsome. Here," she says, handing him a tissue. "Clean me off your face." She leaves the room and Sid wipes away the lipstick. He opens his dresser and slips a half-empty pack of cigarettes into the liner pocket of his tweed sports jacket. He promised himself that he would not smoke during the high holy days. Still, having the slight bulge of the pack in his pocket puts him at ease.

Sid Burns no longer tells himself half-truths, no longer declares absolutes with impossible realizations. If he can't quit smoking this time, he's no longer going to bother. He makes an effort; chews nicotine gum, tries the patch, munches on sunflower seeds. Yoga is his final attempt, at his wife's insistence.

For the first three sessions it has some effect. He dutifully stretches and breathes as the instructor says, "Inhale deep, take yourself to a place where you are content with the world." For Sid, that place is dragging on a Marlboro. He continues with the class until he receives a three hundred-dollar speeding ticket hurrying to his fourth relaxation session. That's when he drives directly to the closest convenience store, buys a pack of smokes, and takes up dowsing himself in Old Spice so that Leah doesn't learn about his failure.

Leah Burns has had enough of being married to a man who smells like an ashtray. "No more smoking, or no more me" is her ultimatum. Sid knows she will never divorce him; that might constitute admitting that she was possibly wrong about something. But if she finds out about his continued habit he might end up sleeping on the couch, as he did fifteen years ago when he refused to call a "professional" and the water heater flooded their basement. Concealing that he still smokes has become more difficult than quitting.

The television is on in the kitchen. Sid pours a cup of coffee, watches an anchor girl smiling. He doesn't care which news channel he watches; the anchor girls are all the same to him: blonde, small shouldered, with bone-thin necks. It's almost as bad as watching baseball on TV. Sid prefers the radio when it comes to sports. For him, instant replay has diminished the responsibility TV announcers have when it comes to actually calling the game. With radio, Sid has to imagine the game, and that seems to be more exciting than watching it these days. The anchor girl cocks her head, clamps her bleached-white teeth together, and the screen cuts to the morning sports anchor, Joe Jacobs.

"He's Jewish," Leah says.

"No, he's not," Sid says.

"Thank you, Cindy," Jacobs says. "Today's biggest news in baseball comes from right here in Seattle. The Mariners' clean-up king, Steve Solomon, is not playing in today's final American League pennant series game against the Angels because it is Rosh Hashanah, the Jewish New Year. Solomon and Angels slugger Javier 'Jimmy' Espinoza have both led their teams into a dead heat.

"With the trade for Solomon from the Dodgers it seemed that this was to be Seattle's year. Fans are outraged, saying that Solomon is giving the pennant to Espinoza and the Angels. Solomon released this statement: 'My place is with God and my family, baseball can have me the rest of the year.'

"Today's game is expected to be close. Both Espinoza and Solomon have had at least one dinger each game of the series. Nobody has seen the likes of this since Sandy Koufax sat out game one of the World Series because it fell on Yom Kippur. Twenty-two years earlier, Detroit Tigers legend Hank Greenberg did decide to play on Rosh Hashanah, hitting two home runs that day. Solomon says that he will be spending the day at Temple Beth Israel in Bellevue."

Sid pulls a breath and stops sipping his coffee.

"Well, sports fans, I don't know about you, but I would play on my New Year's holiday," Jacobs adds.

"Feh," Sid groans. "If that guy's Jewish, then I'm an Eskimo."

Leah takes the remote and clicks off the television. "Eileen said she heard his real name is Liebowitz, that his middle name is Jacob." She shrugs, then pauses. "Sidney, isn't it great that Steve Solomon will be attending our temple today?"

"He's a jerk. Who the hell does he think he is, some new Sandy Koufax? Most guys would give anything for the life he has and he's pissing it away to some Communist from Cuba."

"Solomon is making an important statement. I wonder if there will be television cameras at shul."

"Screw Steve Solomon," Sid says. "That jerk went on strike with the rest of those spoiled brats, cancelled the World Series on us. The players these days are all about money. Guys like Koufax put their team above themselves. In sixty-six Koufax was offered twenty-five grand just to have television people follow him around, do a story on him. He only agreed to it if it was thirty-five thousand and had the money divided so that every Dodger got an equal amount. Bet you didn't know that, Leah. Koufax never even accepted endorsement offers. Solomon blows away a shot at the pennant for some publicity stunt? What's next, a Steve Solomon kosher candy bar?"

"Enough, Sidney. Not today, please."

"Jerk," Sid mumbles. "I was in the military protecting that shmuck's freedom before he was even born."

"I think it makes an important statement," Leah says.

"You would."

"What's that supposed to mean?"

"You never played ball, Leah. That's all."

Sid maneuvers the Buick off the freeway. Leah sees that he is taking the exit just before the one for the synagogue.

"Why are you taking this exit, Sidney?"

"Faster this time of day."

"Uch," she sighs. "I can't believe this. You need to drive by there now? For God's sake, it's Rosh Hashanah." Leah slumps in her seat.

Sid sold the pawnshop two years ago, but still drives by the building every opportunity he has. He and Leah never imagined they would end up raising a family in Seattle. San Diego State University offered Sid a baseball scholarship at the same time the Dodgers were recruiting him for their bush league. "Think about your education," Sid's father pleaded. "There's always time for baseball." Sid thought that there was always time for college and went straight into the Dodgers' farm system. The organization even pulled some strings to keep him out of Vietnam. But after four years Sid tore half the ligaments in his right arm. The arm recovered, but his baseball career didn't. And the scholarship wasn't there when he needed it the most.

Leah pops another diet pill as they reach the intersection.

"You're taking too many of those," Sid says.

Leah says nothing, just stares out the window.

"There she is," Sid says, seeing the sign for Batsheva Pawnbrokers. Leah rolls her eyes. Sid sold the business after conceding that neither of his sons would take it over. It was a blow to his pride, to his vision of the way the world should operate. He closed a deal for the shop with a young Japanese couple, who agreed to keep the name of the business.

Sid hadn't spent almost twenty years building a reputation for nothing. "Sometimes something's gonna come in," Sid had said to the new owners, "something you know you can move fast, make a big profit on. But you want the kind of business that keeps the riff-raff out. You'll get regulars who trust you, who'll take your word, know that they aren't part of anything fishy. Stereo items and jewelry are the hardest, let me tell you. But you can spot it; there are ways to know. Sometimes it's just a feeling, you have to go with your gut every so often."

"They need to replace some bulbs," Sid says, passing the neon Batsheva Pawnbrokers sign, remembering how he came upon the name for the business.

After his arm recovered Sid needed a job; he had a wife and two kids to support.

Marty Bloom called him into the farm league office. "Listen, Sidney, I know you need work. I got a friend in charge of personnel at Dodger Stadium. I told him I'm sending you up to help work the scoreboard. I know it's not the kind of call up you hoped for, but what's done is done. Take this job. Hey, not everyone gets paid to see Koufax and Drysdale pitch."

Sid took the job. Not long after that, his cousin visited from Israel. At the seventh inning stretch Sid rigged the scoreboard to read: "A Dodger greeting to Batsheva Birkowitz...from Haifa, Israel...seeing her first American baseball game." It was almost as exciting as working the scoreboard for the 1966 World Series, when Sandy Koufax pitched the Dodgers to victory. Batsheva was killed in a bus bombing outside Tel Aviv shortly before Sid enlisted in the service.

Sid hadn't felt right about being exempt from Vietnam, thought if it weren't for America his parents would have never made it out of Europe, that he might never have been born in the country he loved so much. His arm injury landed him on a base near Seattle instead of infantry duty in Southeast Asia. Honorably discharged after three years, he and his buddy, Sam Lobe, started the pawnbroker business, which needed a name. They settled on Batsheva. Sid's cousin got closer to having her name in lights than he ever did. When Sam died from a heart attack the night of the 1980 presidential election, the business became Sid's alone.

"We're going to be late," Leah says as the car slows past the shop. Sid sees the man from Tokyo looking at a shotgun somebody has brought in. "Sidney!"

"Okay, okay," Sid says, and floors the accelerator.

"Look, Sidney, I told you there'd be television cameras."

Near the entrance to the temple the camera crews are in place: men drinking coffee, while toothpick-shaped women talk to each other. Across the street some fifty protesters with picket signs denounce Solomon's decision not to play. Sid is inclined to join them. He was disgusted with the hippies protesting the war in Vietnam when he was in the service, but this is different, something real, more akin to union workers demanding their rights. Still, he doesn't think it's any good for the Jews that it has come to this.

"Anti-Semites," Leah mutters as they drive past the protesters. She pulls down the visor mirror to reexamine her makeup. Sid will drop her off at the turnaround so that she does not have to walk from the upper lot with her swollen ankles. She steps out of the Buick, trying to appear as if she is not looking at the cameras. Sid drives the Buick to the upper lot. He parks near a cluster of Douglas firs, then uses one of Leah's bobby pins to fasten a yarmulke to his head. He takes his prayer shawl, locks the car, and walks toward the temple just as it begins to drizzle. As he passes the camera crews, he imagines Leah and her Sisterhood friends hoping to be interviewed. "It makes an important statement." "How could they schedule a baseball game on Rosh Hashanah?" "I've known his mother for years."

Sid steps into the lobby of the synagogue, flashes his high holy days ticket to the hired security officer, who nods his head, which is not covered by a yarmulke. Goy, Sid thinks, and takes a prayer book from a stack in the lobby; kisses the corners of his tallis and drapes it around his shoulders. He doesn't like that the security officer is not wearing a yarmulke. It's only the lobby, not the sanctuary itself, but he expects some respect. It's bad enough that he is required to have a ticket to pray.

Entering the sanctuary, Sid sees Leah on the corner of an aisle and makes his way toward her, shakes a few hands as he nears—old friends, people who once came into his shop. Leah rises, moves to the next seat over, shifting her inflamed ankles that she hopes the diet pills will reduce. Don and Eileen Hershfelt smile from their seats beside her. The stench of urine emanates from Don, who now requires a catheter to relieve himself. Sid takes his seat as the rabbi greets the congregation, then leads everyone into the first Hebrew prayer.

Sid looks about the sanctuary. The women of the congregation are dressed more for a fashion show than for worship. Sid has never understood people getting dressed up to talk to God. He is disappointed that Leah wears fake pearls in hopes of impressing her wealthy Sisterhood friends. The only real piece of jewelry is her hundred-dollar engagement ring, which she still won't allow Sid to replace with a larger diamond, something he has never understood.

Shit, Sid thinks, remembering that he forgot to set the VCR to tape the game. He begins to wonder where Steve Solomon is sitting.

Solomon is only a few rows in front of the bimah. Great, Sid thinks, he has to be even more the center of attention than God. On one side of Solomon is his mother, whose hair is cut into a manageable perm. To his other side is another woman: blonde, small shouldered, red dress accentuated with a silk scarf. The wife. Sid guesses both her ankles together wouldn't come close to the size of one of Leah's. Girls these days, he thinks, so skinny. Where's the meat? The wife holds the prayer book dreamily, as if it were a romance novel. A white satin yarmulke rests on Solomon's gelled hair. His posture is impeccable, his back stretched toward the ceiling as if ready to launch his head into orbit. So, Sid thinks, those are the arms that could have led the Mariners to the pennant.

Sid sees that the eyes around him are also observing Solomon. That putz is letting some Mexican take the Angels to the World Series, he thinks. Or is Espionoza from the Dominican Republic? Or Cuba? Oh, well, guess we Jews are getting our butts kicked again, this time by some third-world border-jumper: probably a Jesus freak. The last thing baseball needs is another Jesus freak.

Damn publicity stunt, Sid almost whispers under his breath. What? Solomon expects us to put him on a pedestal for not playing today?

Sid leans back in his seat. Although he often daydreams in services, he enjoys attending shul, loves the soothing sounds of the cantor's chanting as it fills the sanctuary. God has been good to me, he thinks, trying to subdue his animosity. Maybe I was never a baseball star, but I have had a good life. He thinks back to the retirement party Leah and the twins threw for him after he sold the business.

Sid never thought he would stop working, although he had been putting money into a life insurance policy for a number of years. He was leaving Leah taken care of. "A man has responsibilities," he always said. His retirement party was one of his life's sweet surprises. For Leah, it was fancy-shmancy: expensive invitations, tiny baseball bats and gloves for centerpieces. She had never cared for baseball, but this was her Sidney's special day. She gave her husband a leather bound book with blank pages, the cover titled: "What I know About Running a Pawnshop by Sidney Burns." He had no idea what to write in it. Yes, Sid thinks, I have had a good life. What a wife I got. Who else would throw a guy a party just because he's not gonna work anymore?

The rabbi prepares to begin his sermon: nobody dares leave before or during. Skipping out on the last few prayers following it, just before the intermission between the morning and afternoon services, is generally acceptable, although Leah frowns upon those who do so. She finds the rabbi's sermons inspirational. Sid tries not to fall asleep.

The rabbi greets the congregation. "The New Year brings new challenges and new hopes to embrace. Someone once told me that he never let his children miss a day of school. I was proud of this man's belief in the pursuit of knowledge, one of the oldest Jewish traditions. But when I asked him if he insisted that his children attend school on high holy days I was saddened. 'Of course,' he told me. And so, I see a man in our congregation today who made a difficult choice."

"I bet he's gonna talk about Don's decision to have his surgery," Sid whispers.

"Shh," Leah says, knowing Don and Eileen are to her left.

"I see a man in our congregation who made a decision against expectations," the rabbi continues. "When he has children, I am confident that he will take them to shul and not to school on high holy days. That man is Mr. Steve Solomon."

The congregation stands and applauds. Solomon rises, pans his skyscraper-like body around, and waves. He sits, but the applause does not cease. Sid is motionless; his hands folded in his lap. He's expecting the television crews to barge through the door any minute.

"This is a disgrace," he tells Leah, who is standing, clapping joyfully. "One of the holiest days of the year and I'm in the middle of a campaign speech. Is Solomon running for office?"

"Be quiet, Sidney."

"I'm not sticking around for this hullabaloo. This is worse than the synagogue president asking for our money." He stands and begins to make his way into the aisle.

"Sidney," Leah gasps, grabbing her husband by the sleeve. "You can't leave before the rabbi's sermon ends."

"Watch me." Sid walks down the aisle, reaches the silence of the lobby and needs a cigarette. What a shmuck, Sid thinks. Sandy Koufax never went on strike. He never cancelled the World Series. Sid remembers the strike, his disgust at the players: grown men making millions of dollars saying, "We need to think about our families," as if a few years of playing ball meant that they didn't need to contribute to society any longer. "Feh," Sid had said, "those jerks don't know what it's like to worry about your family's security." That's when he gathered every baseball cap he ever wore and tossed them in the trash. "They go on strike, I go on strike." The strike ended, but Solomon's trade and the Mariners' chance at winning the pennant was what finally brought Sid back to the game. He would never forgive the strike, though.

Sid grinds his molars together. Steve Solomon doesn't know about troubles, he thinks. It wasn't Solomon who humiliated himself when his kids were little, taking an extra job as a custodian at his boys' grade school because money was tight; he wasn't the one who could only afford to give his boys crayons one year for Hanukkah. It wasn't Steve Solomon who watched his son declare bankruptcy at twenty-seven. Damn kid wouldn't even let me help him out; I had the money. You can lose your wallet, but you should never lose your name. Solomon probably doesn't know loyalty, either. He doesn't know how Don Hershfelt needs a catheter to go to the bathroom since his surgery.

Sid knows a place where he can escape for a few moments and have a cigarette. At the end of the hall, around the corner, is a staircase with a glass door at the bottom. He descends the stairs and opens the door. Keeping his body to the side, he lights a cigarette, finally relaxing. He hopes Leah does not detect the odor of smoke when he returns. Sid bends down, takes a rock from the gravel. He stares at that empty space separating the synagogue's walls from the wood-planked fencing. He cranks back his arm and pitches the rock into the shadows, losing sight of it. He drops his head. Over three decades have passed since his dreams were flushed away as quickly as water down a drain.

The door opens. Sid drops the cigarette to the ground and smothers it beneath his loafers, looks up.

"Oh, I didn't mean to startle you," Steve Solomon says, stepping onto the gravel. "Here," he says, holding out a silver case, his cigarettes placed in neat rows. "Have one of mine."

Sid looks up at Solomon, the man's enormous shoulders towering over him like a goalpost. I can't believe this putz had the brains to sneak away from all his worshippers in the sanctuary, he thinks. Solomon smiles a mouth of capped teeth. "Thanks," Sid says, taking one. He looks at the filter. "English smokes?"

"Uh huh," Solomon says, lighting Sid's cigarette, then his own. Sid would never buy English smokes, for the same reason he will only drive an American-made car. "Steve," Solomon says, extending his enormous hand.

Sid forces a smile and takes the hand. "Sid," he says.

"I really didn't mean to scare you," Solomon says.

"It's okay, I just thought you might be a kid."

"I hear ya," Solomon says, as if he and Sid are old pals. "I shouldn't be smoking anyway, been telling myself to quit for years. I dread the thought of some kid seeing me. Then again, I don't need lungs to hit the ball." He smiles. Sid says nothing. "Interesting, what the rabbi was saying," Solomon continues.

Great, Sid thinks, this jerk's gonna start talking about himself. Those protesters should see this guy smoking. Sure, back in my day all the players smoked, but now? Some role model. "I guess so," he says.

"Yeah, tzedakah, charity. I don't entirely agree with everything he said, but it was interesting."

"You don't give to charity?" Sid asks.

"I give money to baseball camps for kids, stuff like that. But handing people free money doesn't help them a bit. I never give money to bums on the street."

"How about buying them a meal?"

"I don't know," Solomon says, grinding the butt beneath his Italian leather shoes. "My agent usually takes care of what I'm supposed to support." He taps another cigarette against his silver case. "Have one more," he says.

Sid drags his cigarette to the filter. Solomon lights Sid's next cigarette, then his own. It begins to drizzle again.

"Damn," Solomon says, stepping closer to the door, "I still haven't gotten used to this. Nice place to live, but when I was with the Dodgers I could practically wear sunglasses year round. Thank God we have a domed roof up here."

"I used to work at Dodger Stadium," Sid says, unable to stop himself, wishing he had.

"Really?" Solomon says in a tone that conveys he believes Sid was selling peanuts.

"I worked the scoreboard in the sixties," Sid says.

"Wow, I thought back then they only let minor league guys whose careers were washed up run the boards."

Sid smiles. "Well, I was one of those guys."

"Oh," Solomon says. "You really played ball?"

"Three years in the bush leagues, left field."

"So, you just hung up your glove or was it an injury?"

"Injury. I tell you, one day I'm throwing the ball to third from deep in left field with no problem, next day I can't even toss a game of catch with my kids."

"I'm sorry, Sid."

"Don't be," Sid says.

"No, I really believe you. I run into guys all the time who say they used to play ball and you never believe them. But I see you have the passion."

Patronizing shmuck, Sid thinks. "It wasn't so bad," Sid says. "I got to see Sandy Koufax pitch. Even met him once. It was fun to play ball then, to make it as far as I did. I probably didn't have the talent to compete at your level."

"You never know. Another season or two in the minors and you might have been sent up."

"Maybe." Sid takes a long drag.

Silence.

"You really met Sandy Koufax? What was that like?"

Sid smiles. "An honor, just to shake his hand, you know? Only had a few words with him, but he seemed like a down-to-earth guy. He was real polite, had a very soft voice; not many people know that. But seeing him pitch was something else. He had a kick to his delivery, first guy to really know how to push off the mound. I swear, when he reached back to throw, the ball was as low as the top of his left ankle. The guy used the whole weight of his body like a slingshot. He even had the habit of tipping off batters; had his elbows out in his windup when he was about to launch a fastball, had them tucked in when a curveball was coming, stuff like that. But it didn't matter because batters still couldn't hit the suckers. Willie Stargell always said that trying to hit against Koufax was like drinking coffee with a fork. I mean, the poor guy had terrible arthritis in his elbow and still threw better than anyone. I'll never forget this one thing I overheard Koufax say. He said baseball was the closest thing to chess. See, the guy was all about strategy: outsmarting the other team. I think that's really why he was the youngest player ever inducted into the Hall of Fame."

"Well, Sid, that's—"

"But you want to know the truth, what Sandy Koufax was for guys like me? All this hullabaloo about Koufax refusing to pitch game one of the series because it fell on Yom Kippur and having rabbis kiss his ass wasn't what it was about. He wasn't even an observant Jew. Seeing Koufax pitch was like watching the left arm of God. He represented the same thing for Jewish guys that Dimaggio did for the Italian fellows I knew. Every time Koufax hurled the ball the whole world had to recognize that we finally made it: the Jews were going places, we were Americans now. He was the most dominant player of his time, won three Cy Young Awards, five ERA titles, was the first guy to pitch four no hitters—a Jew! America was cheering for a Jew, and this was our country as much as it was anyone else's. That's what Koufax was." Sid pauses. "At least to me. I don't cry often, but I have to admit, the day Koufax retired, I wept. Lots of guys did. He had that effect on people."

"That's great. I hope that's what I'm doing for us."

"No," Sid snaps, as if talking to his sons. "You can't do that. We aren't a bunch of greenhorns anymore. You think we need guys like you? You want to know what I did for the Jews? I got up in the middle of the night and bottle-fed my kids, made sure they went to college. I didn't pressure them like other fathers did after it was obvious that they weren't born ball players. I paid my taxes without complaint, I put food on the table. I've been faithful to my wife for almost forty years. I did the best I could. You want to do something? Look at yourself in the mirror every day of your life and tell yourself you're the luckiest guy on earth, because that's what you are. And stop going on strike."

Solomon forces a smile. "Well, Sid, you don't really know the intricate details involving a forty-million-dollar contract. We have to think about our interests."

"I'm sure," Sid says, more annoyed with Solomon than the petty thieves who used to bring in stolen items to his shop. "I don't think my family could possibly make it on forty million dollars, we might have to go on welfare or even food stamps.

Solomon looks coldly at Sid for a moment, then glances at his watch. "I better get back." They smother their cigarettes into the gravel. "Here," Solomon says, holding out a roll of breath mints. "I'm sure your wife is as itchy as mine about smoking." Sid takes one. The two men walk up the stairs: Solomon towering over Sid like a shadowing rain cloud. At the end of the hall the crowd sees them, rushes toward Solomon like sea gulls assaulting a beached whale. Sid steps aside as the people converge, hands reaching out to touch Solomon.

Sid makes his way to the lobby, thinking that he should have told Solomon about lighting up his cousin's name when she saw her first American baseball game. He turns back, sees the people clinging to Solomon. Sid wants to shout out at everyone that they are worshipping a man who is throwing away the pennant, a man who makes millions of dollars and doesn't believe in charity. He wants to scream out to everyone that Steve Solomon is no Sandy Koufax. He turns, goes to a water fountain and spits out the breath mint. Sid wants to find his wife.

Sid navigates the Buick. Leah is skeptical that she will be able to tolerate being in the same car with her husband for the short drive to the coffee shop where they are meeting Don and Eileen Hershfelt. Don suggested a delicatessen, but Sid insisted on the coffee shop. Leah's patience is dissolving. She knows the reason Sid insisted on the coffee shop.

"Don wanted deli," Leah says. "The poor man can hardly take care of himself anymore and you don't even have the compassion to let him eat what he likes." Leah sighs, thinking of Eileen, who had to have a motorized chair lift installed into a minivan so that Don could at least leave the house. "He can't even go to the bathroom normally anymore, Sidney."

"You don't think I know that?" Sid snaps. "If we go out for deli Don will order pastrami. He'll be dehydrated the rest of the day. They have more options for him at the coffee shop."

"Oh, please. You were thinking of yourself."

"There she is," Sid says, seeing the brightly lit sign for Batsheva Pawnbrokers. Leah rolls her eyes as Sid slows the Buick to a snail's pace. "Closed? It's only three-thirty?"

"It's not your store, Sidney."

"The hell it ain't. Those slant-eyes are playing with my reputation."

"It's their business now," Leah shouts.

Sid clicks on the radio. Leah immediately clicks it off and folds her arms over her sagging bosom, her fake pearls clanking against the buttons of her dress. "You can find out the score of the game when we get home. I'm not letting you ruin my holiday." Sid frowns, but says nothing.

There is no sign of the Hershfelt's minivan in the coffee shop parking lot. Leah slams the passenger door, clicks her heels forcefully. Sid is still back at the Buick, walking to the passenger side of the car to make sure Leah locked her door, as he always does. Maybe she smells the smoke, he thinks.

The hostess seats them. Leah takes a handful of Sweet N' Low packets from the condiments tray and stuffs them into her purse.

"You don't need those," Sid says. "We have plenty at home."

"Sidney, why don't we just look at the menus."

"Fine, be that way," Sid says.

Once Don and Eileen arrive Leah will need to be pleasant. She worries that Don will not be around much longer, hears about people making it through the holidays and then letting go. But she knows Don loves talking with Sid when so many other friends abandoned him after he got the catheter. Leah is certain that these same people who are offended by the stench Don carries will be the first to arrive at the funeral, sit righteously with Eileen at the shiva. Leah knows that Don can talk about baseball with Sid, and for those few moments he feels normal again. Don and Sid's favorite subject: Sandy Koufax trivia. "Bet you don't know Koufax was twice as likely to throw a shutout as he was to hit a batter every time he stepped on the mound," Sid might say. "The guy practically lived off fastballs on the outside corner," Don might add, more in conversation than retort. It is a completely foreign language to Leah and Eileen.

Sid's eyes begin to drift, glancing about the restaurant. Not too many people, generally older couples. Some snip coupons from the newspaper, others sit in silence. At the counter Sid sees a slouched man dressed worse than his own parents were in Poland. A length of rope is strung through the loops of the man's trousers instead of a belt. He wears mud-covered Velcro sneakers. Sid looks at the scraggly beard, the dirty hands, the grime under the fingernails. A plastic garbage bag is tied to his torso to shield him from the Northwest drizzle. A large knapsack rests at the man's feet as he drinks coffee.

"Don't worry about him, sir," Sid hears, looks up and sees a young woman with her hair in a bun. From the bulge under her apron she is obviously in the third trimester of pregnancy. Sid looks at her left hand: no wedding ring. He already knows he will leave a generous tip. "He's harmless. The boss lets him come in for free coffee. What can I get you folks?"

"Coffee for me," Leah says.

"Coffee for you, sir?" the waitress asks Sid, who is still staring at the man at the counter.

Sid swings his head toward the waitress. "Yes, please."

"Make his half-decaf," Leah adds.

"Has he eaten anything?" Sid asks the waitress.

"Not here. The boss only gives him free coffee. Don't worry, he'll probably leave soon."

"You don't feed him?"

"No, just coffee."

"You give that man a menu and tell him he can order anything he wants. Charge it to my bill."

The waitress looks at Sid quizzically. "You sure, sir?"

"Yes. But don't tell him who's buying. Just say it's a one-time-only thing so he doesn't expect it again."

The waitress shrugs. "Whatever you say."

The waitress leaves. Sid waits until he sees her hand the man a menu, then returns to deciding what he wants to eat. Leah's shoulders fall; the contorted muscles in her face relax. Her husband is beginning to please her again.

The waitress returns with the coffee.

"I must ask," Leah says. "How far along are you?"

"A little over seven months," the waitress says.

"Is it your first?"

"Yeah," the waitress answers, smiling this time, patting her stomach with the palm of her free hand.

"Oh, wonderful," Leah says. "Do you know yet if it's a boy a or girl? I hear you can tell before they come now."

"The doctor said he could tell me, but I decided it would be more exciting to find out when the baby arrives."

"That's what I say," Sid pipes up. "Half the fun is finding out."

"I don't care if it's a boy or a girl. I just hope it's healthy, that it has all ten fingers and toes, you know?"

"Good for you," Leah says, thinking of her great-niece who must walk with the assistance of orthopedic canes.

The waitress smiles, leaves again. Sid instantly makes a mental note to give her an even bigger tip. No wedding ring doesn't mean there isn't a father these days, he thinks, but you never know. Both his sons taught him that.

"Hello," Eileen says, her arms balancing Don, who has left his four-prong walker at home for the day.

A walker is nothing to be ashamed of, Sid thinks.

"We got a parking space right in front," Don says as he squeezes into the booth with Sid beside him and Eileen next to Leah. Don is growing a beard, shaving being too difficult now. His blood-red lips protrude through gray whiskers, his breath strained and heavy.

"How lucky," Leah says, smiling at Eileen. Everyone but Don knows that Eileen used a handicapped parking space and simply clipped the tag with a wheelchair symbol to the rear-view mirror after her husband was out of the minivan.

"So, Sid," Eileen says, "everyone was saying that they saw you walking down the hall with Steve Solomon, that you actually got to talk with him, alone. Is it true?"

Leah's face brightens. She leans into the table.

"Great player," Don says. "What a season that boy had."

"Well," Sid says, talking more to Don than their wives. "He's terrific at the plate, but not the best I've seen in the field. Could be a better glove man."

Leah cocks her head, raises her eyebrows at Sid, wanting him to be especially pleasant to Don. For Sid though, it's just sports talk.

"But is it true, Sid?" Eileen continues. "Did you really get to talk with him, alone?"

"Yeah, we talked," Sid says, leaning back.

"He's such a wonderful example for all those children at temple today."

"I agree," Leah declares.

"How long did you speak together?" Don asks.

"Maybe ten minutes," Sid says.

"Must be because you were a ball player, too," Don says.

"Did you, Sidney?" Leah presses. "Did you let him know you played baseball, too?"

Sid shrugs. "It came up."

"What was he like?" Don asks.

Sid looks to Leah. Her eyebrows rise, almost begging.

He releases a slight sigh, then, says reluctantly, "He seemed like a regular guy."

"I knew it," Eileen exclaims.

"You're so lucky," Don says.

"It was no big deal," Sid says. "People are people."

Don laughs. "Easy for you to say. He probably talked to you like another player. Real lucky, Sid. Then again, you've always had good luck. Seems like God's always on your side."

"Maybe," Sid says.

"Maybe? You played ball, had a successful business, both your kids went to college, got yourself grandkids, you still have your health. No maybe about it, you're the luckiest guy I know. Real lucky."

Sid smiles. "What do you two feel like eating?"

"Do they have pastrami sandwiches here?" Don asks, taking a menu in his shaky hands.

Sid and Leah look at each other. Leah tilts her head, reiterating to Sid that they should have gone to the delicatessen. Sid smiles and shrugs. She smiles back, knows this is her husband's way of acknowledging that she had been right, as usual.

$\mathcal{A}$ PLACE TO HIDE

$\mathcal{T}$WO YEARS without so much as a birthday card, but within one month of my split from Adam my mother is sending me e-mail every day. First, she began with Feng Shui instructions, believing I can remedy my life by altering the arrangement of my furniture. Now she wants to chat daily over cyberspace, as if we're as close as a sitcom family. Usually, I don't respond, just casually click Delete, the way I have taken to placing pictures of my life with Adam into shoeboxes. But like my mother's e-mails, I respond to the good pictures: Adam and me at my sister's wedding or backpacking on Mount Hood. I even kept the Polaroid of us arm-in-arm at his medical school graduation, more because I had had a good hair day than for the memory of the event—being subjected to an entire weekend with his family.

Today's e-mail is as general and ambiguous as a fortune cookie prediction. "The stars are aligned in positive arrangement for you," my mother writes. "Since you're a Cancer, you will be emerging from a period of reflection. Your astrological number is also strong this month. But be cautious. Mercury is in retrograde, so communication is likely to be down. Love, Mom." Her messages are almost annoying enough for me to take up smoking again. Thank God she's living in Arizona or she might insist on me having my palm read. At least my father's lighting candles every Friday night and praying for me at his new wife's temple have some semblance of normalcy. After my parents divorced my freshman year of college they both decided to explore their spiritual sides: Mom wearing crystals around her neck and believing fruits and vegetables have feelings, Dad becoming so damn traditional about his Judaism that he now makes my grandparents look like club-hoppers.

I click Reply and type. "Thanks for thinking of me. –B." I don't even tell her my plans for the evening. It would inevitably lead to another one of her birth control talks, as if I'm still seventeen. Or worse: a phone call. Back in my high school days my mother had brought the term "condom mom" to new heights.

At least my father knows what makes me momentarily happy. The only thing we have ever had in common is a love for fifties rock n' roll. Lately he has been mailing me CDs: Chuck Berry, Bill Haley and the Comets, Eddie Cochran. It makes me feel like I'm ten years old again, dumping his vinyl records across the carpet and spinning them on the turntable. I enjoy the distance of my mother in Arizona, but lately I want my father to stop sending CDs and actually visit. He's not an affectionate man. As a child I would pretend to be asleep in the car just to have him carry me into the house and tuck me into bed, relishing those few minutes when I could wrap my arms around his neck and get a whiff of Sea Breeze. I just want a hug right now, from anyone really.

Enough e-mail. I shut down and leave for Sandy's.

∘ ∘ ∘

"Visitation rights?"

"Yes," I tell Sandy, my face flushing. We already had this conversation last week over tea, but Sandy likes to drag things out, especially now that I'm letting her fix me up.

"You've got to be joking, Becca," she says. "For God's sake, it's just a cat." Sandy hates animals, always has. She even squirms at the sight of fish.

"Bud is not just a cat. He's a friend."

"Listen, I know it's tough, I've been there."

Sandy's been there all right. But for her, breaking up is a monthly ritual practiced after becoming bored with the Adonises she dates. It's not Sandy who was with the same guy since she was seventeen. At twenty-nine, I find myself dropped into a life so completely foreign that I now enjoy sleep more than being awake.

"You can't hold on like this," Sandy continues as she perfects my hair. "It's over, make a clean break from the creep. Trust me, it's the best thing you can do for yourself. Join my gym, great way to meet guys. But let it go. You can get another cat."

"Maybe," I say as she pulls my scalp back like a slingshot. I've stopped insisting that Sandy not refer to Adam as "the creep." It's her nature to take sides. She can turn shoe shopping into a competition, which probably accounts for her footlocker full of them. But I don't consider Adam a creep, not anymore. The initial damage has subsided. It's difficult to simply write off a person who was the center of my life for well over a decade. I'm not pissed off; that bothers me, because I have every right to be, should be.

I don't want another cat; I want Bud. I can live without Adam; after eight months of not having his body beside mine at night I've accepted that. But the absence of Bud's tabby tail curved around my neck when I wake each morning is more heart-aching than Adam's confession that he had met his "soul mate," or whatever it was he had referred to Emily as. We're together for twelve years and he's engaged three weeks after meeting her. During my last visit with Bud, Emily even showed me her goddamn wedding dress.

"When you know, you just know," Adam told me. I knew that I deserved better than that. I didn't cry, didn't even fight to keep him. The next week I moved in with Sandy, taking all of my houseplants, while Emily started unpacking boxes into what had been my apartment since Adam received his medical degree from the University of Washington. I took the plants and Adam kept Bud, not exactly a fair division of assets. I found a studio apartment quickly. Since then I've been decorating and rearranging my new place as the perfect place to hide from the world, mostly with new ferns and spider plants from work. I've even taken up cooking.

∘   ∘   ∘

"It's time," Sandy told me over a cup of Earl Gray at the Russian Teahouse in the U-District one afternoon. "You need to get back out there."

Get back out there? I couldn't recall having ever been there. Dating was a bewildering concept; Adam was the first and only guy I had ever kissed. We met at a B'nai B'rith youth meeting at my parents' Reform synagogue, when they were still married, before my mother decided to "find herself" though tarot cards and before my father started believing that using electricity on the Sabbath was a mortal sin. Adam had just moved from Portland and I snagged him first, the only guy I had ever snagged. We didn't even sleep together until my sophomore year at Seattle Community College, just before I dropped out. That was when my virginity was a cherished possession that had to be coaxed away from me. Now I've been thinking of sex constantly. Sometimes at work I'll be stacking bags of potting soil and fertilizer and see a man—any man—walk in. He'll remove his jacket, I'll take one look at his shoulders and all I can think about for the remainder of the day is going to bed with him. I can't stand it.

"You've spent eight months doing crossword puzzles," Sandy continued, sipping her tea. "Pu-leeze! If I have to hear about you spending another Friday night watching the Discovery Channel I'm gonna start telling people you've become a dyke. I can't imagine there's a video left at Blockbuster you haven't rented." I could still name a few. But she was right. In nine months I had rented *The Lion King* enough times that I could recite the dialogue and the songs verbatim. "Watching videos alone, fine. But stop mortifying yourself by going to the movies without a date, especially on the weekends. It's time. I have the perfect place to take you."

This should be good, I thought as Sandy squeezed lemon into her tea. I imagined myself being dragged in borrowed spike heels to some hole in the wall near the Space Needle to dance robotically to thumping electronic music while men inspected us like choice cuts of meat. Sandy's excitement over a singles function at the Jewish Community Center on Mercer Island let me know that she was becoming desperate for a man. After all, it had been six weeks, a significant dry spell for her. I guess she had depleted the selection at her gym. It was a bit surprising; Sandy was a three times a year Jew at best, only attending temple on high holy days, which was certainly more of an effort than I ever made.

"You'll have a blast, I hear it's all Jewish singles in their twenties and thirties, just like us."

"I'm not thirty," I said, "yet."

"You might as well be. It's this Thursday."

"I can't, that's the night I get to see Bud."

"Forget the cat!" Sandy raised her voice. "How humiliating. You actually go over to your old apartment and sit there with the creep and his concubine just to pet the fucking cat for an hour? I can't even fathom what you talk about."

"Listen, Friday is Lisa's bachelorette party, baby shower, whatever it's going to be. That's depressing enough. I'd rather get some sleep."

"We won't be out late. Come on, it'll be so much fun. We shmooze for an hour or so and you give out your phone number."

"I'm not giving anyone my phone number."

"Becca," she said with a certain authority, "it's time to get off your ass."

"I don't know. I want to see Bud." I sighed. "Sandy, I'm starting these technical classes next month, I just don't need this right now. I'm concentrating on me for once."

"Enough, you're coming."

And that was it.

o   o   o

Sandy goes to work on me as if I'm a science project. She begins with my nails, then moves to my face. I haven't worn makeup in years. "The trick about wearing makeup is to look like you don't need it and aren't wearing any," Sandy says as she paints me like a canvas. So what's the point of wearing it at all?

Although I've never been fond of Sandy's taste, we are both relatively small-boned, only I have the larger breasts she has always envied. But that doesn't hinder her from insisting on dressing me up like a mannequin. After an hour of changing me in and out of her clothes, she finally finds my attire suitable. I had been content with the first outfit, but I have to admit that I like her ankle-length skirt with tiny rose prints, the white blouse, and the cardigan sweater, all of which Sandy hasn't worn in ages. "Keep everything," Sandy says. "You look like a librarian." She pauses. "A cute librarian," she adds. "Sit. I'll put your hair up, I do the best French braid," she declares after I sift through the footlocker and find some simple one-inch heels. They're a bit tight at the toes, but not terribly uncomfortable. I get to keep them, too.

I still think I'd be more satisfied making popcorn and renting movies, but I actually enjoy the attention, and I know Sandy loves every minute of it. If anything, I'm doing this for her. I don't know how to thank her for taking me in when I split with Adam. How was I to know I'd find an apartment of my own the following week? Sandy would have let me sleep on her couch indefinitely. Besides Lisa, she's really the only girlfriend I still have. In twelve years of building my life around Adam, I hadn't made many friends, just acquaintances. Even my coworkers are relative strangers.

"God, I wish I had your hair," Sandy says as she works on the French braid. "You don't even do anything and it's incredible. Not one split end." I had always wanted to chop my shoulder-length curls, but Adam made it perfectly clear that he dislikes women with short hair. "You get the big boobs, you get the hair, you get the long eyelashes. What do I get? Straight teeth, that's it."

"Stop it, you're beautiful," I say, staring at myself in the mirror and having to admit that Sandy has made me feel pretty. Even the gloss, which makes my lips stick together, looks good. Chap Stick is usually sufficient for me, but not for Sandy. "Becca, you're no longer in the seventh grade." The eyeliner and mascara are a bit too much, but I don't complain.

Typically, I look at myself in the mirror and still see a young girl. Sandy makes me feel undeveloped. She's already a woman. For God's sake, she won't even leave her apartment unless her fingernail polish coordinates with her purse and her blouse. Tonight, with her flared slacks and silver halter top, she's more prepared for dancing than going to the JCC. In her spike heels she towers over me, and I'm only an inch shorter to begin with.

"I know her getting knocked up had a lot to do with it, but I still can't believe Lisa's getting married," Sandy says. "Who would have thought she'd be the first to go? Everyone always said it would be you." She pauses, smiles at me in the mirror. "Sorry."

"Don't be."

"I hear Alex does all the cooking and cleaning. Since he found out Lisa was pregnant, he won't let her lift a finger. Supposedly it's driving her crazy. Wish I had a man like that. Lisa has nothing to complain about. She can't even put cereal and milk together for the kids she teaches."

"I like Alex," I say. "I think he's a good guy, good for Lisa."

"Yeah, me, too. He really is perfect for her. I guess this is going to be the all vegetarian wedding. I'm sure the main course will be sprouts and seaweed."

"We'll hit Burger King before the ceremony, just like her bat mitzvah."

Sandy smiles. "Her sister is planning this party tomorrow night, so don't expect any excitement. Who would have thought Fran would become the spiritual type?" She's almost finished with the braid. "Lisa's so disgustingly happy. She only knew Alex, what, two months? 'It just felt right,' that's what she said."

"Yeah, there's a lot of that going around."

Sandy looks at me in the mirror, even more apologetically than before, until I burst into laughter. She follows.

"I can't believe how well you're holding up," she says. "I would have cracked."

"Life goes on, isn't that what I'm supposed to say?"

She finishes the braid. "Exactly. That's what tonight's all about. Come on, let's go find you a man, and maybe one for me, too."

God help me, I think, and stand up to begin my first night out as a single woman.

"What do I tell people?" I ask as we walk the length of the JCC parking lot.

"Just be yourself."

"At least you can say you're in advertising. I'm a twenty-nine-year-old college dropout who works at a flower shop. I'm sure that will be incredibly impressive."

"You're the manager, tell them that. You're going back to school, that's conversation."

"I'm taking computer classes. Shit, it's not even a school, it's an office skills center." I turn around. "This is stupid."

"Oh, no," Sandy says, tugging me back into step. "No sulking tonight, you promised."

"I am going from being with a doctor to this. I feel so small right now."

"You are small," Sandy says. "Just with bigger boobs than me."

I loop my arm into hers.

If Sandy makes me still feel like a little girl, those in the JCC gymnasium must make her feel like a spinster. "Singles in their twenties and thirties" is a slight exaggeration; it's a sea of college kids who probably still treasure fake IDs. One look at the young girls on their husband hunts wearing their uniforms of women's black sports coats, white blouses, and buckled shoes is enough for me.

"I'm leaving," I say.

"Just relax," Sandy says, as she makes eye contact with two boys standing under a basketball hoop who probably aren't even old enough to vote. "Hi," she says giddily, jerking her head flirtatiously as they approach. I stare at the ground.

"I'm Kyle," one says in a silky voice. "This is Ron."

"I'm Sandy. And this is Becca." She tugs my arm.

I receive a cordial, acknowledging head nod from Kyle. Ron is still sizing up Sandy as if she were a magazine cover. Since we were kids boys have been sizing her up and ignoring me.

"So," Kyle says, "where are you from?"

"Seattle," Sandy says. "Born and raised." She pauses. "Both of us," she adds. "You?"

"We're from Cleveland. We go to U-Dub."

"Oh, my God," Sandy says, jerking her head again, her hand pulling a coiled strand of black hair from her face. "I've always wanted to see Cleveland."

That's it. I can imagine Sandy wanting to visit Cleveland as much as her asking me to go backpacking at Mount Rainier. I don't even bother excusing myself, simply leave for the refreshment table in the corner. I can use a stiff drink about now. Sandy doesn't even notice my departure.

Punch is what I find, four different variations, not even coffee. I sigh and settle for the kosher cookies arranged in a fan formation. I grab several with the intent of taking a walk and coming back to retrieve Sandy in an hour. That's enough time for her to hand out her phone number. Kyle probably already has it plugged into his cell phone.

"Hi," a deep voice says.

I turn, seeing only a torso. I crane my head upward and find a towering boy who looks barely out of high school.

"What's your name?" he asks pleasantly, adjusting his silver-framed eyeglasses. I can't believe he has such a deep voice with that peach-toned face. He's cute, in the kind of way I might have fantasized about when I was thirteen, but I have no idea if it is even legal to kiss such a boy. Then again, the whole art form of kissing anyone besides Adam is beyond my comprehension.

I pause, contort a fabricated smile. "Rebecca," I say, giving my real name.

"I'm Jack."

Great, not a John, but a Jack, as if he owns a hardware store.

"So," Jack continues. "Where do you go? What's your major?"

I know I look young, but he can't possibly believe I'm anywhere near his age. "How old are you?" I ask.

"Eighteen. You?" He pours himself a plastic cup of the red punch. His arms are unusually large, bulging at the sleeves of his patch-brown sports jacket. He reeks of tobacco. I want a cigarette.

"Twenty-nine."

Jack pauses. "So, what was your major in college?"

It takes a moment to recall. In actuality, my major had been seeing Adam on weekends. "History," I finally remember, having declared it two months before dropping out. "You?"

"Pre-law."

Now I really want to leave.

"I'm a freshman at U-Dub."

No shit. I think Sandy and I are perhaps the only ones in the room who aren't enrolled at the University of Washington.

Well over six feet, he's taller than Adam. Twelve years ago, had Adam never come into my life, I might have been interested in Jack. But now I just want to take my cookies and go for that walk, maybe undo this ridiculous French braid that is pulling at my scalp and giving me a headache.

"You from Seattle?" Jack continues.

No escape.

"Yeah. Where are you from?"

"Indiana."

I can't help giggling.

"Yes," he says, "we do have electricity out there now. Even paved roads."

At least he has a sense of humor.

"I had no idea there were Jews in Indiana," I say, more relaxed. I take a bite of cookie.

"Well, you're looking at one. The rabbi that bar mitzvahed me doesn't ride his covered wagon on Shabbos."

I don't respond.

"That's a joke," Jack adds.

If nothing more, at least I'm being amused.

"I guess I'm not doing very well, am I?" he asks.

I like him; I had forgotten that there are still innocent people with undamaged, inexperienced hearts. This evening is a lost cause for finding a date, but talking with Jack is by far better than hanging out with Sandy's new friends from Cleveland.

"So, you're not in school anymore?"

"No," I say. "I manage a flower shop."

"Wow, you have your own business?"

I wish.

"No, I'm just the manager."

"I want to get some plants for my dorm room, but I think they would die."

"Come by the store and I'll set you up. You could get some very forgiving plants, ones you can let go a month without watering that will sprout right back up. The shop's called The Wallflower. You know Capital Hill yet?"

"Sure, I'll remember."

I've heard that before. In twelve years, Adam hadn't remembered my birthday once. I had had to remind him of his own parents' anniversary.

"Well," I say. "It was nice talking to you, Indiana Jack. Good luck at U-Dub."

"Thanks. Say, maybe I could call you. We could go out for coffee."

He's endearing all right, in a cousin way. "You don't think you're a bit young for me?"

He contemplates this for a moment. "No," he says, and grins.

Still, I'm not giving out my number to anyone.

"Good night, Jack." I take my cookies and walk.

"I can't believe you didn't give Indiana Jack your number," Sandy says, as we approach Fran's apartment complex the following evening. I shouldn't have even told her about him, but it feels good to brag about being hit on.

"He's a year younger than my little brother," I say.

"So what? Boys supposedly reach their sexual peak at eighteen. Women don't get there until they're thirty-five or so. You could school him."

"What are you saying, I should have given him my number for the sex?"

"He could be the perfect rebound man. Becca, no offense, but you need to get laid."

I'm not arguing with that. I can't even recall the last time Adam and I had sex, probably months before he even met Emily. But Jack would be more like a rebound boy.

Fran Berman's place is the apartment I only dream of: a spacious kitchen, a bedroom with bay windows and a vaulted ceiling, an adjacent office, and an enormous living room for the party. It makes my studio seem like a cat carrier. Her patio view of Lake Washington must cost her three grand alone every month. My mother has always loved Fran. I hate her. More so because of the fact that even with Fran's trust fund income, her apartment is a waste. The living room is a clutter of beanbags, Indian pillows, and imported carpets, none of which match. Sanskrit posters hang on the walls with tie-died tapestries suspended from the ceiling. Even her lamps are probably environmentally friendly. The bedroom is filled with nothing more than Mexican blankets on a bamboo mattress with Fran's bong resting on the hardwood floor. Candles and incense burn everywhere among the most withered plants

I have ever seen. Even Sandy could water them better, and that's saying a lot.

Fran offers us couscous, green tea, and nachos. At least this mystical crap she's into has compelled her to learn hospitality for the first time in her life. After I decline both mineral water and freshly squeezed citrus, she shrugs and asks me if I want a rum and Coke. When she runs to answer the door for the last arriving guests, I add another hefty splash of Bacardi and move to one of the beanbags.

"Who wants to keep a ledger of the gifts?" Fran asks, walking barefoot across the room with Lisa. Fran and Lisa, although three years apart, could be mistaken for identical twins. But Lisa's kindergarten-teacher draw towards denim skirts and sneakers makes it obvious that the two have little in common besides vegetarian diets and occasionally donating their rare AB negative blood to the Red Cross.

"Me, I will," Sandy volunteers, rushing to find paper in Fran's office, where a "Free Tibet" poster hangs above a computer. Sandy lives for these rituals.

Although we had never discussed it, I had always assumed Adam and I would marry one day. Perhaps it was the thought of living through a séance-like, New Age wedding shower in the Arizona desert hosted by my mother that subconsciously told me to never bring up the subject. But at least Sandy would have taken me to Vegas for a real party, not subject me to this bullshit.

I haven't seen Lisa more than a few times since she got pregnant and Alex proposed. The fifteen or so women sit around the living room as she thoughtfully unwraps gifts. Fran gives her a set of dream-catcher earrings and a turquoise necklace I am certain Lisa will never wear. "This necklace has a lot of positive energy," Fran says, then spoons rice from a pottery bowl. No wonder my mother loves her.

Some of the gifts are nice. Debbie Kaplan gives Lisa a beautiful blown-glass menorah and Staci Olofski gives her the most incredible crystal vase I have ever seen. Lisa loves the negligée I bought with Sandy. Not surprisingly, Miriam Klein gives Lisa the tackiest bagel slicer on earth, complete with a bagel-shaped knife. I haven't seen most of these girls in years and thankfully nobody has yet to ask me about Adam. They all know, I'm certain of it.

At least a few of the girls come prepared to roast Lisa. There is soon an impressive collection of penis-themed items: penis-shaped tampons, penis-shaped chocolate bars, and a penis-shaped flashlight. "This is actually really good chocolate," Fran admits, taking a bite from the end of one of the bars. Jan Hershfelt, knowing of Lisa's love for office supplies, brings a fountain pen in the shape of a penis that also squirts whiteout, bringing the room to a roar, while Barbara Cohen, who is probably still a virgin at thirty, gasps and dashes to the kitchen for more orange juice. Sandy uses the fountain pen to keep the gift ledger for the remainder of the evening.

After examining Lisa's new battery-operated "climax enhancer," I still can't figure out how Susan Allen's gift is supposed to work, let alone which end of the contraption is inserted first. The edible underwear seems more practical. Most of the gifts are accompanied by something for the baby: clothes, toys, a stroller. Lisa even gets a changing table. In all, I'm bored.

Then the speeches come; two hours of tears and clapping and hugs and reminiscences of "we've been through so much together" that I'm compelled to refill my rum and Coke so often that, by the time I'm the last to speak, I haven't realized how drunk I've become. Trying to stand, I lose my balance and fall back into the beanbag to the giggles of the girls, as if we're at a slumber party. And that's when I'm saved by the doorbell.

"Oh," Lisa says, "maybe Jennifer could come after all."

"You should get another drink for this," Sheila Waskow mumbles, leaning to me from her own beanbag. "The entertainment has arrived."

Great, Fran hired a klezmer band, or maybe a sitar player.

The girls begin screaming. Lisa's face flushes as if it were a glass being filled with wine. "Oh, my God," she gasps.

"Girls," Fran says. "This is Jack, the performing cat."

I turn around. Standing at the door, handing his raincoat to Fran, is Indiana Jack from the JCC, dressed in a striped g-string with a matching cottontail hanging from his exposed butt cheeks. He also wears a striped vest over his bare torso and motorcycle boots. Atop his curly brown hair is a clip with striped felt ears.

"I can't believe Fran got a stripper," Sheila says. "Who would have guessed?"

I face the wall and down the rest of my drink. While Jack starts strutting towards Lisa, I make a quick beeline for the kitchen. I mix myself another strong rum and Coke as Sandy inserts the *Saturday Night Fever* album into Fran's CD player after the girls reject the *Grease* soundtrack. The situation is bad enough; the last thing I need is this cheesy, seventies retro crap. The stereo is cranked as Sandy yells, "Start working it, baby!" I'm thankful she doesn't recognize Jack from the night before, probably due to his Lone Ranger mask.

I have no idea what to do. I certainly can't leave, let alone take a bus back to my apartment by myself as drunk as I am. I've never learned how to drive; Adam always drove before and Sandy brought us here. There's no way I can find a cab in Fran's neighborhood. The patio's my only hope; I don't care if the girls think I'm a prude.

Quietly, taking my drink, I stare at Fran's ridiculous Persian rug and inch towards the patio door. I get halfway across the room when Barbara Cohen, of all people, screams out, "Becca, take a seat," then cheers on, "take it all off, gorgeous!"

I glance over and see that Jack is jiggling to "Stayin' Alive" right in front of the pregnant guest of honor, flexing his washboard stomach into Lisa's face as he twirls the striped vest over his head and lets it fly into Barbara's lap. And I have to admit that, at this moment, I'm turned on. It's his calves. I've never given much attention to men's calves, not even Adam's. But Jack's look like toned pears I could bite into. I imagine wrapping my ankles around them. I creep back to the group.

"You've got the right idea," Sheila tells me as I sink into the beanbag. "I'm gonna get a drink, myself. This is too good."

Jack's motorcycle boots are now being held by Sandy, clutched against the penis-shaped fountain pen. He jiggles barefoot with his zebra-painted toes, thrusting his groin back and forth, twirling the cottontail in his hands, his g-string and butt-cheeks facing me. He's shaved every hair from his body like an Olympic swimmer; all except that Brillo pad atop his scalp. It looks as if somebody has placed a soup bowl over his head and shaved whatever sprouted from the edges. I imagine combing my fingers through those curls.

Strangely, I smile looking at Jack's clip-on tabby tail. He reminds me of Bud. I feel myself blushing; I'm nervous that somebody might notice.

And then Jack, slowing to a gentle rhythm, tears the g-string and tail from his body and is dancing completely naked, tan-line and all before Lisa, who buries her face in her small hands. He slips the felt ears onto her head.

"Show all of us, little boy!" Jan Hershfelt shouts, pounding her fists on the floor.

Jack skips slowly around the circle of girls, and that's when I see it. Adam's may have been the only other one I'd seen besides those in *Playgirl* when I was in high school.

Jack circles by me twice. I put down that final drink as if it were a shot of tequila. And on his third circle, he sees me through the slivers of his costume-mask. He freezes; his muscular, toned arms drop to his sides. He stares. I can't turn away, can't stop rotating my glances from his eyes to his groin.

"Keep going," Fran yells. "I'm paying you for all fifteen minutes."

Jack smiles, lifts his arms over his head, flexes, and jumps directly in front of me. He shakes it so close to my face that I can smell his sweat, and the girls cheer on. For the final two minutes he wiggles in front of me only. And I just stare at it, right until the end of the Bee Gees' "Jive Talkin."

The girls clap and holler as Jack puts his outfit back on; Lisa is now wearing the felt ears as a souvenir. Sandy hands her a glass of wine. "Wear them for the big day," Jack says, slipping into his raincoat. "Mind if I step outside for a smoke before I leave?" he asks.

"Stay as long as you like," Fran says, removing the wrapper from another penis-shaped chocolate bar. He smiles at me and leaves for the patio. Fran then collects money for his tip.

"Okay, girls, everyone get a partner to make TP brides," Sandy says. "Who wants ice cream?"

That's my limit. I can handle seeing Jack nude, but I'm not letting anyone wrap me in toilet paper.

"Here," I say, taking the wad of cash from Fran, which also includes a check for the service. "I'll make sure he gets it."

"Oh, Becca," Fran teases. "I know what you're thinking." I'm so loaded I don't care, not even about having to pee.

I contribute five dollars to the tip and step out to the patio. Jack's back is turned to me, his elbows perched on the railing as he looks out over Lake Washington.

"Hi," I say, after taking a moment to enjoy examining his backside.

He turns. I see that he is once again wearing his silver-framed eyeglasses.

"Rebecca, right?"

"You got it," I say, attempting indifference.

"See, I remembered."

"I believe this is for you," I say.

"Thanks." He stuffs the money into his raincoat pocket.

"So, I have to know—"

"This is how I'm paying my way through college, at least my living expenses," he says. "My loans takes care of tuition. Don't worry, I only take my clothes off, I don't…you know."

I smile. "A Jewish stripper. You do bar mitzvahs, too?"

He smiles a mouth of endearingly crooked teeth, nothing like the manipulated perfection of Adam's mouth, which suddenly seems boring. He flicks his cigarette over the railing and lights another. "Want one?"

I swallow, let out my breath. My throat is dry from the alcohol, as if cotton balls have been lodged into my flesh. I haven't smoked in three years, not since Adam aced pathology and threatened to break up with me if I didn't quit. "Oh, I'm so drunk at this point I could smoke anything. Why not?" I take a cigarette and he lights it for me, posing like an old black and white movie conception of a gentleman, his palm shielding the breeze from the flame. With that first drag I recall how much I enjoy smoking. I feel that I have reclaimed something I lost; I should have started again the minute Adam left me for Emily.

"You smoke grass?" he asks.

"Nope. You a pot-head?"

"No, not anymore."

"You're a college freshman, we'll see." I take a long drag, almost stumble from the slight head rush and place my free hand on his shoulder to balance myself. "Don't get the wrong idea," I say, and lift my head, even though I'm still thinking of it. For the first time I notice how nice his brown eyes are. He's cuter than I originally thought. I hope it's not the influence of the booze. "How long have you been doing this?"

"About three months. A guy at the campus gym did the same thing last year. He said I could make good money." Once he's out of college he'll learn that there is no such thing as bad money.

"You're already a pro. I love the cat getup."

"You need to have a theme. I miss my parents' cat, so I went for this."

"You like cats?"

"Yeah, I guess it's kind of wimpy. I wish I could have one in my dorm room. Guess I'll have to wait until I move off campus."

I smoke the entire cigarette with complete pleasure. Through the open patio door I hear the girls laughing as they wrap each other in toilet paper like mummies.

"I guess I should go," Jack says.

"Okay." And I'm not wanting him to leave.

"So, can I call you sometime?"

"My my, you certainly have no shame, at all."

"Does that mean I can have your number?"

I think for a moment. I enjoy being wanted again. "You remembered my name, so you have a good memory, huh?"

"Yeah. Just tell me your number, I'll remember."

I laugh. Not nervously the way I do with Sandy, but a real laugh, a pleasing, unforced laugh I have not felt inclined to release for a long time. "How about this. Last night I think I told you where I work. If you can remember that, come see me. Then you can have my number." What the hell, I think, and tip myself up on my toes and kiss his cheek. "That's my word of honor." And I blush.

∘ ∘ ∘

Adam e-mails me the next morning asking when I will be making up my visitation time with Bud. I don't respond, just click Delete. I go to the salon next door to the flower shop that morning and say I will pay extra to have my hair cut right then and there without an appointment. The beautician suggests that I get highlights, but I decline.

That afternoon, I take my first smoke break at work in three years. I step outside. Sunlight has made an unexpected visit to the Northwest. I take the pack of cigarettes I proudly bought that morning, a choice all my own, and I light up. I even bought lipstick for the first time since college. The neighborhood is unusually calm. And I feel well. After my father's phone call this morning saying he and his new wife want to come for a visit, I'm considering going to the Humane Society after work to adopt a cat that needs a good home. It's time to start making new friends. After all, my mother says my astrological number is strong right now, whatever that means.

"Hi."

I turn. It's Indiana Jack, dressed in blue jeans and sneakers. He wears a sweater with a print of Buddy Holly over his chest; that same chest I fantasized about in bed last night, imagining pressing my palms against. The sleeves are snug around his biceps. The booze must have had the opposite effect, because he's more handsome than ever.

"Hi!" I say, startled by the excitement in my voice.

"I thought you could suggest some plants that not even I can kill." He adjusts his eyeglasses.

I'm surprised to find myself nervous. "Sure."

"Hey, I remembered where you work."

"Yeah, you did." I pause. "You know, I was thinking of getting a cat later today. Want to help me pick one out? I could use another opinion." Does he even understand that I want him: that he doesn't have to try any longer, that we don't even need to bother with picking out the cat?

"I think I'm free. Does this mean I can have your phone number?"

I smile. "I think you've earned it. Besides, I know you have enough cash to at least buy me coffee." I take a quick drag. "So, you like Buddy Holly?"

"Yeah. He's my favorite. You like fifties rock n' roll?"

"I prefer Chuck Berry, funkier than Buddy Holly, more sensual."

"I love your hair," he says, noticing my new pixie-cut.

That's enough for me. "So, what kind of plants were you thinking about getting?"

"Why don't you suggest something?"

I don't care anymore. If I need a rebound man, I can't imagine a sweeter one. I can start watching movies in bed now instead of on the couch. I might even ask him to teach me how to drive a car, after I "school him," as Sandy says. I take a drag from my cigarette, intentionally forcing my lipstick to stain the filter. "I'd love to," I say, and offer him a smoke.

THE INVOLVED CONGREGANT

RUTH SCHNEIDER was one of the most involved members of her synagogue. She and her husband, Judah, now well past their child-raising years, had settled into an unknown dimension of their marriage: life with only each other. Finally retiring from her secretarial position, Ruth had submerged herself in every aspect of synagogue life she could find.

She had been representative of the synagogue Sisterhood, assisted at the Jewish Home for the Elderly, occasionally baked desserts and challahs for Oneg Shabbats and bar mitzvahs, volunteered to inventory the shul library, put together fund-raising auctions for tzedakah, taught private Hebrew lessons to struggling students, and even put in a few hours a week at the synagogue preschool. You name it, Ruth did it. However, her most cherished work was as a fourth-grade religious school instructor every Sunday.

Then there was Ruth's husband, Judah. Having a wife who was so involved in synagogue activities inevitably drew a certain mystique about the man. Judah, over the course of his marriage and fatherhood, had detested every religious aspect of his wife's involvements. The social dimension was a different story, though. There had never been a more personable man than Judah Schneider. When not concerned with his dental practice, he was accompanying Ruth to one or another of her engagements. Like his wife, he could never participate without throwing himself completely into whatever function he was involved with. But when it came to religious functions, Judah conjured quick alternatives.

His flight from "Godly rituals," as he called them, had always been discreet. To escape sitting through services every Friday night and Saturday morning, he would assist with preparing receptions in the back of the synagogue. To be spared boredom during high holy day services he would act as an usher, assisting the elderly to their seats. He volunteered to pick up Chinese food for the entire congregation who gathered to share Jewish company on Christmas Eve, shelling out his own money for everything to be prepared without MSG, then keeping the receipt to use as a tax write-off and finishing a small personal order of shrimp before returning to the synagogue. He was even on a bowling team with Cantor Geller and two of Rabbi Grossman's sons, having his championship fourteen pound ball blessed before each frame.

Ruth had always been angered by Judah's abandonment of her in any religious context of their membership to the congregation. However, through thirty-six years of marriage, she never once complained. For all of Judah's efforts to escape these religious experiences, his alternative endeavors gave him the reputation of being one of the most involved members of the synagogue, which delighted Ruth. And because of this, almost two-thirds of the temple's membership came to Judah for dental work, which gave him immense pride. Still, Ruth longed for her husband to be something more. She met converts who were more knowledgeable of Talmud than her Jewish-born husband. What she wanted was for Judah to become respected for his devotion rather than his participation, just as her Uncle Harry had been.

As always, Judah was awake early Sunday morning. He wanted to get an early start trimming the hedges around the front yard since he was scheduled to bowl a few casual frames with his optometrist friend, Stan Pritzler.

Ruth sat in the kitchen reading the Sunday paper while eating a toasted poppy seed bagel. She was in a pleasant mood, having detected no signs of breast tumors during her monthly self-examination in the shower. She had just spread out the front page of the paper, which contained another editorial concerning the race for Oregon governor. The article ridiculed William Henderson's outspoken wife, from her stance on abortion to the racy eyeliner she used. Ruth read the article, letting out slight giggles between picking bits of poppy seed from her teeth with her fingernails. She had made up her mind to vote for Henderson more than a month ago, because of his wife, not the man himself. Even though Henderson was a Catholic, he did fit Ruth's simple one-word criterion: Democrat. She had been raised with her Uncle Harry's doctrine that voting Republican was the equivalent of voting for fascists. "How can you vote for an exclusive party when you are part of an historically excluded people?" Harry had always proclaimed. Ruth loved Henderson's feisty wife and would have surely voted for her instead of her husband if given the chance. After all, Henderson's wife was also named Ruth. Such a strong biblical name, Ruth thought. Judah didn't see too much difference between any political parties, although he liked to please his wife by praising Democrats. If it weren't for Ruth, he probably wouldn't even vote.

Because of Henderson's wife, Ruth was also toying with the idea of hyphenating Schneider with her maiden name, Horowitz. This made no sense to Judah. "What's this name changing hullabaloo? You've been Ruthy Schneider for thirty-six years now, and all of a sudden you wanna go changing things?" That's when she considered dropping Schneider all together.

Ruth looked at her watch and gobbled the last bite of bagel. She was due to teach religious school at the synagogue in less than an hour. She folded the paper and slid on her blue summer coat, being sure her collar did not cover the Henderson campaign button she had made herself, which read, "Vote for Ruth's Husband." She swung her bag of teaching supplies over her shoulder and walked to the front door.

Judah was furiously cutting the hedges that bordered the yard. The flap of hair he combed over the top of his bald head now hung down the right side of his face, occasionally taking flight with the breeze. Sweat trickled from the top of his scalp to his neck. Ruth had once bought Judah an electric hedge-clipper for their anniversary, but he wouldn't have anything to do with such things.

"What," he had said, "you think I don't know how to clip a hedge anymore?"

Ruth had laughed, knowing her husband liked to think of himself as an artist in certain ways. He could turn replacing a light bulb into an abstract endeavor. He also liked to occasionally think of himself as "working class," like his own father and Ruth's Uncle Harry. But he knew better. Judah's only comfort against shame for his financial success was a continual affirmation that he made his living by working with his hands, like all the previous generations of Schneider men.

Ruth, a good three inches taller than her husband, walked past Judah, patted the damp top of his scalp affectionately with her free palm, and proceeded to walk the four blocks from their home to the synagogue. "Be back at three," she hollered over the grunting sound effects Judah was applying to his art. He lifted his hand and waved good-bye without turning around. He was deep in concentration. Occasionally he had the inclination to shape the larger bush by the front door into a bicuspid or lower molar, but feared Ruth's reaction.

When Ruth arrived at the synagogue she noticed the usual slew of minivans and station wagons revolving around the front entrance. There were young parents holding their children's hands as they escorted them inside. Ruth thought fondly of her son, Leonard, and how hard it had been to leave him that first day of preschool so many years ago. It wasn't the season, but she made a mental note to bake hamantashen for him when she returned home and mail them off to Seattle first thing in the morning.

She calmly made her way past the temple doors and into the extended hall that had been recently remodeled because of her fund-raising efforts. She walked into the tiny room at the end of the hall that now served as a staff room for religious school instructors.

"The nerve of him," Ruth overheard Sylvia Stockenheimer saying to her sister, Miriam. Ruth poured herself a cup of coffee and sat down at a table to relax. She removed her jacket and swung it over the chair. The Stockenheimer sisters had been the co-directors of the religious school since Ruth had been hired sixteen years before.

"Well, what's he going to do," said Miriam, "is he still running for reelection?"

"Who knows? Oh, probably. That man always was an ass. It wouldn't surprise me in the least if he did."

The two women sat down with Ruth at the table.

"How are you, Ruth?" Sylvia asked.

"Fine," said Ruth, blowing lightly on the surface of the mug, then taking a sip of coffee.

"He won't run," said Miriam, "I'd place money on it." This was Miriam's tactic for drawing Ruth into the gossip. Ruth was fully aware of this because Miriam was an outspoken opposer to gambling of any kind. She wouldn't even allow her husband, Lyle, to come over when Judah put together penny-ante poker games.

"Oh, tell her. You must," said Sylvia.

"Oh," Ruth humored her. "Tell me what?"

"George Finklestein," said Miriam.

"What about George?"

"Well," Miriam lowered her voice, looking over her shoulder, "it turns out that George..." She glanced once again, then whispered, "had an affair."

"No. Not George."

"Yes. Married twenty-seven years and gets caught with his legal assistant in the file room when Gail comes down to his office to surprise him with a homemade lunch. Who knows how long it's been going on."

Ruth turned to Sylvia. "Such a shame. George's brother, Glen, he still works for Max Ollen's investment firm, right?"

"Ruth," Mirium gasped. "You're missing the point."

"So they're getting divorced, that's the point?"

"No, although I assume Gail's leaving the S.O.B."

"Well, then, what is the point?"

"Is he running for reelection?"

It had completely slipped Ruth's mind; George was the president of the synagogue. She now understood that the Stockenheimer sisters were concerned with the potential of an adulterer being reelected to such a prestigious position.

"So what do you think, Ruth?"

"I don't know. I mean, did he actually have the affair or is this just talk?"

"Oh, he did it," said Sylvia. "I heard the whole thing from Linda Cole. She plays bridge with Joyce Leiberman every Tuesday. You know how close Joyce and Gail are."

"So what's the problem?" Ruth said, pushing the sisters a little further.

"What's the problem?" Sylvia practically shouted. "Ruth, the man put his you know what where it didn't belong."

Ruth looked up to the wall to check the clock. "Listen, you two shouldn't go around talking about this till you know everything. Especially since George is still president."

"What, us say anything? We're just talking. Isn't that right, Miriam?"

"Yes, what makes you think we would spread things, Ruth? We're just talking."

"Fine," Ruth said as she stood and pulled her jacket back on. "I'll see you both after class."

"But what about George? He's held the office for eight years. Who else will be president?"

"I don't know," said Ruth. "I'm sure somebody will come along if George decides not to run again."

Ruth was cleaning her room after class when Miriam poked her head in the door.

"Hi, Ruth."

"Oh, hello."

"That was pretty good, you pulling us along like that this morning. You're such a comic. Just wanted to say, we're all with Judah, one hundred percent. Gotta run though, give me a call."

Ruth always thought Miriam to be a somewhat loopy-minded woman. She could usually interpret her language, but this was perplexing. In sixteen years she could not recall speaking to the woman over the phone once. She finished cleaning the room, then went to the staff lounge.

"Ruth, just the person I was looking for." It was Stan Pritzler, blocking the door to the lounge with his goal-post legs. "You tell Judah to give me a call before we bowl. I got a few ideas to throw at him. Glad there's somebody with balls around here. Oh, excuse my language."

"That's all right, Stanley."

"Gotta run, Ruth, April's waiting. Be sure to have Judah call me before we bowl, and let's all get together for dinner soon. It's been a while."

"Sure," Ruth said, even more perplexed. She stepped into the lounge.

"Ruth, I'm so excited. Everyone always knew Judah was a mensch but this is a real surprise." It was Doris Sessman, who had stopped speaking to Ruth three years ago when she and Judah had forgotten to invite her and her husband Bill to a barbecue.

"Okay, Doris. Will somebody please tell me what's going on?"

Doris laughed. "Ruth, you're always such a game player. This is great. I'm sure Bill would love to help. Call me tonight. If you can't, I'll buzz you first thing in the morning." She then tapped Ruth's button with a glossy red fingernail and brushed past her.

Ruth paused and looked down at her "Vote for Ruth's Husband" button and thought of George Finklestein. She stood motionless for a moment, till a large grin stretched across her face. She immediately called Judah to tell him not to go bowling with Stan Pritzler. Something urgent had come up.

"What is it?" asked Judah. "Are you sick? You don't look sick. Maybe I should call Dr. Hastert."

"I saw Doris Sessman today."

"So you saw Doris Sessman. You see her every Sunday. You're sure you feel all right? Do you have one of your headaches? Sit, I'll find a thermometer."

Ruth put her bag down and sat at the kitchen table. "She talked to me, Judah."

"Who talked to you?"

"Doris Sessman."

"So she talked to you."

"Judah, the woman hasn't spoken to me in three years. Don't you want to know why she talked to me, why every person on the earth wanted to talk to me?"

"You're not sick?"

"No."

"And I still can't go bowling?"

Restraining her frustration, Ruth finally relayed the entire story, including as many of the details she could put together. The gist was instantly clear to Judah: everyone had been convinced he was running for synagogue president.

"What? You're out of your mind."

"You're already getting support and you didn't even make an announcement," said Ruth. "You can win."

"Because of a silly button? Please, then what if I do win, then what?"

"You've shmoozed this long, what's the difference?"

"Ruthy, I'm a dentist, not a politician. I don't even pay attention to real politics, remember? You're the one who tells me who to vote for synagogue positions each year. Heck, you even told me whom to vote for governor this time. What's that woman's husband's name again?"

"Henderson."

"A Democrat, right? I am voting for a Democrat I hope. It's bad enough we have two Republican presidents in a row." Judah thought that that comment would appease his wife. He paused at Ruth's silence. "Is Henderson a Democrat?"

"Don't try to change the subject. This is your big chance. I want you to run."

"You've flipped this time. It's your chance not mine." He turned his head to the ceiling. "What did I do to deserve this?"

"God has blessed you with this, not cursed you."

"You're the most impossible woman sometimes, you know that?"

"Fine," Ruth said indifferently. "Don't run, see if I care. Sure, my husband could be synagogue president, but he doesn't feel it's his duty to help anyone, always thinking of himself, how to make his own life easier."

"Ruthy," Judah said with tender affection, "don't be that way."

She stood from the chair, turned her back, and walked towards their bedroom.

"Ruthy, please."

Ruth, standing in front of their closet, slid off her dress and stockings, exposing the web of varicose veins blanketing the loose skin of her legs. After thirty-six years of marriage, Judah still lusted for her with the intensity of their first meeting at a bus stop in downtown Portland.

Judah stepped behind Ruth and placed a hand on each naked shoulder, gently caressing her skin. Ruth shrugged him away and stepped aside to hang up her dress. She then pulled on the sweat pants and denim shirt she gardened in every Sunday. Judah sat down on the edge of the bed. He looked around their bedroom and noticed that it was practically a shrine to their son, Leonard. There was a framed picture from every possible achievement of his life, and every age, for that matter. Ruth even still had the finger-paint self-portrait Leonard had drawn when he was four framed on the wall next to her and Judah's ketubah marriage document. Judah often wondered if it was possible that the infrequency of their sex life had paralleled Leonard's aging. It had seemed that as more pictures of their son were placed about the room, the less sex they had. It was as though Leonard might be watching them from all directions.

"Fine," Judah said. "I'll do it. But I'm not making any speeches, and I'm not doing one damn thing that requires me to miss my bowling night."

Ruth picked up the sneakers she wore for gardening, held them in one hand by the laces, and patted her husband's bald head with her free palm, then walked to the kitchen.

"It's a mitzvah. Be proud you're doing a good thing for others," she said as she walked down the hall. Judah put his head down in his hands, still wondering if he was doing the right thing.

That night Ruth and Judah made love for the first time in months. She normally pushed him away when his hands would make their way over her body every night out of habit, but things were different this time; Judah was running for synagogue president. Ruth even allowed him to watch television on the Sabbath, so long as he turned on the tube before sundown and used the remote control for volume purposes only.

Judah, although strongly urged by Ruth, still did not sit with the congregation during services that next Friday evening. As always, he spent his time in the back of the sanctuary, helping set up the oneg.

After he heard the final verse of "Adon Olam," he found himself bombarded with handshakes and cheek-kisses, showered by wishes of good luck and declarations of support. Ruth observed with immense pride, certain that she was soon to be the wife of the next synagogue president, perhaps would be asked to sit with the rabbi's wife on high holy days, at last to be seen as the great woman behind a prominent man. She reveled in overhearing the conversations surrounding her as congregants stuffed their mouths with challah and grape wine.

"So lucky, that Ruth," a woman's voice proclaimed. "I've always liked Judah, such a caring man. My son, Loran, the younger one, he was so afraid of getting his teeth cleaned. You should have seen Dr. Schneider, so good with children."

Judah's shaking-hand ached by the time he and Ruth were ready to leave.

"Good Shabbos," said Rabbi Grossman, startling Judah with an extended hand. Judah took the rabbi's hand and squeezed as firmly as he could muster, the blood no longer circulating down to his fingertips.

"Good Shabbos," Judah repeated. He was tired. They never stayed long at temple if he could coax Ruth away. And tonight he wanted to catch ESPN late-night bowling for the first time without Ruth's intervention of the observance of the Sabbath. She normally made him preprogram the VCR.

"I suppose I'll be seeing you on Tuesday." The rabbi smiled, showing off six decades of hardware in his mouth.

"Yeah, we'll hopefully get those gums taken care of for good."

"Cantor Geller tells me you're quite the bowler."

"I do okay."

"Two thirty-nine average, okay? Don't be so modest."

Just then Ruth approached. She was with the rabbi's wife.

"It'll be such fun," Ruth said.

"Oh yes," said the rabbi's wife, "let's get together soon. Oh, Dr. Schneider, good Shabbos." She practically skipped onto Judah's feet. "I want you to know I've been brushing twice a day and flossing every night, just as you told me to."

"Excellent," said Judah. "A woman as beautiful as you shouldn't let her teeth go bad, such a pretty set of whites."

"Oh," the rabbi's wife blushed, "you're so silly."

"Well, good Shabbos," said Ruth.

"Good Shabbos to you both," said the rabbi's wife.

Ruth held tight to Judah's numbed shaking-hand as they walked the four blocks home from the temple. Judah thought of freeing her grip to ease the stinging of the muscles. But when he looked over and saw Ruth so happy with that smile he had fallen in love with so many years before, the pain seemed to dissipate.

When they reached the house, Ruth wrapped Judah's hand in a dishtowel and ice, then sat him down with a blanket to catch the last of ESPN bowling while she fixed him a gin and tonic. That night in bed Ruth snuggled herself around Judah's body with her head resting in the pocket of his shoulder, just as she had done when they were first married. She rubbed her fingers in tiny circles over the dense hair protruding from his V-neck T-shirt. Judah affectionately stroked his left hand over her varicose veins, thinking of touching her in that same way she always resisted but had surprisingly not only a few nights ago. Instead, he lightly stroked her skin until they both fell asleep.

The next Monday at work, Judah had to soak his hand in hot water after each patient he saw. Oh well, he thought, I suppose this is the life of a politician. It was almost noon, only one patient to see before lunch. He went to the back of the office and opened the cabinet he kept the stereo in, slid a Benny Goodman cassette into the tape deck, and turned on the speakers that ran into the reception and examination rooms.

"Dr. and Mrs. Pritzler are here," Judah heard the receptionist announce. "I'm taking my lunch." He had already let his hygienist leave, knowing that his last morning patient was only a cleaning. He walked to the door of the reception room.

"Stan, good to see you. Come on in."

"Hello, Judah," said Stan's wife.

"Hello, April, you look lovely as always." He immediately noticed the "Vote for Ruth's Husband" button she had pinned to her blouse.

"Thank you, Judah." She turned to Stan. "It's too bad some other men don't know how to recognize such things."

"Hey," said Stan, "what do you want from my life?" He turned to Judah. "Women."

"Come on Stan, let's see about that cleaning."

"Yeah, I can handle that, cleaning's good, but not this drillin' and fillin' stuff." He laughed. "Hey, April wants you to have lunch with us."

"Sure," said Judah, "that would be great. Oh, sorry about having to cancel our bowling game Sunday."

"Not a problem."

"Okay, Stan, sit right there." He peered into Stan's mouth for a quick overview. "Ah, been brushing and flossing."

"What did I tell her. That wife of mine says I never take care of my teeth." He shifted himself up in the examination chair. "Hey, April," he yelled to the reception room, "you owe me, I told you...." He looked at Judah and received a smile.

Judah held up a tiny metal instrument with a miniature mirror attached to its end. "How about that cleaning, Stan?" Stan eased back into the chair, relaxed, and let Judah start cleaning, right in syncopation with the rhythm of Benny Goodman's clarinet.

"It's nothing, Stan," said Judah. "Just a little cavity."

"Little, huh? You said I'd been brushing good."

"Only needs a little filling, it shouldn't give you any problems. Just don't eat on that side of your mouth till we fix it. It can wait till next week."

"Next week?"

"Don't worry."

"Afraid, me?"

"I didn't say you were afraid."

"No, I'm not afraid, next week it is. I don't know a better dentist to do the job. We'll do this tooth thing, then go bowl a few frames."

"Judah," said April, "where should we go to lunch? I'm famished."

"I'll decide," said Stan.

"Hush you. We never come downtown, Judah will tell us a decent place to eat."

"I know plenty of good places to eat down here," Stan insisted.

"We're paying, not choosing."

"Paying?" Stan gasped.

"Please," said Judah, "it'll be my treat."

"See," said Stan, "he said it's his treat."

"Stanley Pritzler. Judah is going to be the next synagogue president. We are paying."

"Well," said Judah, "it's not really—"

"About time somebody took on that adulterous bastard," April declared.

"Come on now," said Judah, "George is a nice guy."

"Nice guy that cheats on his wife. A shiksa no less," she added. "That's what I heard from Linda Cole."

"Things happen," said Judah, "people change."

"I see, said Stan, don't want to run a negative campaign. Smart move."

"Campaign?" said Judah. "I'm not running a campaign."

"Of course you are," said April. "You just cleaned my worthless husband's teeth, we're taking you out for lunch. Sure you're campaigning."

"I do that stuff anyway. We have dinner together, I bowl with you."

"Oh yeah," exclaimed Stan, "I have an idea, we can get together with David and Ben and—"

"Listen," said Judah, "you two should know that I'm not really—"

"Oh," April interrupted, "I'm so hungry. Come, Judah, you can tell us both about all your ideas for improving the shul."

"That's the thing, April, I'm not..."

The reception room door opened and a man in gray slacks and a blue sports jacket walked in.

"Can I help you?" asked Judah. He knew all his patients by name and face, and this was not one of them.

"I'm looking for Dr. Judah..." The man looked down at a piece of paper. "Shneeder."

"I'm Dr. Schneider."

"Hey," piped up Stan, seeing the briefcase. "Couldn't you read the sign? No soliciting."

"Stan, it's all right." Judah turned to the man. "How can I help you?"

"Dr. Shneeder—"

"Schneider," Stan corrected.

"Dr. Schneider," said the man, "I have instructions to hand-deliver this notice to you." He held out a large envelope. Judah took it. "Good day." The man turned his back and promptly left the office.

"How rude," said April.

Judah fingered the fold of the envelope and pulled out the notice. He read aloud in the quiet tone he often fell into when writing out checks for monthly bills at the kitchen counter. "Plaintiff, Eloise McCafferty, first consulted the defendant as a patient in July 1988...regarding her dental evaluation, diagnosis and treatment...plaintiff remained under treatment of and as patient of the defendant until November 1989." Judah paused. "That was last month." He continued to read in that quiet tone. "From and after the commencement of the defendant's treatment of plaintiff's teeth...defendant breached his duty and was negligent... on information and belief...as direct and proximately result of said conduct of the defendant, plaintiff contracted an HIV virus, directly from defendant." Judah's eyes bubbled. "Malpractice!" he exclaimed. "Eloise McCafferty is suing me for supposedly giving her HIV?"

"AIDS?" said Stan.

"Hush, Stanley," said April.

"Malpractice?" Judah said. "I don't get sued for malpractice. I've never even gotten a parking ticket."

"Hey," said Stan, "we won't take this sitting down. we'll—"

"Stanley," April interjected. "Can't you see that we should leave Judah be?"

"Oh."

"I'm sorry," said Judah. "I can't go to lunch."

"That's perfectly fine," said April. "We'll see you at temple Friday night. Come along, Stanley. You can buy me lunch."

"Hey," Stan said, "give me a call. We'll still talk about your campaign, go bowl a few frames, you know?" April tugged at his arm.

They left the office and Judah found himself looking over the first legal assault on him in his entire life. He did the most sensible thing he could think of. He picked up the phone and called his older brother, Irving, the attorney.

Ruth was with her friend Ellen, who baked desserts for most bar and bat mitzvahs at the temple. They pulled the station wagon to the back of the synagogue and began unloading the goods into the small storage room behind the sanctuary.

"Be back in a few minutes," said Ellen, excusing herself to the restroom.

Ruth began separating the cookie tins by category when she overheard the voices of two women outside the room walking through the back of the sanctuary.

"And that horrible excuse for a brother of his is the one representing him."

"That filthy Irving?"

"Yes, the one who weaseled Herman Eisenberg out of any responsibility for what he did."

"But AIDS?"

"How many times do I need to repeat myself?"

"Not Judah Schneider."

"Yes."

"Ruth's Judah?"

"Please, I'm not going to repeat myself."

"But AIDS, he has AIDS? How did he get it?"

"It's passed by homosexuals, you know."

"Judah, queer? No. Ruth and Judah have a son."

"That doesn't mean anything nowadays."

"You really think he's queer? I mean, this is Judah Schneider, not one of those lesbian people at that Reconstructionist temple across town."

"Nobody knows if he's gay for sure. But he's being sued for giving this thing to some girl."

"I heard the girl was a shiksa."

"Why am I telling you all this if you already know?"

"Oh, well, I don't know. You hear things, that's all."

"Feh, you probably know more than me."

"Okay, all I heard was that Judah might have been having an affair with this girl, and that she's probably young enough to be his daughter."

"Had an affair, Judah?"

"Might have. Not had."

"Do you think Ruth has it, you know, AIDS?"

"HIV, Ruth?"

"AIDS, not HIV."

"Aren't they the same?"

"I'm not sure. But we all know Judah's type. He probably won't let her sleep. I'm sure he demands sex three, maybe four times a day. At his age, can you imagine?"

"He's such a flirt."

"Really?"

"Haven't you seen the way he oodles over Lillith Zimmer?"

"Oh, my, you're right, I've never looked at it that way. Do you think he'll still run for president?"

Ruth stood motionless. She knew about the lawsuit and was even concerned that this McCafferty woman might have infected Judah, not the other way around. But she had not thought about the situation in this way.

"What are you talking about?" asked Judah.

"You should get tested?"

"Ruthy, of course I'm getting tested. Irving says it's the best way to prove I didn't give it to this McCafferty woman."

"Since when does Irving know anything?"

"That's not what I'm talking about. What's this affair hullabaloo?"

"Did you?"

"Did I what?"

"Have an affair with her?"

"Ruthy, I can't believe you're saying this. I would never do that to you."

"You did it to her, not me. I might have this thing now?"

"I swear I didn't do it."

"How do I know? I mean, you're always flirting at temple with Lillith Zimmer. Everyone sees it."

"What? I've never been anything but faithful to you. This is ridiculous."

"They're saying things, Judah."

"Who?"

"People."

"Not people I care about. Listen, I'm in danger of losing my practice over some loopy woman who's out for a scapegoat. I'd have better chances of getting hit by another car on my way to work than giving her AIDS. Ruthy, we could possibly go into serious debt if this doesn't clear up. I've been asked to stop bowling with the team, even Stan canceled his next appointment. Stan Pritzler canceled his next appointment for God's sake! I've known the man more than twenty-five years."

"Well, at least April and he are still helping with your campaign."

"My campaign? Ruthy, every congregant I know has canceled their appointments with me, even the rabbi."

Ruth gasped. "Even Rabbi Grossman? What about his wife?"

"Yes, even his wife. Now how am I supposed to become synagogue president when I got this mess on my hands? Besides, I was only doing it to make you happy."

Ruth let out an exasperated huff and marched into the kitchen. She took an onion from the fridge and began chopping it into small slivers.

"You'll have to run then," she said. "It's the only way you'll prove you're innocent."

"Going to court with Irving is how I'll prove I'm innocent."

She sniffled as a glossy film began to cover her eyes. The same thing had happened to her earlier in the week when the parents of every student she tutored Hebrew lessons for called with fabricated apologies for deciding to no longer send their children to Ruth, all stating that even though they were certain Judah was innocent they had to think of the safety of their children.

"Oh, Ruthy," said Judah, wrapping his arms around her shoulders from behind. "It'll be all right."

She shoved him back and turned around with the knife facing him. "Get away from me. Go back to your mistress."

"I don't have a mistress."

"Maybe not anymore you don't. I know how you look at other women."

"I don't look at other women. I only have eyes for you."

"Liar. You read that Playboy smut, still, even after all these years. I tried to understand when we were first married, but you still look at those sleazy pictures. You keep them piled on our nightstand, how is that supposed to make me feel?"

"Ruthy, I read them for the articles, they have good articles."

"Articles," she cried as the film in her eyes began to form into tiny lakes. "You are having an affair, aren't you?"

"Ruthy, what do I have to do to prove to you that this is all absurd? Come on, don't cry."

"I'm not crying, it's this stupid onion." She marched to their bedroom and slammed the door.

That night Judah made his own dinner for the first time since Ruth's hip surgery four years before and began an extended nighttime residence on the couch in the living room with his bowling trophies. Ruth no longer put out his clothes to wear each morning to insure he matched well, and Friday night ESPN had been a short-lived toleration.

That first night on the couch, Judah finally wondered if Eloise McCafferty might have been able to infect him with the HIV virus. He had vivid memories of the blood that had flowed from the inflammation of her gums as he ran floss through the crevices separating her coffee-stained teeth. He tried to recall if there had been anything different about the appearance of her blood as it was sucked out of her mouth by his hygienist with one of the many instruments he personally sterilized.

Nothing had ever frightened Judah in over three decades of practicing dentistry. He had seen it all. But this was different. However, he could not risk sharing his concern with Ruth. He decided then to make it his mission to run for president of the synagogue as best he could. And he was determined to win his trial; not for the salvation of his reputation or practice, but for the love of his wife.

The weeks before the election were growing more and more strenuous for Ruth and Judah. Even the old women he helped to their seats at temple were uneasy with him, using handkerchiefs to wipe themselves of any germs they might have contracted. Rabbi Grossman's wife steered as far away from him as possible now and made an early trip to the synagogue every Sunday morning to personally instruct the temple's caretaker as he disinfected the door handles and toilet seats of each restroom thoroughly before the children arrived for religious school.

That last Sunday before the election, Stan was sitting in the faculty lounge of the religious school with Ruth.

"This is bullshit," said Stan.

"Stanley," Ruth gasped.

"Oh, excuse my language, I always forget about the kids. It's just that this is a bunch of crap. I can't believe they won't let you volunteer at the preschool anymore. It's Judah who is being sued, not you. You can teach fourth-grade religious school but can't supervise finger-painting?" Stan was occasionally reaching up to feel the left side of his face where that cavity had still not been treated by Judah. Ruth wondered why Stan was so quick to cancel his appointment but still be so adamantly supportive of Judah.

Then, Sylvia Stockenheimer and her sister Miriam entered.

"Now he's got that big shot brother of his trying to get him off the hook just like he did for that horrible Herman Eisenberg," said Miriam.

"No," gasped Sylvia, "not that filthy Irving?"

"I would get your girls tested if I were you," said Mirium.

"I haven't taken them to get their teeth cleaned in six months."

"But you don't know how long ago he contracted this from that girl."

"I thought he gave it to her?"

"Well, does it make a difference? I heard he might actually be queer."

"No!"

"Well, I mean—" They finally saw Ruth sitting at the table.

Stan couldn't restrain himself. He launched to his feet, his presence bringing the staff lounge to immediate silence.

"Let me tell you something about Judah Schneider. I've been living in Portland for over twenty-five years—"

"Stan, it's all right—"

"No, Ruth, I'm gonna say my piece." He turned back towards the Stockenheimer sisters. "The first night I was here in Portland I met

Judah. April and I went to temple. Halfway through the Kaddish I get this awful ache in my mouth, like a hammer's coming down on my teeth or something—far worse than the pain I have now. I go out to the lobby because I think I'm gonna scream. I'm sitting with my hands clutched to my face and the only person I see is this guy helping an old woman take off her coat. There's Judah Schneider, helping this old woman. He sees me and the first thing he does is introduce himself. How was I to know he was a dentist. He takes me to the restroom where there's better light and looks in my mouth. Sure, he could have told me to see him first thing Monday morning. But not Judah. I don't even know the man, don't even know a soul in this city, and he insists on getting his car from his house to drive me downtown to his office to fix my tooth. He's willing to drive on Shabbos to help me. I told him it could wait, that I should be in temple with my wife. But no, he insisted because he was worried that it could get ugly if he didn't treat me. So then I say I can't pay him because April and I were broke. Judah immediately refused to take my money because it's the Sabbath. What a sacrifice he made. I'd never seen such kindness, surely not back in Jersey. Every time I offer to pay him back for that night he refuses, says it was a favor. A mitzvah, that's what it was. A mensch, that's what Judah Schneider is, a true mensch. And all this talk about AIDS, all this hullabaloo about him being queer. Feh! Let me tell you, I know how this girl got this terrible disease; from being stupid and not being safe, from her lifestyle not her dentist. She's probably a dope fiend, used unclean needles. I've never known a man more devoted to maintaining a respectable business, or more devoted to his wife and family than Judah Schneider. Our boys went to Hebrew school together, he even had an aliyah at my son Michael's bar mitzvah. Queer? An adulterer? AIDS? Please, I don't know a better man than Judah Schneider. And I can't think of a finer man to become our next synagogue president."

Stan then stormed out of the lounge with the intention of having Judah finally look at that cavity that was now almost unbearable, even if it meant having him come over and examine him in his bathroom at the house. But April refused to allow it, not until they could be sure. Stan refused to see another dentist, he would wait.

That afternoon, after cleaning her Sunday school classroom, Ruth gave notice to the Stockenheimer sisters that she would no longer instruct her class for the synagogue. After sixteen years of teaching religious school, she turned in the key to her room and made sure to leave specific lesson plans for the remainder of the year. She then went home to her husband.

Judah had put on a suit and tie and was now carefully combing that extended flap of hair over his shiny scalp. He remembered cutting his boy Leonard's hair when he was young. Judah thought of hair styling as a natural second trade. "After all," he often said, "dentists had also served as town barbers at one time. Not many people know that those red and white spirals outside barber shops were originally where dentists had hung the blood-soaked gauze rags from the more sophisticated of their two lines of work." It was painful for Judah when Leonard eventually insisted on being taken to a "real" barber once he reached early adolescence and began primping his hair in the morning, hoping to impress the girls at school. Judah reluctantly succumbed to his only son's wish and the next day took him to see the same man who had been trimming his own hair for the past twenty years. The special hair trimming set and clippers Judah had bought came out of retirement when Leonard decided to grow his hair down his back and to his waist in late high school, when he bashfully asked his father to snip off the split ends. It brought Judah pleasure to assist his son, almost as much as the two free dental examinations he gave him each year.

Ruth entered the bathroom as he was applying the special hair spray his barber had given him.

He had been sleeping on the couch for weeks. The test results would be ready the next day. But tonight was what Ruth had been waiting for. The congregation would vote on the next synagogue president. If Judah won, she said she would consider allowing him to sleep on top of the covers on his side of the bed until the results of the test came back the next day. She had been reading about AIDS, but was still skeptical of the ways the informational brochures said it could be transmitted. She was suspicious of such things, just as her Uncle Harry had taught her to be. Judah had already thrown away the collection of *Playboys* he had compiled for more than three decades and canceled his subscription in hopes of demonstrating to Ruth how much her feelings meant to him.

"Do you have your speech ready?"

"Speech, what speech?" said Judah.

"Your speech, the one you're giving tonight."

Judah, although officially running for president, had not made one pledge or been asked one question concerning any stance he may have had even on what type of bagel he preferred. Yet the congregation had divided into separate camps: those who believed Judah was innocent and those who believed he was guilty. Stan had even printed buttons that read "Judah Was Framed." This didn't help the fact that Judah was still angered that his dear friend had been skeptical enough to cancel his appointment, just like the others. He said nothing of this, though, and graciously accepted whatever support was offered.

Ruth still needed the test results for her own assurance, but she had already joined in support of her husband's innocence. She had made calls to the local Jewish Review, the B'nai B'rith, and the Anti-Defamation League to inform them that her husband, Dr. Judah Morris Schneider, a respected member of Portland's Jewish community, was the victim of anti-Semitism. The Oregonian wanted to run a cover story but Judah refused an interview. With Irving's coaxing, Ruth had finally ceased making press calls. However, she still made Judah sleep on the couch.

"So?" Ruth said.

"What?" said Judah, finishing the hair flap placement. He had changed his suit three times already at Ruth's request and was weary of the demand for a fourth, more respectable-looking choice. He had put his foot down when she insisted he wear a fedora. She was convinced it would make him appear distinguished, like her Uncle Harry had looked to her. Judah thought it transformed him from a dentist into a Meyer Lansky impersonator.

"Your speech, what about your speech?"

"I'm gonna wing it."

Ruth was not pleased. "What are you going to say?"

"I don't know," said Judah, dabbing his neck with a few splashes of Old Spice. "Maybe I'll suggest that we give up fasting on Yom Kippur and have a buffet table in the lobby so people can come and go with plates during services and not get hungry."

He could see Ruth's approaching reaction.

"Hey, I was just kidding."

Exasperated, Ruth pulled on her coat, made sure her "Vote for Ruth's Husband" and "Judah Was Framed" buttons were secure, then went to wait for her husband on the porch.

The banquet hall in the basement of the synagogue was packed. The caretaker had cleared out the entire room, set up a portable stage, and lined as many metal folding chairs into the hall as possible. Both emergency exit doors were opened for ventilation.

Ruth sat in the front row with Irving to her left and Stan and April to her right. There was an aisle separating Judah's supporters from George Finklestein's. On the makeshift stage sat the incumbent president, Finklestein himself. Then there was Judah, wearing a stylish velvet yarmulke that Ruth had bobby-pinned to his flap of hair.

The congregation quieted. Judah still couldn't believe he was going through with this. He would have felt more comfortable in front of the congregation at a bowling alley. He was too accustomed to sitting in the banquet hall when the rabbi pitched the congregants for financial donations once a year. But when he looked down and saw Ruth's proud smile, he knew he would do his best.

"My fellow congregants," Judah said, attempting to sound as political as possible. "My wife asked me to prepare a speech for tonight. But that's not the kind of man I am."

"We know what kind of man you are," a shout came from Finklestein's side of the audience. "Pig."

"You calling my friend a pig?" shouted Stan, leaping to his feet. "Show your face, let's see who the pig is." Stan was now speaking with a slight slur, which made Judah concerned about how that cavity was treating him.

Doris Sessman stood, her head barely rising above the shoulders of those still seated around her. "I don't want a homosexual representing our congregation, not to mention an AIDS carrier. God only knows what germs he's spreading in this room, or has already spread to our children that he has examined."

"God," said Stan, "you want to talk about God. Fine, let's talk about God and your candidate. Thou shall not commit adultery," Stan shouted. He then turned around to Judah's supporters behind him and Ruth. "Thou shall not commit adultery," he shouted. And that's when all of Judah's supporters came to their feet, and shouted over and over with Stan, "Thou shall not commit adultery," raising their fists in the air as though they were marching in a rally against neo-Nazis.

"Please, please," said Judah, "please sit down." After a few moments and the rising presence of Rabbi Grossman to calm the crowd, everyone took their seats.

"Thank you for your enthusiastic support," Judah began again. "But this is a night for dialogue and debate, not shouts and accusations." A muffled applause followed. "I'll say again: I did not prepare a speech, because I am the kind of man who prefers to say what is on my mind. I hope that you will not judge me or my family based on rumors and unfounded claims that have not been resolved yet. I also do not wish to shower you with promises. I'll just say that as president, I'll do the best job I can do, and if I make a mistake, I'll admit it. That said, I think we can all gain more by having George and me openly answer any questions you may have."

After Finklestein quickly agreed to the sudden change in the debate format, practically every hand in the audience rose. This prompted the rabbi to rise once again, take the spare microphone from the stage, and, as moderator, begin selecting hands.

"This question is for George," said the first man selected among Finklestein's supporters. It was Joel Grossman, the eldest son of Rabbi Grossman with whom Judah had always bowled with until recently. "How do you personally feel about Dr. Schneider's current situation?"

Finklestein took a sip from his water glass and adjusted his slouching posture.

"I sincerely empathize with Judah and his wife. I, as many of you know, have been the victim of rumors myself. But I question the manner in which Judah is handling these horrendous circumstances. Judah is without question a family man. But his decision to seek the counsel of his brother disturbs me. I hope everyone remembers the outlandish acts which Irving Schneider performed three years ago as a licensed practitioner of the law."

A subtle roll of whispers began circulating through the room. Ruth glared at Irving, wishing that he had been adopted or somehow not been related to Judah. The incident Finklestein was referring to was when Irving had represented Herman Eisenberg, the kosher butcher from East Portland who was discovered to have kept an unsanitary business, which had not been certified by a rabbi and had been knowingly contaminated by treif. Irving had helped pull strings to allow Eisenberg to keep his kosher butcher's license, which infuriated many members of the Jewish community. Even Rabbi Grossman had stopped asking Irving to raise the Torah each year during high holy day services, an honor that had been his for almost ten years Since he made the largest financial contributions to United Synagogue Youth.

"I realize that Irving is Judah's brother, but do we want our president associating with a man who has no regard for the laws God set before us? After all, a tree that drops one rotten apple is bound to drop another."

Judah was about to defend what he considered an attack on his late mother, but Stan cut him off.

"Thou shall not commit adultery," Stan shouted, standing once again. That entire side of the hall rose and began chanting in unison, "Thou shall not commit adultery," over and over, until Finklestein's supporters rose and began moving across the aisle. Folding chairs could be heard being pushed aside, crashing to the floor then stomped over as the two coalitions confronted each other. Finklestein's supporters began chanting "AIDS carrier!" repeatedly in response to the adultery chant. Irving finally had to lift Ruth to the stage to avoid the stampede. She rushed to Judah and stood behind him. She then placed her right hand on his shoulder. Judah reached up and held it, squeezing softly, hoping that she understood what he was trying to convey.

When everyone finally took their seats again fifteen minutes later, Rabbi Grossman, convinced that the congregants had already made up their minds as to whom they were supporting, called for a dispense of any more questions and insisted that an immediate vote be taken.

When the numbers were tallied, George Finklestein won his reelection by thirty votes. That night Judah did not sleep on the couch in the living room with his bowling trophies. Instead, he slept on the floor of his and Ruth's bedroom, able to hear his wife's breath as he fell asleep.

The next day the results of Judah's HIV test came back negative. With this information, the lawsuit was dropped. Irving urged Judah to file a countersuit for defamation of character, but Judah, thankful that the ordeal was finally over, simply wanted to reopen his office and resume the practice of dentistry. Most importantly, he was relieved that Ruth could be assured he was indeed the faithful husband he prided himself being.

His real frustration now was that his bowling team, all Finklestein supporters, had asked him to step down after eleven years of league camaraderie. And although he tried repeatedly to assure Ruth that he had never cared about being synagogue president, she never recovered from the thought that she had been so close to sitting with the rabbi's wife during high holy day services, only to fall short by thirty votes. She was certain that there would never be another opportunity for her husband to gain the righteous notoriety that had always bestowed her Uncle Harry. Nevertheless, the ordeal was over, and she once again allowed Judah to sleep with her in their bed.

Judah had paid for a newspaper ad in the local *Jewish Review* and had also put up an announcement on the bulletin board at the synagogue explaining that his office was as sanitary as ever and that he had even had the Occupational Safety and Disease Association run a thorough inspection. Stan arrived that morning to finally have his cavity taken care of, the first patient Judah had seen since being sued for malpractice.

"Hey, sorry about dropping my appointment. We all just had to be sure, Judah. April made me. But she wants you and Ruth to have dinner with us this Wednesday. Really."

"Why don't you sit down in the chair, Stan. I bet that cavity's gotten a little uncomfortable."

Judah went to the stereo in the back and turned on the tape of Beethoven's Third Symphony that he had brought specifically for his return. He then began the awkward new procedure of securing a sterilized rubber glove over each hand. He made a mental note not to use a local anesthetic on Stan, reached for his drill, and once again went about working on teeth, maneuvering his hands in syncopation to the rhythm of the music.

BEING SECULAR

We have just enough religion to make us hate,
but not enough to make us love one another.
                                    —*Jonathan Swift*

*N*OAH STEPPED into the lounge of the office and surveyed the selection of mugs from the rack above the water-filtering tap. He took the white ceramic cup, the words "Marty Cohen, Jewish Community Center Men's Club Man of the Year" lithographed over the front.

A note had been posted on Noah's desk when he arrived for work earlier that morning, scribbled in the office secretary's grade-school penmanship: "See Mr. Cohen in his office—four o'clock sharp. Finish all last week's figures before meeting." Noah had worked throughout the day, even skipped his lunch hour to complete the task. He was a perfectionist when it came to numbers.

He had been with the company for almost a year. And although the three partners of Cohen, Bernstein and Klein Office Supplies rarely spoke to him, he had been praised on several occasions for his accounting work. It was not Noah's last name that had secured his job; the "berg" had been immediately dropped from "Green" the day he turned eighteen. His interview surely wasn't the reason either. He had sweat so profusely during the ordeal that Klein actually asked if he needed a towel. It was one of the only times in his entire life that Noah played up his Jewish background, hoping to save a dismal-looking future and put his dust-collecting college degree to purpose.

"It's my allergies," he said. "This kind of thing hasn't happened to me since I was in Hebrew school." It sickened him, using his unwanted heritage when he detested it to begin with, having sworn to erase all its traces.

He got the job.

It was Christmas Eve, and even though Noah had referred to his religious faith as "secular" since the day he left home for college, he knew Mr. Cohen thought of him as a fellow member of the tribe. After all, Noah had fostered that impression. But that didn't mean that a holiday bonus wasn't a possibility. Noah was well aware of Mr. Cohen's financial generosity; the man boasted of giving ten percent of his yearly income to tzedakah. Christmas Eve had also been a traditional time for such appreciations to be shown at his former accounting job with a frozen French fry company. Noah filled the mug with coffee, mixed in the powdered creamer, straightened his tie, wrapped his fingers around Marty Cohen's name, and walked down the hall to his boss's office, a report of the previous week's figures in hand.

He knocked.

The door swung open and Mr. Cohen motioned Noah inside with a head nod. He was talking into a cellular phone.

"Yeah, of course," said Mr. Cohen. "What, you think I don't hear you? Hey, it's me you're talking to, not that shmuck from the L.A. office. Fine, give me one minute." He cupped the receiver with his free hand and looked at Noah. "Have a seat, Green," he said softly. "I'll be back in a minute." He proceeded down the hall to resume his conversation.

Noah sat down in the seat directly in front of Mr. Cohen's enormous oak desk and scanned the office. It was the first time he had been there since his interview. Behind the desk was a framed poster-size picture of Mr. Cohen and his brother, Marty, standing together at the top of Masada in Israel. Marty Cohen had run a customized toilet seat manufacturing empire in San Diego before retiring to the Northwest. In the three years he had been living in Portland, he had managed to refurnish the bathroom of every member of his younger brother's synagogue with a new customized Cohen toilet product. He truly was "Man of the Year." Noah placed the mug of coffee on the desk and turned it around so that Marty's name would be facing his boss when he sat down. He then saw a white envelope propped against a framed portrait of Mr. Cohen with pro-golfer Peter Jacobson and smiled, certain now about the bonus. He strategically placed the report beside the envelope and waited.

Mr. Cohen stepped back into the office, shutting the door behind him. "Damn Seattle distributors," he said, tossing the cellular on an empty chair near the door, then taking his large swivel chair. "I tell you, I'm gonna place dollars to donuts that guy calls back and wracks my balls at least one more time before I leave today." He paused and looked right at Noah. "You know how it is."

"Oh yeah," said Noah, giving that 'I know where you're coming from' grin.

Mr. Cohen then swung the chair towards the window and looked out over the charcoal Portland skyline. "Well, Green, I guess you're wondering why I asked to see you. First of all, I want you to know that you're a good kid. How old are you, twenty-four?"

"Twenty-seven, sir."

"Twenty-seven," Mr. Cohen sighed. "When I was your age I already had two kids and Mrs. Cohen had our third baking in the oven." Noah gave the slight laugh that he knew was expected. "You're married, right?"

"No, sir," said Noah.

"Huh? Could have sworn I've heard you talking with a Mrs. Green over the phone a few times when I passed by your desk."

Noah hesitated. "I live with a woman."

"Oh? So that's how it is." Mr. Cohen waved his palm forward. "Don't worry, you don't need to explain. I think it's good young people do that nowadays. But Mrs. Cohen and I couldn't get away with that kind of thing when we were kids. Had to drive all over town till we found a dark place to park, know what I mean?"

Noah managed to produce another contrived laugh. The courteous small talk was making him grow impatient. He wanted that bonus.

Mr. Cohen swung his chair back to the desk and his eyelids dropped for a moment. "Well, Green, this isn't my idea of fun, but I drew the short stick, if you know what I mean. Don't take this the wrong way, you're a good kid. But," he sighed and leaned back, "we got ourselves a little situation. Turns out Bernstein's oldest boy graduated from Stanford in June and still hasn't landed a job. The kid's got some degree in international economics. Anyways, we're gonna take him in as the company's financial organizer. Bernstein lives for that father and son crap, wants the boy to start first of the year. I don't like it being this way, but I've known this kid his whole life. Heck, I was at his bris. Anyway, we're gonna release you. You know how it is, right?"

Noah didn't answer.

Mr. Cohen picked up the white envelope. "I know this must be coming as a surprise and all. You're a good kid, got a real head on you, I've noticed. Klein said he thought two weeks' severance pay was sufficient, but I want you to know I pulled for you, Green. Got you the entire two months of pay left on your contract. Bernstein agreed it was the right thing to do. I wish I could do more."

Noah remained silent. He stood, leaving the mug on the desk that had gone completely unnoticed along with the report. Mr. Cohen stood with him and handed over the white envelope, which Noah immediately placed into the liner pocket of his sports jacket.

"I included a short recommendation letter in there for you. You're a good kid, Green. Don't hesitate to put my name down on a résumé." He put out his hand. Noah gave it a firm shake, looked directly into the man's eyes, the way his father had always instructed him to do as a boy.

"Have a happy first night of Hanukkah," said Mr. Cohen. "Too bad it started late this year, the Christians got one up on us again." He smiled.

Noah returned the smile as best he could but did not laugh. He had no idea Hanukkah was beginning, nor did he care. "Thank you, sir." He couldn't believe he had managed the words through his dampening lips.

"Take care of yourself, Green." Mr. Cohen walked Noah to the door, shook his hand once more, then picked up the cellular phone from the chair.

"Thank you," Noah said again, then walked down the hall. He opened the top drawer of his desk and took his car keys, making careful effort not to slam the drawer when he shut it. He turned around and headed for the door. Bernstein and Klein came around the corner discussing invoice records, not even noticing him. The secretary saw him leaving and dropped her head down to avoid eye contact. He opened the door and left the office, the sweats that had always plagued him now returning to his neck and forehead. The pits of his arms felt like the worn bristles of a broom.

Kike, Noah wanted to scream as he stopped and looped the two buttons of his sports jacket to shield the chill. It was only a few minutes past four and already dark. Kike, he wanted to scratch into the metallic-gray paint of Mr. Cohen's BMW with his keys, the same way the water polo players in high school had done to his father's Buick when he had borrowed it once.

He unlocked the door of his car. "That fucking kike!" Noah finally screamed as he shut the door and tore the tie from his neck, ripping off the top button to his cotton shirt in the process. He turned over the car and quickly clicked on the radio.

"It's Christmas Eve," a sultry voice came from the radio as Bing Crosby and the Andrews Sisters singing "Mele Kalikimaka" was ending. "That's right, we're playing twenty-four hours of Christmas fun."

Noah slammed his fist into the torn vinyl ceiling twice, then heard Bing Crosby's voice again, this time singing the first verse of "Silver Bells." He thrust his fist into the radio over and over until the power and dial knobs both broke off, and his hand began to bleed. Bing Crosby still came in strong over the slight static. Noah tried, but was unable to turn off the sound. The metal nubs where the dial knobs had been were too thin for his numbing fingers.

He wiped the perspiration from his brow and calmly pulled out of the parking lot onto the street, taking the first on-ramp for the freeway. His right hand was lacerated, the blood running in tiny streams from his knuckles to his wrist and down his shirtsleeve. He didn't care. All he could think about was how Mr. Cohen had made him complete the report on the previous week's figures before firing him. He then thought of Bernstein's son and floored the accelerator.

"Stanford," Noah huffed. He remembered his own parents' reaction when he received his own acceptance to Stanford during his senior year of high school.

"Too expensive," Noah's father had declared. "You'll go to Portland State University and live here at home with us. Your mother needs you here. What, you want us to die of worry, you being so far away? You'll stay, no more discussion."

Noah then thought of where he was driving—home, to Christine. He had completely forgotten. Had he received the bonus he expected, he would have bought her something. Not a holiday gift, maybe just flowers, an apology for not being capable of becoming the man she needed, even though he so badly wanted to be. He had been planning to break things off with her after the holidays, but this was different than ruts with past girlfriends. He was living with this one. Christine had said that she adored him because, unlike her previous half-dozen "beaus," he had a job.

"It's funny," she said after they had moved in together three months before, "all my boyfriends have always been unemployed or lost their jobs by the time we broke up. You're a real step up, you've got your act together." Noah had laughed at the comment. But now, as much as he despised his mother's superstitious belief in omens and curses, he was convinced Christine was more than simply the flawed human being he had been planning to sever all relations from; she was the deliverer of his punishment.

Noah opened both the driver's and passenger's windows in hopes of drowning out the static-filled sound of Jose Feliciano breaking into "Feliz Navidad". He took the exit off the freeway for the small house he rented with Christine. She was as unemployed as her ex-boyfriends and would be at home watching soap operas and cutting newspaper coupons that they would never remember to use.

He pulled into the supermarket five blocks before their street, circled the lot for five minutes before finding a parking space, then quickly cut the engine as Elvis began to sing "White Christmas." He licked the last of the trickling blood that had not clotted over his knuckles. As he walked towards the electronic glass doors of the supermarket, he thought of Christine and what might be the best tactic for breaking off their relationship.

"Merry Christmas," the Salvation Army man said to Noah as he walked into the market. "I said, Merry Christmas," the man repeated, even though Noah was already a good five feet away. He walked on. Noah had plenty of cash on him, but wasn't about to give away even one penny of the change in his pocket, especially to an emaciated man in a Santa Claus costume ringing a bell.

He strolled through the aisles of the store, past the last-minute shoppers racing to find a few more items for the dinner table. It was difficult to ignore the sniffles of the many children, begging their parents to buy them the cheap plastic toys they discovered, being told that Santa might have already thought of putting such gifts in their stockings.

Noah came to the wine section.

"Do you think Daddy will be able to come to my holiday sing-a-long tonight, Mommy?" The little girl's high-pitched whimper came from the next aisle. The mother's voice was then muffled by the passing of a bag-boy pushing a procession of metal grocery carts. Noah remembered his own grade-school sing-a-long assemblies in vivid detail; how the entire school would perform a dozen rehearsed Christmas carols with the token "I Had a Little Dreidel" slipped in near the end of the program to appease the few Jewish parents in the audience. He remembered how he had kept his eyes towards the floor with embarrassment as his mother held his hand after the recital while his father gave a dissertation to the grade-school principal about the separation of church and state, citing articles of the Constitution from memory. He recalled sitting in the backseat of the car on the way home as his mother said, "Now Noah, you only mouthed the words about Jesus, right? You didn't sing them, did you?" But he had sung them, being told by his music instructor that if he did not his participation in the sing-a-long would be replaced by a library assignment. His father then added, "You know why they have their Jesus, their fantasy, don't you, Noah? Because they can't identify with God unless he's a man, that's why. Small brains, that's the goyim for you."

Noah would prefer any white wine over red. But he knew Christine would want a Merlot. The wine was meant as a peace offering of sorts, to ease the tension of their soon to be dissolved relationship. He took a cheap bottle, then walked to the register, bypassing a group of screaming children in green and red jumpsuits with bells strapped to their ankles. He passed a collection of reduced-priced Christmas knick-knacks: holly, plastic mistletoe, and artificial wreaths. There was even an entire section of lights. Noah believed each bulb was an assault on what he was not and what he had never wanted to be. Most of all he hated the Jewish homes in the suburbs that displayed blue and white lights as compensation to their children. Traitors, Noah always thought as he drove by these houses.

Noah despised candles as well: Havdalah candles, Shabbat candles, Hanukkah candles. He had tried to erase the memory of the Yahrzeit candle he lit with his mother last August on the anniversary of his father's death, but failed.

"Have a merry Christmas," the checkout girl said with a smile, handing Noah his change and the bottle wrapped in a paper bag. She was blonde, maybe seventeen. The bell on the peak of her Santa hat jingled every time she swiped an item across the electronic scanner. A thin gold cross hung between the loosened buttons of her virginal white blouse, brushing the pale skin of her adolescent cleavage. She reminded Noah of the chirpy girls who wore dresses resembling delicate bakery pastries the entire week before Easter in elementary school, the ones who made snide jokes about the matzah and haroset sandwiches his mother would pack in his lunch during Passover. He wanted to pull that Santa hat down over the checkout girl's cheerful smile that was armed with red and green sparkled lipstick.

"Well," the girl said, "have a merry Christmas." She turned away and began helping the next customer in line. "And how's your Christmas Eve been?"

Noah walked towards the glass exit doors.

"Merry Christmas," the man in the Santa costume said again, furiously jingling his bell. Noah stuffed one hand into his pocket as though he were actually about to make a donation, then walked by him. He quickly rushed past the chain-link fence lined in barbed wire that housed the last of the tree selection, making a beeline for his car at the end of the lot.

The Pointer Sisters were singing "Santa Claus is Coming to Town" on the radio when he turned over the ignition, but there was no longer any static, just clear reception.

Driving home, Noah thought of how Christine was most likely one of those little girls in pastry dresses. He thought of how he had only met her six months ago, how mesmerized he was with her rejection of the born-again Christian upbringing her mother had subjected her to. Noah had assumed their reasons for running away from religion were the same when she nodded in agreement and understanding while he declared his faith as "secular." He mostly thought of how naive he had been to move in with this woman solely based on the hopes of more frequent sex and amusement from his mother's reaction to her. But it was not as he had expected. His mother fully accepted Christine with the anticipation of acquiring a daughter-in-law, which would of course increase the potential for grandchildren. Perhaps a baby boy to immortalize her dead husband's name.

"So, Green," their neighbor, Len Johnson, had said the week before. "This will be your first Christmas as a married man?"

"We're not married," Noah had clarified.

"Oh, then this will be your first Christmas as—"

"No," Noah had said, "we don't celebrate Christmas."

"Oh," Len had chuckled, "I completely forgot, you're a Hebe. You know, you don't even look like one, I mean, you'd never know is all. Happy Hanukkah."

"No," Noah had said, "we're secular." And Len looked at him, perplexed.

He drove into the neighborhood slowly, yet still managed to roll through the three stop signs before his turn. St. Paul Avenue was lined with weathered manufactured box-homes built in the 1950s, the kind that possessed the same architectural design every three houses with neatly manicured plastic lawns, but all in different colors providing the illusion of individuality. Noah and Christine's place was at the end of the street, the only house without festive bulbs, only a yellow patio light. Noah had done a successful job of alienating every neighbor who asked why they did not decorate their house. Len Johnson even asked for the power drill back that he had lent Noah after being told that his and Carol's home resembled a Las Vegas casino with its twinkling lights and billboard-size illumination of "Joy to the World" radiating in green and red neon letters from their two-story roof. Len had bought a portable power generator to light the sign every night.

Noah parked the car, immediately cut the engine and Nat King Cole singing "Merry Christmas to You" with it, then took the wine, and walked to the front door. He looked up, proud that there was not a wreath on the door and even happier that a mezuzah did not adorn the frame.

Before opening the door he paused and turned around. The house across the street, Len and Janice Johnson's, was radiating even more so than it had the previous few weeks. Have they added lights on the yard bushes? Noah wondered. He looked closer. Not only was the entire Johnson home lined with festive bulbs, but there was now a small plastic barn on the front lawn with illuminated statues of the three wise men on a revolving track circling the birth of the baby Jesus. To the right of the nativity scene was now a life-size Santa Claus and sleigh, a single red-nosed reindeer attached to the reins with a sheet of white, blanket-cotton over the grass to substitute for the snow that had not fallen that winter. Noah placed the bottle of wine down on the welcome mat in front of his door, then walked to the carport.

When they had moved into the tiny rental they piled an incredible amount of junk left from the previous renters into the carport. Now, tearing the countless items off the pile in the back of the darkened port, Noah finally came across the plastic pink flamingo he had buried with thoughts of his grandmother's Miami retirement home. The paint was scuffed and it was missing a leg, but the post-stick was still attached. He walked to his own flood lamp-lit lawn and stuck the synthetic bird right in the middle, then went back to the front door. He reached for the doorknob but dropped his hand and turned.

He shrugged, walked back to the middle of his grass, uprooted the flamingo, and marched right across the street to the Johnson's lawn. Although it was December, the Johnsons still had fresh bark dust brought in the first of every month to outline their perfectly manicured bushes. The odor nauseated Noah. He picked up the ceramic reindeer and removed the sleigh reins. The plastic flamingo was firmly shoved into Rudolph's place on the synthetic snow and the reins slung over the wings. Taking the reindeer with him, Noah walked back to his carport and tossed it on top of the junk pile.

Going back to the front door, he once again thought of what the best tactic would be to break things off with Christine. He considered beginning the conversation by telling her she was a "good kid," then opened the door.

Christine sat on the Goodwill, brown-corduroy couch that was positioned in front of the empty fireplace drinking a glass of milk and reading a double-sized issue of *People* with Princess Di on the cover. Noah was surprised that she had the television turned off for once.

Positioned five feet from the checkered kitchen linoleum was an undecorated pine tree with a single tattered cloth angel on its peak. The tree was larger than a potted plant, but recognizably among the last of the selection at the supermarket. Several of the needles were already fading into brown daggers.

"What the hell is that?" asked Noah, closing the front door behind him and walking to the kitchen.

"What does it look like, silly?" said Christine, walking over to kiss him with her thin lips. Noah turned his back and opened a drawer to find a corkscrew. "My, somebody's in a bad mood."

No reply.

"It's just a tree, Noah. There's nothing religious about it, it's an American thing."

"I've never had one."

"Of course not, you're Jewish."

"Secular, remember."

"Whatever. Listen, I've always had a tree. It wouldn't be Christmas without one."

"Christine—"

"Oh, come on, everyone celebrates Christmas. Like I said, it's American to have one." She swung her arms around his shoulders from behind. "Come on, we'll decorate it together, string popcorn. It'll be fun, sweety. It's like watching the clock fall in Times Square on New Year's, you know? We can read our horoscopes, drink that bottle you got there. Come on, I rented *A Miracle on 34th Street*. We can watch that and then…"

He finally turned around and she smiled at him, expecting a kiss. Noah was disgusted at how she always addressed him with the affectionate pet names she acquired from daytime melodramas. She stared at him longingly, blinking her almost transparent eyelashes as though she were begging him for sympathy.

"What's that?" he said, looking at the counter. It was a package, wrapped in the same metallic-blue paper he had seen every Hanukkah of his childhood. His mother still had three economy-size rolls in her linen closet that she had purchased during a closeout sale.

"It's from your mother."

"No shit. I told her I don't believe in gifts."

"Well, we got one from her. Just open it." He could see she was excited with anticipation. The contorted ballerina position of her feet and bending knees were a dead give away.

"I want that tree out of this house."

Christine stepped back.

"Listen, Noah, it's just a tree, get used to it. It's not gonna bite. Besides, I made sure not to put it in the window."

Noah said nothing. He was thirsty, but didn't want to open the wine yet. It would only lead to another, more uncomfortable discussion. Besides, he knew it would be easier if he was already well oiled.

He opened the fridge.

"Eggnog, huh? My, aren't we in a festive mood."

"What's your problem?" asked Christine.

"Nothing," he said, "I'd love to have some eggnog for Jesus day, maybe we can bake a ham tonight as well and invite the Johnsons over." He took the eggnog out and put it on the counter, then opened a cupboard. As he reached for a mug he thought of Marty Cohen, "Jewish Community Center Men's Club Man of the Year." He took a tall glass instead. "Excuse me," he said, nudging Christine's bony shoulders aside and opening the cabinet behind her to find the brandy.

"I thought we were having wine? Hey, what happened to your hand? Do you need to see a doctor?"

He didn't answer.

"Noah, are you all right, what happened? You're covered in blood." She took his hand with concern. He instantly pulled free of her, breaking one of her nails in the process.

Neither said a word as he poured a half glass of eggnog and filled the rest with brandy until he had to slurp the lip of the rim before picking up the glass.

"Want one?" he finally asked, breaking the silence.

"You hate brandy."

"It's my New Year's resolution, to grow more tolerant."

She turned, walked to the living room with heavy steps, and kicked off her shoes in front of the coffee table. "Listen, I'm going to take a shower, you build a fire and chill out. Let's just enjoy the fact that we can spend time together without you boiling about work. You have the next two days off, you should be happy."

"Sure," said Noah, "you, me, and our new green friend here, maybe we can invite my mother over to decorate it with us."

"It's just a tree!" She slammed the door to the bathroom.

Noah stood in the kitchen, downed his drink, and mixed another. The eggnog seemed to make the brandy tolerable. He quickly finished the second glass, then heard the shower turn on. He made a third drink as he casually took note of his mother's gift on the counter.

Although he despised the wrapping, he was interested to see what she had sent. He ripped the paper away to discover a set of kitchen knives. His mother had even taped a bag of chocolate Hanukkah gelt to the box. She had also included a miniature menorah with pinkie-size candles. He lifted the box. "Can cut through a tin can as easily as a tomato," he read aloud and laughed. "A must for the experienced chef." Christine and he together could barely prepare a TV dinner. He put the box down and walked to the chairs in front of the empty fireplace, sat down, and stared at the tree. It was empty of any decoration, only that tattered, cloth-sewn angel on the peak.

While he sipped his drink, Noah began to once again think about Christine. "Marry a nice Jewish girl," his Aunt Phyllis had always told him. His mother's sister did not consider Christine to be nice and she definitely wasn't Jewish. Now a Christmas tree stood before him, in his own house. And Christine, a girl who believed that a good collection of National Geographics was the symbol of an intelligent family's home, had put it there. He was ashamed, though he was confused as to what of and why.

Christine was taking an unusually long shower. He knew she wanted him to join her. But he couldn't remember when he was last attracted to her and he had not wanted to even touch her in weeks. Still, sleeping with her always gave him a certain reassurance.

He finished his drink and rose from the chair, walked back to the kitchen counter, then tore open the box of knives. He took the large blade from the decorative display holder, went to the recycling bag by the back door, and picked out an empty Diet Pepsi can. He cut through the aluminum with ease and laughed, then walked back to the living room.

The tree barreled over with one solid kick, the flipped support-dish drowning his shoes with water. Clutching the sappy trunk in his left hand, he began sawing it in half. He imagined the trunk was Mr. Cohen's legs as he chipped through the outer bark; Bernstein's son's arms as he began driving a steady carpenter's arm-sway into the inner body of the wood; finally picturing it as Christine's thin, tightly skinned, ivory throat as he severed the tree in half. He then went about slicing the branches from the trunk and scaling the pine needles off the limbs. He collected several pieces and went about constructing a fire by crumpling newspaper coupons for kindling. But the wood would not light.

He found a container of lighter fluid, which he poured over the messy structure of branches and crumpled coupons. When he tossed in a match, the flames climbed clear over the mantel of the living room. He ran to the fireplace latch and opened the flue. The branches were surprisingly still slightly aflame. Bending down, he gently blew under the wood, the same way he had once blown on the small of Christine's back.

The white paint of the mantel was now scorched with black soot and the room was littered with the remaining scraps of the tree. Pine needles blanketed the cheap gray carpeting, and the smell of smoke filled his nostrils.

Noah smiled at the now crackling fire. He walked to the kitchen and placed the knife back into the display holder with the rest of the set, then made another drink, this time only filling the bottom fourth of the glass with eggnog. He pored out the rest of the brandy and returned the empty bottle to the cabinet. Picking up the gelt his mother had sent him, he sat in a chair by the fire. He put his drink down on the glass of the coffee table without a coaster, making sure to spill just a splash so that there would be a permanent ring-stain for Christine to see, then began tearing the golden tin foil away from the chocolate. He dipped the candy into his drink and gobbled it.

After pulling his necktie from his pocket and tossing it into the fire, he carefully removed the white envelope from his sports jacket and fingered it open. There was a check for two months severance pay and the shortest letter of recommendation he had ever seen.

> To Whom It May Concern:
>
> I am sure Noah Green will be a valuable asset to any business he applies himself to. Feel free to contact my office if you have any questions concerning this fine young man's capabilities.
>
> Regards,
> Raymond P. Cohen
> Cohen, Bernstein and Klein Office Supplies

Noah crumpled the letter and envelope in his blood-dried hand and tossed them into the fire, then stuffed the check back into the pocket of his sports jacket. He sipped his drink, noticing the cutting sound of rushing water from the bathroom. Christine was finished with her shower.

Looking down to his wingtips, Noah saw the tattered cloth angel lying among the pine needles on the carpet. He was still for a moment, then dipped another piece of chocolate gelt into his drink and gobbled it. He picked up the angel and examined it. Seeing a carefully stitched red cross over the chest, he tossed it into the fire, watching the faded white cloth immediately ignite into flames. He finished his drink, left the glass on the table, and went to get the bottle of wine in the kitchen. Taking a glass and the corkscrew, he walked back to the chair, removed the cork, and poured.

Christine opened the door to the bathroom, her lemon-blonde hair drenched and hanging long down her back. She was wearing only a short, thin towel around her body. Noah distinctly recognized the berry fragrance of her perfume. He began to sweat in that same way he had during his interview for employment with Cohen, Bernstein and Klein.

She ran to where the tree had been, frantically throwing the remaining dismembered branches about. Noah downed the glass of wine and stood up, ready for battle.

"Where is it?" she screamed.

"I built a fire with it, you said you wanted a fire," he said, trying to be as smug as possible.

"Not the tree," she shouted, "the angel, my grandmother's angel. Where is it?"

Noah was stunned. He was normally a natural at impromptu lying, had almost made a career out of it in college. But he had no words for Christine.

"Don't just stand there, look for it, Noah."

He couldn't move. Christine stood up and grabbed him by the shoulders, looking into his eyes pleadingly.

"Listen, I'm not mad about the tree, I promise, we'll just forget about this, we'll never have one again. I shouldn't have brought it home. But the angel is the only thing of my grandmother's that I have, she left it to me. Please, just help me look for it." The towel shook loose to the floor and her soap-scented, chalk-toned skin glistened before him.

Noah couldn't believe how good she looked. For all her concern, he was actually turned on by her for the first time in weeks. He put his head down and avoided eye contact. She tried to regain his attention, then looked to the fireplace. She grabbed his shaggy black hair tightly in her hands. He thought of her grandmother he had never known, but heard so much about, so much that it reminded him of his own father. Why couldn't the angel have been from anyone else? he thought. He would have done anything to bring that angel back.

"You didn't, please say you didn't."

"Okay," he said, "I didn't."

She held tight to his hair with one hand and with the other gouged her nails into his right cheek. He screamed and shoved her still glistening, naked body onto the mutilated tree branches and needles on the floor.

"How could you?" she shouted. "How could you? That was all I had of hers, it's the only thing I got." She began to cry, then leaped up.

Noah was leaning over, holding the bleeding side of his face with both hands.

The doorbell rang.

Christine jumped onto Noah's back and dug her fingers into his scalp, pulling out strands of black hair. He threw her off. She landed on the chair and fell over with it to the couch.

The doorbell rang again, and was followed by a knock. Noah stepped over Christine's body and walked to the door. "Don't you dare answer that," Christine said, scrambling for the towel. He opened the door.

"Merry Christmas, neighbor," said a man in a green and red angora sweater embroidered with an American flag design surrounded by mistletoe. The man ran back into the street and stood at the end of a line with ten or so people breaking into "Silent Night." There were children, parents, grandparents, even a German shepherd with antlers duct-taped to its head. Noah felt the urge to sing "I Had A Little Dreidel" over their voices.

Christine pushed him aside and slammed the door, holding the towel over the front of her naked body. Noah noticed the pine needles now stuck to her wet skin.

"You bastard! I hate you, I hate you!" she screamed at him. She fastened the towel around her body and ran to the only other separate room in the tiny house besides the bathroom; their bedroom. She slammed the door shut as the carolers headed down the street, singing "We Three Kings."

Noah took a dishtowel from the kitchen, held it over his right cheek, and walked back to the bedroom door. It was wedge-locked with one of his golf clubs. He knew he could break through if he wanted. He had done so during previous quarrels with no trouble. He decided not to bother and walked back to the kitchen to find a clean wineglass to pour a drink. The one on the coffee table had been shattered in the scuffle.

He looked down to the counter and saw the miniature menorah his mother had sent with the knives and the gelt. He put down the glass, tore open the plastic bag containing the pinkie-size candles, and began working them into the tiny spaces of the menorah. He remembered Mr. Cohen saying it was the first night of Hanukkah. It didn't matter. He simply filled all nine spaces with the candles, then searched through the kitchen drawers for matches. Slowly, he lit one candle at a time. He wanted to say a blessing but could not remember how.

There was another knock, this time hard and followed by a procession of serious thuds.

Noah walked to the living room and quickly began conjuring what to say to the police, wondering how to counter what the carolers must have seen as the type of domestic violence they were told about on the nightly news.

Holding the dishtowel over his still bleeding face, he opened the door slightly enough to see who it was without exposing the disorder of the living room. Len Johnson was standing on the doorstep holding the one-legged plastic pink flamingo in his arms.

TELL ME WHAT HAPPENED

THE GRASS at the cemetery was long that day, much longer than Rose had seen it before. She was accustomed to grass being mowed with the calculated perfection that had always defined her parents' lawn when she was a child. Every Sunday afternoon of her youth her father would be in the front yard of their house, manicuring the lawn to one-inch precision. Occasionally, Rose would remove her shoes and socks when she visited the cemetery to remind herself of the feeling of her father's lawn. But today the grass was uneven, filled with sprouting weeds and dandelions, a few brown patches here and there. Perhaps the Hispanic caretakers are on strike, she thought to herself.

She clutched the enormous bouquet of gladiolas in her arms. They had always been her daughter Sheli's favorite. As a little girl the child had been so easy to please. Yellow gladiolas—that's all she would ask to have for her birthday. So Rose had decided to still give them to her every year.

When she reached the top of the hill, she set the flowers on the ground, then removed the diaper and stone cleaner from the bag around her shoulder. She lowered herself to her knees, feeling the dampness of the grass penetrate the thin fabric of her floral skirt, and began cleaning her father's grave first. It was a modest stone, not one of those ostentatious markers, just a simple rectangular plaque. *Morris Michael Pinsky: Devoted Husband, Father, and Grandfather 1904–1986.*

As she carefully cleaned the stone, Rose thought of her mother, cremated three years before Morris's death. "Spread my ashes over the ocean, that's what I want," Goldie Pinsky had always told her daughter. "None of this funeral fuss, I won't have any of it." So when Goldie died of kidney failure in the spring of 1983, Morris and Rose did exactly what she had asked. Morris actually contemplated the issue for an hour or so, knowing that Jewish law prohibited cremation, not to mention his uneasy conscience knowing that so many of his relatives had perished in the crematoria of Auschwitz. However, the thought of raising his wife's temper, even after she was already dead, was enough for him to grant her last wishes.

"Besides," Morris told himself, "my Goldie always was the eccentric one. Cremation seems to be about as melodramatic as she ever wanted to be." So they did just as she had asked. They cremated her, then chartered a boat used for commercial fishing to take them twenty miles out to sea and dumped her ashes into the Pacific. Morris insisted that a rabbi accompany them. It took them an entire week before they found a retired Reform cantor in West Hollywood who agreed to it. As always, Morris compromised for his wife.

When Morris knew his own death was approaching, he let Rose know exactly what he wanted. "Don't you dare cremate me," he said. "If you cremate me, I'll never forgive you. None of that hullabaloo for me. I want to be buried in a pine box, and I want a traditional Jewish funeral. Is that understood?"

So that's how it worked out that Sheli was buried next to her grandfather and not her grandmother. But Morris had known his granddaughter would be joining him soon. "Make sure you reserve a plot next to mine for Sheli," he told Rose when he was bedridden in the hospital with prostate cancer. "She can't be alone. And no flower vase by my grave; you know about my allergies. I'll be sneezing for the rest of eternity as it is with all that grass around me."

Rose was actually thankful her mother had not been buried—no stone to clean. The woman had been worse than a drill sergeant raising her daughter, meticulously inspecting every nook and crevice of the house after Rose had dusted each week. She would take the same magnifying glass she used for reading the newspaper and creep along the edges of coffee tables in the living room, carefully pointing out the places nine-year-old Rose was required to redust to her satisfaction. "There, and there, and don't forget there, and that spot, the one I know you intentionally neglected. What, you think I don't see these things? Always taking short-cuts, aren't you?" Rose could only imagine the ordeal she would have to go through cleaning a gravestone if her mother had one. Or worse, Goldie Pinsky knowing that the grass around her stone was cut by Hispanics.

Finished with Morris's stone, Rose then scooted on her knees and applied the cleaner to her daughter's marker. It was the first time she had cleaned it since its unveiling five months earlier for the one-year anniversary of Sheli's death. She knew that the cemetery caretakers would not do an adequate job of cleaning her daughter's stone; they never had for her father's. It was a rectangular stone, much like Morris's. But Sheli's was a bit more elaborate, thickly cut with a border and an imprint of a gladiola carved into the corner by an artist Rose and her husband Daniel had commissioned. As she cleaned the crevices of the gladiola, she read the inscription for the first time since the unveiling, when she could hardly bear to even look at it. *Sheli Jessica Heschel: Beloved Daughter, Cherished Granddaughter 1967–1987.* When Rose was finished cleaning the stone, she picked the uneven blades of grass from around the edges and then placed the cleaner and diaper-rag back into her bag. She reached down, took the bouquet of gladiolas, and removed the tissue holding them together. Taking the thermos she had brought with her, she emptied half the water into the flower vase to the side of Sheli's marker. The flowers fit nicely into the vase, much easier than expected. She was thankful that it was not necessary to cut their beautiful long stems, the kind Sheli had always loved.

Before relaxing, she removed one gladiola from the bouquet and placed it over her father's stone, which as he had requested, had no vase beside it. "Happy sneezes to you, Papa," she said, almost giggling, then turned to Sheli's marker. "And happy twenty-second birthday to you, my precious one." She placed the thermos back in the bag and leaned her weight over her arms, her long skirt stretching over the grass.

Mucus was beginning to collect in her nostrils, but Rose quickly sucked it back into her throat. She had promised herself she would not cry. It had always upset Sheli to see her cry when she and Daniel visited the assisted-living center. That's why Daniel had not come today. "It's just too painful," he had said, "I can't do it anymore. I went to the unveiling, that was it. I just can't, not again." Rose did not push the issue. She respected her husband's choice, the same way she respected his insistence that they never attempt to have another child when she felt she was ready to several years back. In fact, she even preferred him not coming, enjoying the time alone to sit by herself with her father and her daughter.

Twenty-two years old, Rose thought. Had it really been that long since that incredible moment when she held Sheli for the first time—a perfectly healthy little girl who from the moment of her entrance into the world was the spitting image of her proud daddy? Rose thought of what her own life had been like when she was turning twenty-two. It had been 1963. She remembered the year well. She and Daniel were getting married, Kennedy had been killed, Vietnam was slowly becoming bigger news, and she had bought her first Beatles album with some college graduation money. The world was exciting, changing, fast, and exhilarating.

She thought of the kind of woman Sheli might have been on this day had she had a more normal life, one similar to the sons and daughters of her and Daniel's friends. Perhaps she would be graduating from college. Perhaps she would be independent, moving to a new city or going overseas. She might have been doing daring things that Rose had never dreamed when she was that age. Times were different now. Perhaps Sheli would be living with a man, not concerned with being married as she and Daniel had been raised to be. Perhaps she would be a women's activist, or applying to graduate school, or volunteering in the community. Maybe she would live far away, or close by, or still live in Los Angeles with her and Daniel. One thing was for certain, Rose knew that she and Daniel would have been proud of her, loved her more than anything. No matter what, Rose knew that Sheli would have still been the most beautiful thing she had ever set eyes upon. She would have been everything to her and Daniel, as she still was.

But as Rose sat and wiped her nose with the handkerchief she had taken from Daniel's dresser, she knew that even if Sheli had lived to see her twenty-second birthday, she would have been and done none of those things. She would have still been in the assisted-living home they had fought for so many years not to place her in. She would have still cried every time Rose and Daniel had to leave her after visiting hours were over; she would still be fed through an intravenous drip. But she would still be able to at least say to Rose and Daniel, "Mobba on Dobba I lub yu," along with the few other words she could pronounce. Even when her responses would be restricted to blinking her eyes once for "yes" and twice for "no," she would still be able to say, "Mobba on Dobba I lub yu." Even at her most unhealthy, she had always been able to say that as Rose and Daniel walked into her room at the home.

Rose gently stroked her fingers over her daughter's stone. She thought of Sheli as a little girl, how exuberant the child had been, how she was full of questions about everything around her. "Mommy, why are there clouds? Mommy, why do apples grow on trees and carrots in the ground? Mommy, why does Grandma yell at Grandpa so much? Mommy, why does Daddy smoke?" Questions, questions, and more questions. Rose recalled how she would sometimes become annoyed and frustrated by Sheli's questions, how she would often tell her to be quiet and not ask so many of them. Rose remembered how Sheli once answered that instruction by saying, "Okay, Mommy, but can you tell me why I grow out of my shoes and have to get bigger ones, can you tell me why I do that and then I won't ask anything else today, please?"

Always a talkative one, that's how Rose remembered Sheli as a little girl. Whereas the other boys and girls she attended preschool with were timid around adults, Sheli could keep an entire room of them captivated for hours, whether she was asking questions or performing cartwheels. Rose was frequently told that her daughter would be an actress or a lawyer someday. Her kindergarten teacher once said, "I'm sure if Sheli had a driver's license and a checking account she'd be leaving home already." And books, Sheli's ambition was always ahead of her abilities—always wanting to read, even though she usually had to have Rose or Daniel read to her. Every other week Daniel would bring home a new Golden book, thinking his daughter was on her way to becoming a great scholar since she wanted to read at such an early age. He would occasionally talk to Rose about her one day accepting a Nobel Prize.

"You're spoiling the child," Rose once argued. "Her birthday, fine. For Hanukkah or even Valentine's Day, fine. But you can't shower her with all these books; she can't even read them yet."

"I can't help it," Daniel would always say, "she likes them so much; she already has a vocabulary of a child two years her senior. She won't even look at the dolls you gave her, why not give her books?"

After a while, Rose and Daniel disagreed so much about how to raise Sheli that they put off having another child. But after that day on the freeway, the thought of having more children was inconceivable for Daniel.

As the police report verified, it had been a beautiful day, not a cloud in sight. Rose would have especially remembered if there had been rain. She was from Oregon, where differing degrees of rain was an almost hourly occurrence. But after they had moved to Los Angeles she learned to cherish the rain. It had been a gorgeous afternoon, the kind that made Rose thankful that they had moved to Southern California. She had just picked her daughter up from kindergarten. They had stayed a few minutes longer than usual so that Sheli could show her the painting she had created that afternoon. Rose had no idea what the painting was supposed to be, but she was convinced it was a work of genius. They waited half-an-hour to let it dry completely so that Sheli could give it to her father when they visited him for lunch at his office. Rose remembered Sheli explaining the painting. It was intended to be a self-portrait of sorts: Sheli standing on top of a large green hill with a dog beside her. Rose knew this was her daughter's way of continuing her persistent begging for a dog, which she and Daniel had said was out of the question numerous times. Rose even remembered the exact conversation between her and Sheli as they drove down the freeway.

"Mommy," Sheli had said, "why can't we have a dog?"

"I've told you, precious. Daddy's allergic to dogs."

"But why is Daddy allergic to dogs, Mommy?"

"Because he just is."

Rose recalled the inflection in her voice deepening with how frustrated Sheli was making her. But that had been the end of the conversation. The only thing Rose remembered after that was the shattering of the windshield, Sheli's scream, and the collision. She recalled the honking of cars, the sound of the sirens, her panic to reach Sheli, the blackness of her vision, the impossibility of her mouth to form speech, and the immobility of her body. Sheli, Sheli, Sheli, was all she kept thinking, even as the helicopter lifted her body into the sky. It was the first thing that came out of her mouth when she awoke from the coma in the hospital over a month later to see Daniel holding her hand and sitting beside her hospital bed.

Rose often wondered who it could have been who would toss a rock of that size from the overpass just before the exit leading to Daniel's office. She wondered why the person, or persons, had done it. She wanted to know why they had not thrown the rock a few more degrees to their right so that it could have been her who was hit by it and not Sheli. She wondered where the rock had originally come from. She even wondered if the anxiety and paranoia that overtook her every time a leaf or raindrop touched her windshield now would ever cease.

"Mexicans, it's those dirty Mexicans that did it," Goldie had always said. But Rose couldn't make such assumptions. She would simply never know. What she did know was that her beautiful, most precious, and only daughter would never be the same again. While she completely recovered within the next six months, Sheli remained in intensive care for almost a year. The rock had crushed her tiny skull and permanently damaged her brain, leaving her mentally disabled beyond rehabilitation. The doctors were amazed that she even lived, calling it one of the most miraculous feats for a child her age they had ever seen. One of the doctors even had an award-winning report on the incident published in a reputable medical journal. Rose refused to allow them to publish Sheli's picture with the article.

Rose often wondered what might have happened if she had not allowed Sheli to stay and let the painting dry. Would things have been different? Would nothing have happened to her daughter, the one person in the world she would have unconditionally sacrificed her own life for? Might another woman's daughter been the victim of such an irrational act? It was Rose who had the questions now.

Sheli would never ask questions again. She would never perform cartwheels or plead for a dog. She would never learn to read all the books Daniel had bought for her or have a younger sibling. She would never be kissed by a boy for the first time, or have her heart broken. She would never have a bat mitzvah, or have her Grandma Goldie teach her how to prepare a decent brisket. She would never be able to pose with her prom date for endless pictures taken by her parents. She would never bring Rose to tears as she graduated from high school and left for college. She would never bring out the overprotectiveness in Daniel by introducing a boyfriend from her university and asking if they could sleep in the same bed. She would never travel the world, or have a career, or get married. She would never have a daughter of her own that brought her as much joy as she did to Daniel and Rose. But worst of all, she would die before her parents, perhaps the most unthinkable of horrors to Rose and Daniel. But she would always be loved, even if the only words she could ever speak were "Mobba on Dobba I lub yu."

Across the grass, Rose could see a group of mourners making their way to a fresh gravesite several yards away. She could see the rabbi leading the procession as though he was a prophet. He looked over and saw Rose. He smiled and nodded his head, giving recognition of her own continued suffering, though he did not know who she was. Rose then saw the Hispanic groundskeepers waiting with shovels by the path a few yards from the gravesite the mourners were walking towards, taking it as a signal that she should leave. She remembered Sheli's funeral; how the groundskeepers waited by a utility truck listening to Spanish disco fuzzing from a portable radio as the family shoveled dirt over Sheli's casket. She recalled Daniel, leaving the gravesite, taking the radio and smashing it to pieces on the asphalt of the path, then his two younger brothers, Sheli's loving uncles, having to run over and restrain him to prevent a physical altercation. It was the only time she had ever seen her husband act upon a violent impulse. Daniel's days of pacifist advocacy, carried on from college, seemed to have ended on that day they buried Sheli. Several months later, Rose overheard him talking in a drunken stupor over the phone to one of his brothers. "I'd murder anyone with my bare hands to have her back," he had said. "No, Dave, I mean it. Yeah, well, fuck you, fuck everyone." Phone receiver slammed. For a long time Rose would often hear these types of statements from Daniel, mostly when he drank, which since Sheli's death had been an almost nightly ritual of Jack Daniel's mixed into his Coca-Cola.

Although they now slept in separate beds, Rose was thankful that she and Daniel had not divorced. She had heard the stories of parents who lose children, then gradually lose themselves and each other in the aftermath. But while their marriage had become platonic, they still had each other, still had something. Daniel made sure they had dinner every night together, and Rose said nothing if he went out for the evening and did not return home until the following night. Yet, there was still love, just a different kind of love than they had expected.

Rose softly pressed her lips to Sheli's stone. "Mind your grandfather, my precious one," she said. "Happy twenty-second birthday. Your father sends his love." She brushed her palm to the gladiola over her father's stone. "Good-bye, Papa." She then removed the two rocks from her bag that she had brought from her garden, and placed one on each grave marker. "We haven't forgotten you," she said aloud. Taking her bag, she quickly walked past the mourners, who were now congregating around the fresh grave, and headed for her car.

She arrived at the Levis' home forty-five minutes later. The entire block of the Reseda neighborhood was filled with cars, most of which she recognized as those of her and Daniel's friends. She noticed Daniel's Chrysler only one house down from the Levi's; he had arrived early. Rose parked two blocks away, but under a streetlight, just in case she stayed after it became dark. Rose had not seen Ron and Helen Levi's daughter-in-law, Pati, since the wedding, but she had come for the baby more than anything. Ron and Helen, proud grandparents for the second time, had invited everyone who had known their son Richard growing up. It had been eight days since the baby was born and they were anxious to have as many people as possible present to witness the bris.

Rose let herself into the house without knocking, just as she and Helen had done at each other's homes the past twenty years since meeting at the JCC swim center. Daniel was in the living room talking with Ron and Fred Zimmerman. He immediately excused himself, extinguished his cigarette, and came to where Rose was hanging her jacket in the closet near the door. He put his hands on her shoulders from behind.

"Are you okay?" he said.

She turned and faced him, then wrapped her arms around his waist, inhaling the imbedded aroma of nicotine from his shirt. "I'm fine," she said.

"Are you sure? I should have come with you, I knew I should have."

"I'm fine," she said, looking up at his face with a smile. He reached down and kissed her. "Where's the baby?"

"In the kitchen. I think that's where they're gonna do the bris."

"It hasn't started yet? Good. I thought I had missed it, I would have felt awful."

"No, Rabbi Kolatch and the mohel aren't even here yet."

"Where are they, a bar?" They both laughed and Daniel led her through the thirty or so people in the living room to the kitchen.

"Rose," Helen exclaimed as she walked into the kitchen. "Daniel said you were gonna be a little late, I'm so happy you made it." Rose wrapped her arms around Helen, not expecting her to remember that it was Sheli's birthday. But she was surprised that Daniel had not told her that it was the reason she was going to be late to the bris. "Come, you must meet my grandson. He's the most beautiful baby I've seen since Richard and Pati had Carrie."

"Hello, Mrs. Heschel," said Richard, seeing Rose approaching. Daniel had disappeared back into the living room to talk with Ron and Fred and light another cigarette.

"Richard," said Rose. "You're almost thirty years old. If you don't start calling me Rose I'm gonna start calling you Richy again. Hi, Pati. How are you?"

"Hey," said Pati. She was a few years younger than Richard, probably in her mid-twenties. She was everything Helen had dreamed of having in a daughter-in-law: maternal, able to cook, Sephardic background. At the moment though, Pati looked ready to fall asleep. Not only had she given birth a week ago, but she was now expected to mingle with all the friends and business associates of her in-laws, most of whose names even Richard had some difficulty remembering.

Rose peered into the travel-bed the baby was sleeping in, noticing that soft, pink newborn skin. "Oh," she said, "what a beautiful child. He looks just like Richard."

"Yeah," said Pati. She said it with a droning tone, as though she had been hearing this the entire day and couldn't wait to go home and let Richard, or her sitter who was taking care of Carrie, watch the child for a few hours.

"Did your parents make it from Portland today?" Rose asked. "Daniel and I are originally from there, that's how I remember. We met them at the wedding, I liked them so much."

"No," said Pati. "They're not here."

"Her parents are coming down next month," said Richard. "Dad's gonna videotape the bris so that they can see it when they get here."

"How nice," said Rose.

"Yeah," said Pati. From her inflamed, droopy eyes, Rose now contemplated asking what medication her doctor might have put her on. Then again, the girl might have simply been stoned. Rose knew that she and Richard had been arrested for growing marijuana plants while they were in college, but it was a forbidden subject with Ron and Helen, as forbidden as mentioning to Daniel that everyone knew he wore cowboy boots to Thanksgiving dinner every year just to look taller than his brothers.

"Yes," said Helen, "wouldn't it have been absolutely grand if we had had video cameras when our kids were growing up. These young couples are so lucky, they don't even know what a good thing those cameras are. Sure, we had super-eight home movies, but they were only three minutes a reel, then you had to reload. And so expensive to develop. With these video cameras you can record for six hours straight and never even press stop. Oh, come." She grabbed Rose by the sleeve of her cardigan. "Lynn Roth is here. Did you know that her husband is the mohel that's coming."

"Congratulations," Rose hollered behind her shoulder to Richard and Pati as Helen dragged her into the hallway. "Glen Roth is the mohel?" she whispered to Helen. "But he owns a bark-dust company. What does he know about circumcision?"

"I guess it's something he's always wanted to do. That's what Lynn told me when she offered for him to do it."

"But I assumed Ron would do it. I mean, not only is he a doctor, but he's also the baby's grandfather. It would be so special for Ron to do it, and a wonderful mitzvah no less."

"That's what I originally wanted, but Ron said he'd be terrified to do it himself, said he'd never forgive himself if he snipped off too much." Both women erupted into laughter as they entered the back room near the patio entrance to the yard. Rose felt good laughing, it put her at ease.

"Rose," Lynn Roth greeted in her squeaky voice. She was looking through a photo album with another woman at the table near the door to the back patio, an untouched plate of chocolate cookies between them. Rose was waiting for the fresh bagels and deli that were almost guaranteed to be served following the ceremony. "Have you met my sister? Barbara, this is Rose Heschel."

"Pleased to meet you," said Rose, sitting down at the table as she took the hand of a very pregnant Barbara.

"I was just telling Rose about Glen being the mohel," said Helen.

"Oh, yes," said Lynn, "he's so excited. He was just certified last month. This is going to be his first real circumcision." Lynn nodded her head with pride.

"Wonderful," said Rose, somewhat apprehensive about Glen branching out his bark-dust manufacturing services into foreskin removal. She couldn't imagine Daniel performing circumcisions on weekends when he was not selling insurance. "So," she said, looking at Barbara's stomach, "when are you due?"

"April," said Barbara, patting the bulge beneath her denim maternity overalls.

"Is it your first?"

"Oh, no. This is my fourth."

Helen tugged Rose's cardigan sleeve again. "She already has three girls."

"Wow," said Rose. "This will probably be the fourth girl then, looks like you're on a streak."

"Oh, don't say that," gasped Barbara. "My husband will absolutely die if this isn't the boy. This one better be the boy, because I can't take another pregnancy. I just don't have it in me."

"I expect there will be a little blood from the circumcision," said Lynn. "That's what Glen tells me, that it's natural for there to be just a smidgen, no big deal."

"Yes," said Helen, "I remember Richard's bris. There was a pinch of blood."

"Well," continued Lynn, tapping Rose on the hand, "if there is we must remember to smear a little onto Barbara's stomach. It's supposed to bring good luck to the next expecting woman, so maybe this time she'll have the boy."

"Oh," said Rose with a slight giggle, "I'm sure this baby's gonna be a girl. Look at the odds."

"Don't say such things," gasped Helen. "Have a little faith, Rose. Here, try these cookies, I made them last night, tell me what you think because I didn't use as much sugar as usual."

Rose took a nibble, wanting to save her appetite for the deli. She smiled and nodded her approval to Helen.

"Here, Lynn," said Helen, "you try one."

"No, I'm on a diet."

"Oh, please, one little bite."

"Fine," said Lynn, taking a cookie and handing another to Barbara.

"So," Rose said, "when is Rabbi Kolatch arriving with Glen?"

"Don't get me started," said Lynn, "they were supposed to be here over an hour ago."

"Here," said Barbara, "look at these pictures, they're just darling." She slid the photo album over to Rose. There were numerous shots of Richard and his younger sister, Emma, throughout their early childhood. Rose liked turning through the pages, noticing the outfits Ron and Helen were wearing from the sixties and seventies.

"Is Emma coming today?" asked Rose. "I didn't see her in the living room or the kitchen."

"Ugh," Helen practically growled.

"What?" said Rose, turning another page of the album.

"That daughter of mine, giving me nothing but a headache."

"I assume she's not coming then?"

"Oh, she was invited, but no, she's not coming. Oh, that's right, I haven't talked to you since Ron and I got back from Tahoe. She wants to get married, Rose. I haven't told you that have I?"

"No, you didn't. How nice, when did this happen?" Rose was humoring her. From Helen's tone she could tell that her friend was displeased with some aspect of Emma's announcement. She thought the girl probably went and chose a gown without Helen present or something even more trivial.

"Nice?" said Lynn, as though she were Emma's mother. "No, Rose, it's anything but nice." She was now gobbling another cookie with two in her other hand.

"What do you mean?" asked Barbara, dipping a carrot into a bowl of ranch dip.

"Okay, fine," said Helen, "everyone's gonna know soon enough, they might as well have the story right." Rose tried not to laugh, as though Helen wasn't going to tell her anyway. "She brings this boy home last winter. Sure, he's way over six feet and has really dark skin, but I'm willing to give him the benefit of the doubt. They go to school in Arizona, it could just be a tan. But no, his name's Ricardo. So of course I want to get to the bottom of this. I mean, I can live with that, I'm open-minded, I've known plenty of colored people in my life. And with all this talk about there being Ethiopian Jews I figure this might be a nice way to bring one of them into our family. No, he's from Cuba. He's probably a communist. Did you hear me, Rose? Cuba."

"Uh huh," said Rose, turning another page of the photo album. Her eyes instantly gravitated to the picture at the bottom of the next page with Helen's red penmanship underneath: "Hanukkah 1979." It was a picture of Richard and Emma, both leaning to one side each of Sheli, who was strapped into the special mechanical chair the hospital had taught Rose and Daniel to put her in. There was Sheli, her hands securely fastened to the armrests, head uncontrollably cocked to one side and that half-smile she always managed to muster for pictures, even with the incredible lack of control she had over her facial muscles. Helen's children appeared as healthy as they ever did, Richard with his strong swimmer's physique and Emma with that slender, toned figure she eventually lost in college. Rose remembered that Hanukkah well. It was the last holiday Sheli spent with them before they had to move her into the assisted-living home for disabled children. In the background of the photo she could see the menorah they had used. Sheli had made it herself in kindergarten, a simple slab of wood painted blue with gold glitter and glued bottle caps to place the candles in. Sheli had been five when she made it. In this photograph, her daughter was almost fourteen.

"So," Helen continued, "I knew there was no way this boy was Jewish.

But when I finally got Emma alone she tried to pull this story on me about how his grandmother was really Jewish but that when she married his grandfather in Cuba—a strict Catholic mind you—the family lost all connection to their Judaism. Emma then starts spouting all this mumbo jumbo about if the grandmother was Jewish and had his mother, and if Judaism is passed through the mother's bloodline, then this Ricardo is technically Jewish, even though he was baptized and admitted to me when I met him that he still takes communion. Yes yes, at least the boy didn't lie to me. But it's not as though Emma really thinks I'm about to fall for this charade."

Rose kept staring at the picture, kept thinking of Sheli, her precious daughter who would have been twenty-two today. She looked up and saw Lynn listening to Helen's anguish over Emma, a perfectly healthy daughter, possibly marrying a boy that was not Jewish and Lynn's sister fearing that the baby she was carrying might actually be a daughter.

"Then," Helen went on, "Emma comes up to me while I'm making the bed in the spare room for this Ricardo and asks me if it's okay if they sleep together."

"No!" Lynn gasped, even though she had already heard the story.

"Oh, yes," said Helen.

"The nerve," said Barbara, as if she had been having lunch with Helen and Rose for years and knew Emma intimately.

"Yes," Helen continued, "in my own home. So we have the first screaming fight since she was in junior high and it ends with her and this Ricardo leaving the house and getting a hotel room." She paused and sighed. "So, that's why she's not here to be at her own nephew's bris, because she wouldn't come unless she could bring this Ricardo, and after what she pulled while they were here I just won't have that filthy boy in my home."

"Good for you," said Lynn.

"Yes," said Helen, "but I just don't know what to do. Now Emma's talking about going to beauty school. Beauty school for God's sake. Ron and I didn't send her to college so that she could use her degree as a place mat and go to beauty school. I'm sorry for keeping all this from you, Rose, but I just wanted to forget about it. See, I thought Emma would get bored with this Ricardo and date other people. But when Ron and I got back from Tahoe to call and wish her a happy birthday, she told us she's going to marry him. I think she might actually go through with this wedding, just to spite me. I can't believe it, the boy isn't even circumcised."

"How do you know that?" said Barbara.

"I asked Emma. It was my right to know."

"And she actually answered you?" said Lynn.

"Yes, and quite flippantly, too. She hasn't talked to me with this kind of disrespect since she was a teenager."

"Wow, I could never have asked that. I wouldn't want to know if he had foreskin or not."

"What does Ron think of all this?" said Barbara.

"He said the same thing about the boy that I've been saying," said Helen. "What kind of child no longer speaks to his parents? That should say it all."

Rose closed the photo album and stood, thrusting back her chair. "I gotta go," she said.

"What?" said Helen. "Why, Rose? Glen and Rabbi Kolatch haven't even arrived yet."

Rose didn't say anything more, she ran her hands through her short, graying hair, and made her way down the hall, through the kitchen where Pati was busy breast-feeding the baby, and shoved her way around the herd of people in the living room to get to the front door. Daniel saw her as she was opening the closet for her coat and excused himself from Ron and Fred.

"What's going on?" said Daniel as he approached her.

"I need to go," she said, pulling on her jacket and clawing through the pockets for her keys. The front door opened. It was Glen Roth and Rabbi Kolatch. The smell of whiskey emanated from them like cologne. Rose found her keys and shoved both men aside, practically running across the driveway.

Daniel pushed through Glen and the rabbi and followed, tossing his cigarette into a planter of marigolds by the garage. He finally caught up to Rose two blocks away at her car, her hands shaking as she attempted to slip the key into the lock. Daniel swiped the keys from her.

"Give them to me," she demanded, and began to cry, tearing at his arms with her nails. "I'm leaving, just give me the damn keys, I don't want to be here anymore."

He threw the keys into the bushes of the yard behind them and locked his hands into vices around her wrists until she calmed and stopped trying to pull away.

"What is it?" he demanded. "Tell me what happened."

She finally managed to look up to his face. He did not need an explanation. He pulled her close to his body and wrapped his arms around her. He held her as she cried. And when she could no longer cry, he continued to hold her.

REPLACEMENT

REUBEN could still detect her scent from the sheets, particularly as he pulled them from the bed and carried the bundle to the washing machine in the garage. After lifting the lid of the machine, he brought the sheets to his face one last time, smothering his nose into the fabric and breathing heavily for traces of Debbie's perfume, then dropped them into the half-load of whites left unfinished from the previous week. He set the cycle and returned to the living room, maneuvering around the five unopened cardboard boxes blocking his way back to the bedroom.

"Ha," he shouted with pride. Sure, some men in his situation—mid-fifties and recently divorced—might not have known how to set a wash. But not Reuben. "That's right," he said to himself, "it was me that always did the laundry, not Janey."

He stepped back into the bedroom and scoped the floor for the condom and its wrapper, finally discovering both at the foot of his bed where he placed his slippers every night. Taking an enormous wad of toilet paper from the bathroom, he surrounded the prophylactic and wrapper, then flushed everything down the toilet. He quickly washed his hands, scrubbing furiously with the soap bar, disgusted by the thought of one drop of semen or spermicidal lubrication having touched him. As he scrubbed, the nakedness of the finger on his left hand that had once held his wedding band became apparent. That was the first thing he noticed the most after the divorce; all the men he saw each day wearing wedding bands, men not giving even a casual thought to it. He knew this because he had shown a similar mentality for over three decades.

Debbie's undeniable cosmetic smell still filled the bedroom. She had been the first woman he had been with since Jane. She was nobody special, just a girl he had been dating from the grocery store down the street; only twenty-five, a checkout girl without even a high school diploma. This did not bother Reuben, though. He knew the relationship was nothing serious, just dinner and a show every so often, somebody to go out and do things with in a town that was slowly becoming familiar to him. He was dumbfounded when she removed the condom from her purse the night before after they had been fooling around on the bed. Reuben had never used a condom, had never been with another woman in that way other than Jane.

His son, Zachary, was driving down from Eugene to visit him for the first time at his new place and the bedroom was infested with the scent of recent sex. Zachary was a college student, already receiving job offers, diligently applying himself to an internship, giving his father immense pride. Reuben remembered his own college years at UCLA as he fumigated the room.

The windows above the bed opened with a slight creak. Reuben liked that, the way he could open windows in California during March without any worries of a chill. He had been born and raised in Los Angeles, but had lived in Oregon the past thirty-three years, raising his family, building his business. When Jane asked for the divorce he did not even bother fighting it, not as he had fought answering her when she asked him if he had ever slept with another woman when they first made love shortly before getting married. He wanted the divorce over as quickly as she did. Neither of them needed one of those prolonged separation periods, for the divorce to be finalized in the distant future after excruciatingly expensive negotiations. Jane kept the home in Portland and Reuben took his full retirement plan early with no future obligations to his former spouse. Within six months the marriage was dissolved and within another three he had moved back to California. They had not even bothered to initiate a Jewish divorce. It had been years since they had attended temple or considered even Yom Kippur anything more than a holiday on par with Labor Day. By the time their three children had moved out of the home they were even exchanging gifts on Christmas morning. But neither one of them was going to blame those things for the divorce. They knew better than to substitute those particulars for what had really become unsalvageable.

Reuben had decided that a change was in order. While visiting his older brother, Saul, that last summer, he had impulsively made a bid on a small two-bedroom in the quiet town of Ojai. "California's never been better," he often said to himself as he sat in isolation every evening to watch a movie or maybe the news on the tube, diligently scarfing a microwave dinner. "I should never have left." Then he met Debbie at the grocery store, only a few weeks after finally deciding it was time he removed the white gold wedding band that had adorned his finger for over thirty-five years.

He predicted that Zachary would not arrive until later that night. There was plenty of time to clean the house, maybe do a little more work on rearranging the furniture or change the alignment of the vintage art on the walls. Debbie had recently given him a book on Feng Shui to help him design his life with the ancient art of placement. According to Debbie's belief, Feng Shui conveyed the theory that life forces flow through all things, that the manipulation of those forces through the proper orientation of physical structure could enhance a person's luck, wealth, and even health.

Had he still been married to Jane, she would have nailed a mezuzah to the frame of the front door and said, "There, stop worrying. Enough of this hippie-skippy stuff." He knew Jane would have done that, even if she was far from being the observant Orthodox girl he had met when he was nineteen. She would definitely have never tried to coax him into taking up yoga, as Debbie was now doing on a daily basis.

Debbie had mentioned several weeks before that the wall separating Reuben's bedroom and the front room was "blocking the flow of energy" to him while he was sleeping, thus resulting in the nightmares that had been waking him. She had earlier mentioned that the moon's seasonal rotation was possibly off that year, giving a direct justification for Reuben's high cholesterol count. "Then again," she had said, "you are a Sagittarius." It was then that Reuben knew he could never introduce this girl to his children, especially his daughters, Polly and Adrienne, since Debbie was close in age to both. How would he ever explain Debbie's decision to move his great-grandmother's menorah into the bathroom medicine cabinet, where its "energy" would not be a disruption to the front of the house?

After going on a few casual dates, Reuben was having urges he and

Debbie had still not acted upon. In hopes of finally getting her into bed, he had borrowed an ax and sledgehammer from his neighbor and had completely obliterated the wall that separated the bedroom and living room. The remnants of the wall were still in a pile out on the driveway. Scraps of siding and insulation now dangled from the various sections of the ceiling, which itself seemed to have slumped slightly lower than it had been when he bought the house. "Oh, well," Reuben said to himself, "welcome back to California." He feared the smell of the previous night's lustful escapade would drift through that open space into the rest of the house. A father had to keep a certain image for his children. He opened another window near the front door.

The idea of soup seemed delicious. He went to the kitchen, pushed aside the abdominal exercise machine Debbie had bought for him that was positioned in front of the counter as a tie-rack, and removed a can of clam chowder from the cupboard. It was a rarity that he cooked. Reuben had begun to enjoy eating out, something that had been a fading occurrence in Jane's and his relationship. Debbie could barely prepare toast, so eating out had become almost a necessity. Unlike Jane, who had cooked the same dish for its particular night of the week all during their marriage, Reuben was now enjoying the fine tastes of Thai, Ethiopian, Vietnamese, and other never before tasted cuisines. "None of this fish on Tuesday, chicken on Wednesday nonsense anymore." He now ate what he wanted. But he had still not taken the time to purchase proper items for his new kitchen. Jane had kept everything with the house.

Reuben removed the Swiss Army knife from his slacks and turned out the can opener, carefully jagging it along the edge of the soup can. "Clam chowder here I come," he proclaimed. He would be happy to never see another matzah ball so long as he lived. Every Friday night for the past thirty-five years he had been served the same meal, no surprises or alterations to the menu, ever. And they had not even observed the Sabbath for the latter half of their marriage.

He dumped the soup from the can into the pot and set it on the burner, tossing the leftover tin into the garbage can beneath the sink. "None of this recycling nonsense anymore either." Reuben knew he would be eating out of the pot, since he did not own bowls.

Christ, he thought, Zachary is coming. How could he possibly host his only son in his new home without owning a set of plates and bowls? It was bad enough that he would have to explain the missing wall between the living room and his bedroom. "Yes," he said, "after I eat, I'll go buy plates and bowls. Time to start treating myself right." He would take Debbie with him, to insure that he purchased kitchenware with the proper energy.

The living room, aside from the wall, was actually quite elegant. With the divorce, Reuben had taken all of the antique furniture that his mother had left him after her death. His new home seemed to display it far more impressively than the large house in Portland, where each piece had been lost to the composite aesthetics of Jane's eccentric floral decor. Yes, living in California again was not so bad; it even made Reuben's mother's furniture look tasteful. But the boxes in the living room had to go before Zachary arrived.

Reuben bent down and looked at them; five large cardboard boxes delivered the day before. He wondered what they could possibly contain. Jane had sent them. She had been sending things C.O.D. mail for several months now. Nothing important usually, just little things she would come across that were his. She never included a letter though, never mentioned anything concerning how she was getting along, only the packages with the contents carefully protected in crumbled newspaper. His children had also made a commitment to not discussing their mother during his weekly calls, which often unsettled Reuben.

He had been overwhelmed to find the five boxes on the porch when he arrived home from a pleasant afternoon walk the day before. But he had to wait until it was dark to move them inside; they were excruciatingly hot to touch after sitting in the sun all day. It surprised him that cardboard could retain such heat. Because of his date with Debbie they had remained unopened.

The boxes were numbered in Jane's familiar calligraphy. He opened the first and was ecstatic to find that there was actually a letter at the top. But even more surprising, he realized that the boxes contained his entire record collection, acquired since high school. Reuben had brought his stereo system with him to California but had intentionally left his records, thinking that with the fresh start he would begin to rebuild a new collection. So far, he only had the few Michael Bolton and Gloria Estefan CDs that Debbie had given him with the Feng Shui book and the abdominal exercise machine.

He was genuinely touched, certain that this was Jane's way of sweeping the animosity behind them. She knew how important his records had been to him, that over the years he had taken impeccable care of each album. When they had first met at UCLA during a function between his fraternity and her sorority, she had been impressed by the fact that he had a record collection and turntable. Until Reuben, Jane had never known anybody her age who owned more than a few forty-five rpm singles to play on the communal turntable in the back room of her sorority house.

Reuben put the letter aside after rubbing his rough fingers over his name, scrolled beautifully across the front of the envelope in Jane's perfect calligraphy. He began removing albums from that first box, amazed by Jane's consideration. Each album seemed to have been placed in perfect order from the cabinets in their Portland home to the shipping boxes. The Beatles, the Big Bopper, Nat King Cole, John Denver, Neil Sedaka, the Drifters, the Kingston Trio, the Christi Minstrels, Cole Porter, Kenny Rodgers, the Temptations, Willie Nelson. She had even paid for the postage herself this time.

He then came across the only Seekers album he had ever bought, which contained "I'll Never Find Another You," his and Jane's song while dating in college. He pulled the record from the jacket and removed it from its protective liner sheet, holding the vinyl gently in his hands by the edges. Something did not feel right, though. With a careful inspection, he noticed that the vinyl was no longer flat as when he had bought it and kept it in mint condition for so many years, but was now curved and wavy.

"No!" Reuben shouted. He began pulling albums randomly from the box, one after another, frantically removing them from their jackets. Every single record was warped, as though a hair dryer had been held to each one. "No, that bitch, that goddamn bitch!" He tore open two other boxes, removed a few more random albums. His collection was ruined. He then remembered how the boxes had been sitting on the porch in the sun all day before he arrived home from his walk, and then even longer until he took them inside the night before.

He dropped to the hardwood of the living room, album jackets and warped records scattered around him and his mother's antique furniture. He then ran his hands though his thinning hair.

At his side was that letter, still sealed in the envelope with his name written in Jane's beautiful calligraphy across the front. He tore it open. It was handwritten, also in calligraphy.

Dearest Reuben,

It's been ages since we last spoke. I wanted to write sooner, but waited till I felt I was ready. I wish things had been different between us these past few years. It seems horrible that two people who have shared so much of each other's lives no longer speak. I hope that will change with time. We have three beautiful children between us, something that will always give us a special connection. It would be so nice for the two of us to be able to be pleasant and friendly with each other, especially now that Polly will soon give us our first grandchild. I'm sure you are as excited as I am. We should talk soon, maybe even come up with a gift for the baby to be given from both of us, as grandparents.

Here are your records. A few nights ago I pulled several out to listen to and thought of those good times we used to have listening to albums in your fraternity house during college, laughing and talking all night. I want you to have them, knowing they mean so much to you. I am sending them because I will be moving soon. I have sold the house and plan to move to Seattle by June. I have met a wonderful man—James. He is a widower and has a five-year-old daughter, Kelly. I think you would like Kelly, she is very much like Adrienne was at that age. James is sixteen years my junior, but we have lots in common.

I sincerely hope you will come to my wedding in August. You always used to say how noble it was of George Harrison to attend the wedding of his ex-wife to that guitarist I can never remember the name of. I have put the past behind me and it would mean so much to have you there, with the other important people throughout my life. It is James' second marriage as well, so we plan on only having a small reception with a judge to perform the ceremony. It would also make the children so much more comfortable if you could do this.

I am very excited. I have not been a mother to a five-year-old for a long time. This is certainly going to be an adventure. Enjoy the records, Reuben. From everything the children say of your weekly phone calls, it sounds as though you have made a wonderful new start with a beautiful new home for yourself.

With the best of friendship, Janey

Reuben set the letter on top of the box and sat motionless. Looking down, that Seekers album was still beside him, still warped beyond recovery. Taking the record, he walked to the entertainment center beside his mother's antique hutch, and placed the vinyl on the turntable. He set the needle carefully onto the edge of the record and sat down on the love seat that had once been in the living room of the house Jane was now selling.

The song began, first clean, then warped and static-laced, then clear, going back and forth between clarity and warped heat-distortion. For some reason though, the chorus of "I'll Never Find Another You," his and Jane's song from the time they were nineteen, seemed to play perfectly each time the record turned between the warped sections of the vinyl.

Reuben dropped his face into his hands and began to cry. He could not remember the last time he cried. Perhaps it was when his mother had died, eleven years before. Even then, he had hidden himself in the bedroom so that the children would not see him. A father must keep a certain image for his children. As the tears flowed from his eyes, puddling in his palms, he thought of sitting in his fraternity house at UCLA with Jane, listening to that same record. It had been their song since the night they sat with a bottle of wine an older fraternity brother had bought for them, listening to it only an hour after purchasing it at the record store a few blocks off campus. Reuben missed the way storeowners were back then, allowing the kids to listen to albums before they were bought, the way people trusted each other in those days, the way he and Jane would neck in those listening booths. But he knew now that, for the first time since the divorce more than a year ago, he missed his Janey. He remembered the night they were drinking wine to that album, how he had not even kissed her yet, but after several glasses was able to lift her off his bedside and dance her around his room, slowly maneuvering back and forth to avoid the textbooks and dirty laundry blanketing the floor, until he mustered enough courage to finally press his trembling lips against hers. Yes, he missed that, wanted it once again, or something like it.

He sat on the couch. Only one year and Jane was getting married to another man. Reuben could not comprehend it. He had been Jane's first and only. The thought of another man touching her infuriated him. The thought of another man sharing her life was too much to bear, especially when all he had now for companionship was Debbie, which he knew was temporary.

Glancing to the opposite end of the couch, he noticed the Feng Shui manual. He threw it across the room, then buried his face again in his hands.

"I'll Never Find Another You" was still playing, drifting back and forth between distortion and clarity.

The front door opened. Reuben looked up and there was Zachary. He had not heard the car pull into the driveway, nor expected him to arrive until that evening. He buried his face back into his hands and began to cry uncontrollably. He couldn't believe it, he was crying in the presence of his only son.

"Dad," exclaimed Zachary, "what's going on?"

Reuben controlled himself and looked once again to his son, who was now removing the needle from the warped record. Reuben then looked about the room, noticing the scattered records around the boxes and the dismantled wall between the bedroom and the room they were in, knowing the debris from the wall was piled out on the driveway, the aroma of the clam chowder emanating from the kitchen, the taste of Debbie's skin still resonating upon his tongue.

"Dad, are you—"

"I'm sorry," said Reuben, burying his face back in his sticky palms. That was the only thing he could manage to say, over and over again. "I'm sorry, I'm sorry."

"Dad," said Zachary, kicking aside albums, making his way to the couch to comfort his father. "What's going on?"

Reuben did not respond, he simply turned away from Zachary, attempting to conceal his moist eyes and swelling face. Faintly, he could hear the rushing of water. It couldn't be the soup, he thought, it wouldn't make that type of sound.

"Just sit here," said Zachary, touching his father's shoulder affectionately, "I'll be right back." He then walked to the hallway. "Shit, Dad. I think your toilet's overflowing." He opened the door to the bathroom and quickly stepped back as the water began to pour over his sneakers. "Shit," Zachary said again. "Dad, where's your plunger? I'm gonna clean this up for you." He stepped farther back from the hall as the water continued to flow from the bathroom. Zachary then looked down, startled. Floating over the hardwood of the hallway was the condom and its wrapper Reuben had flushed down the toilet.

THE TEMPORARY LIFE

Ribono shel olam,
I hereby forgive
Whoever has hurt me,
And whoever has done me any wrong;
Whether by word or by deed.
> *Medieval prayer, adapted by Jack Riemer*
> *The Mahzor Hadash, Yom Kippur evening service / Kol Nidre*

I STAND in the living room of my parents' house, silently staring at the light coming from under the crack of the kitchen door, still feeling the bourbon Ari and I swiped from his father's liquor cabinet, still wondering if I'm capable of defending my position or not. I'm not drunk, I think, maybe a little tipsy, but not drunk. I tell myself lots of things I want to believe. But even so, the light slipping through the kitchen door's crack is captivating me. It's like the headlights of a large semi creeping up on the tail of my car on a highway. The glow frightens me, but I'm still compelled to keep taking glances in my rearview mirror, just to see if it has the empathy to back off from my much smaller, much more fragile vehicle.

Cautiously, I open the door, making sure to stop just before it will creak. Same house for seventeen years: same kitchen door, same creaks.

Composure is important. I glide my tense, nail-bitten fingers through my stubby curls, attempt to straighten my shirt as if I'm dressing for picture day in grade school. In a matter of minutes I plan to announce my refusal to attend Yom Kippur services, knowing I'll get as much understanding as when my older brother, Josh, decided to drop out of college. The difference is that Josh was able to release his bomb on the telephone with over three thousand miles of the North American continent separating him from our parents.

I blow a quick breath into my palm and inhale deep for traces of the bourbon I tried to dilute with a breath mint, then step into Mother's kitchen, her sanctuary, her fortress. This place is hers.

The blue of the walls is particularly glowing this evening. I notice the one wall that is cluttered with framed photographs, Mother's historical museum of the whole extended family. Aunts and uncles, grandparents, great-aunts and great-uncles and great-grandparents, first cousins, second cousins, third cousins once-removed, family friends we affectionately refer to as aunts and uncles. There is even one of Mother and Dad under the chuppah at their wedding, and a whole collection of pictures taken over the years of Josh, me and our younger brother, Neil. There are so many pictures that the blue of the wall is barely visible. Aged black and white photos with creases and ripped corners, some with faded sepia-tones, Polaroids, and even a few brilliantly colored snaps. The faces in those frames never leave, always keep Mother company during her endless hours of solitude in this compound, the living along one half of the wall, the deceased along the other. The front room originally served as this immortalizing monument, but Mother eventually transferred them to the kitchen. She likes them there, even if the majority of the faces on the living portion have never come up north from California and Arizona to visit. It's her own rendition of Jerusalem's Wailing Wall. If she had it her way, I'm sure she would have Dad tear down the wallpaper and paneling to reconstruct it with ancient stones.

Mother has recently moved a portrait of Grandpa to the deceased portion of the wall, where he now joins his own parents, her grandparents. I can't believe it has taken her only seven months to shift his position. It's a beautiful picture, a clean black and white taken in Los Angeles during the late 1940s. One might think Grandpa had been a movie star with his wavy hair slicked back with olive oil. He is so handsome in that picture, so young, so distinguished. Alive. I have another picture of Grandpa in my bedroom, taken on the day of my bar mitzvah. He does not look the same as the man in that picture framed on

Mother's kitchen wall, although he could still be mistaken for a movie star. If the Jews had a face for God, I would place His photo alongside Grandpa's with my other dead relatives on that wall.

At the end of the kitchen, right where I have entered, is a brick-mantel fireplace that my parents utilize more for incinerating paper waste than for heating the house. We live in Oregon of all places and they still don't recycle. Directly above my head are wood support beams cluttered with hanging pots and pans, Jell-O molds, and a few souvenir mementos from family vacations. The continuous heat from Mother's oven has added a thickness to the air tonight that complements the burning trash in the fireplace. Mother's kitchen is always a good twenty degrees warmer than any other section of the house. When I look at sketches of medieval dungeons in my history text, I can't help but think of where I now stand.

Mother is cooking, filling the air with secrets; marking her territory. It's almost twelve-thirty in the morning. She can cook any time of the day or night and is now bent over the oven peering into the beast, not yet noticing that I'm here.

I test the air. Brisket, nothing new. But I know it's intended for Yom Kippur. Mother's been cooking nonstop for almost a week, preparing for the feast she will be serving in four days to celebrate the end of the annual fast. Yom Kippur, "the holiest day of the year," Mother always says, "the day of forgiveness." Tonight she will easily be cooking until three. She would never think of serving food she is not proud of. There are never more than ten people at our holiday dinners, but Mother cooks as if she'll be supplying a starving infantry platoon with their last home-cooked meal before heading off to battle.

Dad is concentrating on a stack of bills at the kitchen table; a bowl of sunflower seeds to his right and a fresh cup of black coffee to his left. He's chasing the coffee with a can of Coca-Cola. My parents suck down caffeine even before going to bed, just to add a little edge to their suburban dreams.

A thick gold necklace hangs from Dad's throat, barely skimming the chest hair creeping up his Adam's apple from the collar of his V-neck undershirt. It's that same gold chain that ruined Mother's Passover seder last year. Grandma had presented it to Dad the day before—a thick, braided gold necklace with a gold chai the size of a small paperweight. It had been Grandpa's. With no sons of her own, Grandma thought it appropriate to give it to her son-in-law, the man raising her daughter's sons—her precious grandsons. It was the comment Dad had made that did the damage. Leaning close to his brother, Harold, he said, "They don't call it JEWelry for nothing." It was a response to my uncle's facetious question as to why Mother's side of our family had so many precious metals in their surnames. I will never forget Mother's silencing glare during that seder. I doubt that Dad has either.

Dad still wears the chain, but the chai is now tucked away under the socks in his dresser in the same manner that my younger brother, Neil, hides issues of Hustler and Maxim from Mother. "Safer there," Dad once said about the chai being taken off the chain. But I know better. Mother knows better. "Safer there." He had said it as though it were a code for "Why advertise?"

He looks up at me, takes a quick glance at his watch, and smiles. I'm home before my curfew, which means there's nothing for us to talk about tonight. He spits out a sunflower seed shell into a soup bowl and brings his attention back to the bills. He's been spitting that same way since his junior varsity baseball days in high school.

My parents don't talk much lately; they argue more than converse. He who yells the loudest wins. My best friend, Ari, says the only time he's aware of his own parents arguing is if his father leaves for work in the morning without kissing his mother good-bye, twice or so a year supposedly. Ari once asked me how I know when my own parents are fighting and I told him that no member of my family has ever learned sign language.

"Benjamin," Mother calls from across the kitchen. She refuses to call me Ben. I let her get away with it, but not for the same reason I allow Grandma to still call me Benny. "Come here," she says, waving a flour-dusted hand.

I walk to the opposite end of the kitchen, toward that blazing oven, then notice a bottle of Manischewitz on the counter behind her. I panic slightly. I know she has a refined canine scent, but can she actually detect the bourbon on my breath from that far away? Or even worse, smell the bacon-cheeseburger I ate with Ari three hours ago?

"Try this," she says, forcing a forkful of kugel to my lips. She fluffs the side of her black-dyed permed hair, then scratches an itch under her right eye with her forefinger. A line of flour smears across her cheek, her maternal war paint.

"I'm not hungry," I say.

"Just one bite," she says, "just to taste it for me."

"No," I say.

She cocks her hip to one side, still holding the fork to my lips, but now plants that other fist on her waistline as if she carries a hip-pistol.

"But I made this kugel especially for you," she says.

"Okay, okay." I take the bite.

Mother pulls away the fork and waits. "What do you think?" she asks. But she's not asking. I've known since infancy that this is her technique for extracting a compliment.

"Needs more cinnamon," I say, just to see her eyelids narrow.

"Hmph," she exhales through her nostrils, "just like your father."

"I told you it didn't have enough cinnamon," Dad says.

"Be quiet, Bernard," she says, then starts to place plastic food-wrap over the kugel. She must still be upset with Dad for using her favorite kugel pan to marinate chicken in last summer.

I lean against the counter. I've planned this moment since Rosh Hashanah, putting it off until I had carefully crafted my declaration. I start fidgeting with my fingernails because I need her to start it somehow. Beginning it myself is impossible; I don't have the guts.

But Mother is not talking, not to Dad or me. And this makes me nervous because it's usually a challenge to escape her presence, as she is typically speaking to anyone in the same room. Heck, she's been known to have hour-long conversations with complete strangers at the post office.

I stand silent for a few moments, then begin to back away, thinking that I can wait until tomorrow. It'll be far more difficult if I'm completely sober, but maybe I'll have time to work out exactly what I want to say, refine my declaration, or perhaps catch Dad alone and talk it over with only him.

I walk past Dad, not even saying good night, just heading for the hallway as fast as possible. He doesn't notice.

"Oh, Benjamin," Mother calls out just as I step from the linoleum of her kitchen to the carpet of the hallway. She's got her back to me, but can still pinpoint the exact moment my body leaves her presence. It's her sixth sense of sorts: Jewish mother's intuition.

I turn and face her.

"Yes," I say.

"I completely forgot to tell you, your grandmother called this morning with the most wonderful news. It turns out that airline rates are the lowest they've been in ages. So, she's purchased a ticket and is flying in from Phoenix tomorrow to celebrate Yom Kippur with us. Isn't that just wonderful?"

"Yeah, great," I hear Dad mumble through a swig of Coca-Cola.

I'm beginning to sweat. It doesn't surprise me at all that Grandma would come to sit through services in Portland, just so she can stand and recite the Mourner's Kaddish for Grandpa with Mother beside her. I know about prayers, the ones I made that had not saved Grandpa. I also know that the Mourner's Kaddish cannot bring him back. Grandma can't come for Yom Kippur, not now that I've made this decision.

"She must have confused you," I say. "Grandma's terrified of flying, she'll never get on the plane."

"That's exactly what I thought," Mother says, "but Rabbi Weiss, you know, he married your Uncle Harold to his first wife, Molly. Ugh, what a horrible woman, thank goodness you boys were too young to remember her. Well, you know how your grandmother is. However, she's going to get on the plane with no worries at all because Rabbi Weiss has agreed to bless her at the terminal before she boards tomorrow morning."

Dad lifts his head from the bills and stares at me. "Silly old woman," he says, "she'd be better off having the rabbi bless the plane's mechanic or pilot."

"Bernard," Mother shouts over my restrained laughter. Dad is instantly quieted and returns his attention to the bills. Mother puts down an oven mitt and stands slouched to one side, her right fist once again planted on that cocked hip. "Now Benjamin, I'm having your father take me to the synagogue early before Kol Nidre services begin." Great, I think, she's arriving early to scope out the prime seats, as if the closer to the front of the sanctuary she sits the more faithful she'll feel. "So," she continues, "we'll need you to drive Neil and your grandmother in my car."

I take in a long breath. "They'll have to go with you and Dad," I say. "I mean...I mean that I'm not going to services."

Mother pauses. "What do you mean, you're not going?"

My glorious speech had melted away from memory, or the brain cells containing it had been short-circuited by the bourbon. "I mean just what I said, I'm not going to any Yom Kippur services. Not Kol Nidre, Yitzkor, Mincha, or any other service, ever again, all right?"

There's now a lovely amber red seeping between the crinkles of her eyes, almost matching the color of her baking apron.

"Bernard, do you hear this, do you hear what your son is saying?" Dad is still concentrating on the bills. "Bernard!"

"What?" Dad says.

"Your son, he says he's not going to services with his family."

"Hmm," Dad sighs and takes off his reading glasses to rub the bridge of his nose.

"Do you hear me, Bernard, do you hear what your son is saying?"

"Yes, Rita," Dad says with recognizable annoyance, "I hear you just fine."

"Why?" Mother continues. "Why are you too good to go to services with your family? Tell me Benjamin Daniel Bregman."

I lean silently against the wall, staring at the floor to avoid her eyes.

"Bernard," Mother says after a short silence, "Yom Kippur is the holiest day of the year, it's the day of forgiveness."

"I'm not going," I say.

"Oh, yes, you are," she shouts, marching to my end of the kitchen. "You don't see your father going to work on Yom Kippur, do you? No, he takes the day off to be with his family, he closes his business so that his customers know what's important to him. But you don't care about anything at all, not even your own mother. I only carried you for nine months. I only endured thirty-one hours of labor for you. And this is how I'm rewarded? Maybe you're so self-centered that nothing is important to you but yourself, huh? Well, explain yourself."

"What good is going to services? I can't understand anything they're saying. I didn't even understand one word I was chanting at my own bar mitzvah. What good is that?"

Mother's eyes now become slivers, her nostrils slightly flaring. "If you think that the day you turned thirteen was the day you didn't have to be Jewish anymore, then you must have been raised by another woman, not me."

"I just don't want to go."

"Do you know what it means if you don't go? It…oh, I can't believe I'm hearing this." Mother is practically shaking; her fists clutched tight, fingers wrapped around her thumbs. "Why…why…why look at Sandy Koufax!"

"Huh?" Dad says, his face coming alive at the mention of the unforgettable sports legend.

"Sandy Koufax refused to play in the World Series because he knew his presence at services was more important than any silly baseball game," Mother professes, forgetting that even the slightest mention of sports at the dinner table irritates her. "He made a statement to the entire world about how important his heritage is to him." The skin of her neck is now stretched, her jaw lifted high.

"What are you talking about?" I say. "You hate baseball."

"So what?" she snaps, chin curling, molars grinding, her hands running down the bib of her apron as if it were chain mail.

"So what? You have no right to talk about something you know absolutely nothing about, that's what."

"I can say whatever I wish. This is my house, and you live under my roof, and you're going to services, whether you like it or not."

"Fine," I shout, standing right in front of her. She takes a few steps back but I persist, looking down a good eight inches into her lava-brown eyes. "If you think you know so much, then you might as well get the story straight. Sandy Koufax didn't make any statement at all, even though you would like to think so. His manager, Walt Alston, scheduled him to pitch game two of the sixty-five series. Don Drysdale pitched game one while Koufax went to temple. They knew in advance that Koufax wouldn't play. A statement? Please, that's all a bunch of bull. I bet you don't even know what team Koufax was playing for."

Dad answers: "Easy. The Dodgers."

"Bernard," Mother snaps.

"All right," I continue, "if you're so smart then tell me Koufax's earned-run-average for the series, huh? Were the Dodgers in the National League or the American League, or do you even know the difference? Please, you don't know a thing about Sandy Koufax, and you wouldn't care at all if he wasn't Jewish."

"Even your brother, Joshua, goes to services," she says. "Who knows why that boy won't go back to college, but at least he goes to services."

"Well, I'm not Josh. And I'm not Sandy Koufax. And I'm not going to services anymore."

"Feh, you're drunk. What, you think I can't smell the liquor on your breath?" She looks over to Dad. "Bernard, please."

Dad sighs, then leans against the kitchen table, the way the entire family does. We all seem to lean. But he's also breathing heavily, the way he does when he wants a cigarette. He's tired tonight. "Apologize to your mother," he tells me.

"Why?" I say, "I'm right."

Then, I notice that Mother's beautiful brown eyes have begun to moisten, but she contains herself with the strength of a gladiator. If she cries I'll surrender, but I know she would rather leave the room than let me see her do so. "Why do you hate your family?" she asks. "I want to know, why do you hate us so much?"

"I didn't say I hated you," I say softly. "I just don't want to go to services anymore."

"Well," Dad says in an exhausted tone, "if you don't want to go to services, then maybe you're not welcome at our table to break the fast." This, coming from the man who refers to a yarmulke as a beanie.

"Dad," I stutter, "it's not about that, it's not the same thing."

"You're ashamed of us, is your mother right, is that it? Is it?"

"Where do you two come up with this stuff? I simply don't believe in God anymore, all right? There it is. There is no fucking God."

There's a long moment of hesitation. It's as if everything has turned into cotton—soft and silent. The timer for the brisket pings, but Mother doesn't budge. She's making an immense effort not to cry. If she lived in the desert with Grandma, she would rub sand in her eyes just to save face.

"Who said anything about God?" Dad asks.

Silence.

"Name one time you ever heard me speak about God?" Dad asks, the rage beginning to form in the wrinkle of his brow.

"Exactly," I say, "you don't believe in God, Dad, I know that."

"I believe in God," Mother says.

"But he doesn't," I say, pointing to Dad.

"I attend services because it pleases your mother," Dad says, "because it's a time for our family to be together. Because you don't have to believe in God to be Jewish."

"What?" I roll my eyes in the manner I know they despise.

"Do you know what your grandfather would say if he heard you talk like this?" Mother says, pointing at that handsome picture on the wall as if he's actually in the room, alive, breathing beside us. "He lived his entire life as God commanded us to."

I look directly at her and effortlessly speak what I have known for the past seven months. "When Grandpa died, the same thing happened to God."

"You're going to services and that's final," she shouts.

The moment had come, the one children know well. It's that invisible pocket of time when there's a line drawn in transparent dirt that the child knows never to cross.

"Go to hell," I shout at Mother, then begin to turn my back to go to my bedroom.

The blow of knuckles colliding with my jaw comes out of nowhere. I feel no sense of falling or my back colliding with the linoleum of Mother's kitchen floor. I lie looking at the cluttered wood beams stretching across the white plaster of the ceiling. One side of my face is completely numb. Dad is holding the reddened fist of his right hand in his left, the skin of his neck flushed. I had never been spanked, had never been in a fistfight, had never known the sensation of being struck other than the half-efforts of my older brother.

Dad is staring at me. It's that look every child knows, the incredible amalgamation of anger and the only thing worse: disappointment. He takes a step forward and looks down at me.

I begin to smell the brisket burning in the oven as Mother sobs in a chair at the kitchen table—crying in her own fortress—face buried in the flour-covered palms of her shaking hands. And I know that there's no possible way to change what I said.

Dad continues to stand over me menacingly in that Zeus-like omnipotence that I have not sensed from him since grade school. "Think what you will of God," he says. "Think what you will of your mother. But know one thing. That is my wife you are speaking to."

∘ ∘ ∘

Three days later I come home from school and immediately crawl into bed with no intention of sleeping. From the shade of the blinds I observe sundown approaching, slowly casting a shadow over the framed picture of Grandpa with me on the day of my bar mitzvah that I keep propped on my dresser. I see his smile. How could I ever forget that smile—so proud with his arm clutched around my shoulder?

I hear the front door of the house shut and a car pulling out from the driveway. It is almost five o'clock. Dad is taking Mother to the synagogue early, before Kol Nidre services begin. Even though my parents have not spoken to me since that awful night, I know that Dad will be returning shortly for Grandma and my younger brother.

I lie awake for a half-hour incapable of removing my eyes from that picture of Grandpa and me, wishing what I know is impossible. Slowly, I bring myself to rise out of bed, put on my only suit and tie that was handed down from Josh, then wait in the living room for Dad to return. I sit beside Neil; Grandma simply smiles at me. I am ready to attend services with my family.

It is the beginning of Yom Kippur, the holiest day of the year. As Mother says, it is the day of forgiveness.